DEAD SILENT

Also by Dean Fetzer

The Jaared Sen Quartet

Death in Amber

Death After Midnight

Book of the Dead

Dead Silent

Edited with Gordon Butler

Fancyapint? In London

DEAD SILENT

Dean Fetzer

First printed in this edition 2024

GunBoss Books, 3rd Floor, 207 Regent Street, London, W1B 3HH, England

www.gunboss.com

No undead beings were harmed in the writing of this novel and
all dogs and cats are extremely well looked after.

ISBN 978-0-9573977-7-4

F2

To Debra, Ross and Chris

– I wouldn't have finished this without you.

ONCE UPON A TIME...

The little girl sits in the middle of a broad meadow, picking wild flowers amongst the tall grass.

Her long, straight black hair glistens in the sun, her vibrant emerald eyes watch as her hands carefully weave the stems of the flowers together.

It's raining, it's pouring, the old man is snoring...

She looks up suddenly, a dark cloud visible on the horizon. A look of concentration on her face, her left eye closes, squints and then opens again.

The dark cloud is gone.

A stiff breeze starts up, causing the long grasses to sway and dance, loose petals raining to the soil in a multi-coloured rain.

...he's coming, he's coming, he's coming...

She's confused for a moment before continuing to sing.

...he bumped his head and went to bed and couldn't get up in the morning...

A hint of rain appears on the wind, thrown here and there. The little girl concentrates again and the rain vanishes. The wind drops to a murmur in the grass and the sun beams down, warming the earth.

The little girl smiles up at the sun, closing her eyes and basking in the glow.

*...raining...pouring...snoring...*she singsongs.

A big orange cat wanders into the meadow, meandering towards her. When he reaches her, he slumps down beside her, purring to beat the band.

The little girl strokes the cat absently, leaning against his flank and feeling his purr course through her.

*...he's coming, he's coming, he's coming...*she sings contentedly. The other rhyme has finished and she concentrates on the new one, pulling petals from the flowers in her hands and dropping them on the ground around her.

Her petting becomes more vigorous and the cat opens one eye, daring her to continue, his purr gaining a hitch. She finishes petting him, giving him a quick peck on the nose. He smiles a cat-smile, his fur practically glowing in the intense sun.

...he's coming, he's coming, he's coming...

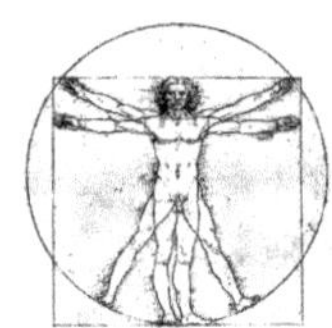

AP: An earthquake in Uttar Pradesh has left 269 people missing, feared dead, after a hospital collapsed. Rescue attempts have found no survivors so far...

221B Baker Street

I hit the wall as a projectile smacks the bricks in front of me. Flinching, I duck back, trying to make as small a target as possible.

Nick's body impacts the surface behind me.

"You okay?" I hiss.

"Of course," he replies.

I shake my head in exasperation, catching my breath, wiping the sweat from my forehead. He's still immaculate.

"It helps they do not know how to use projectile weapons," he continues.

Laughing under my breath, I take a quick peek around the corner. Another bullet kicks up some brick dust near my face and I flinch. "I think they're learning."

It's been a long time since I've been in this kind of firefight. Thankfully that kind of training never quite disappears. I'm carrying a modified late generation Heckler and Koch MP5 (MP5SD5-XXD, for the gun nuts out there). It hasn't really changed that much since I first used one (cautiously, as I had lost my eyes before they came into common use) but its fewer moving parts requires more technology now.

I actually have a readout in the corner of the Heads Up Display (HUD) running in front of my eyes, telling me barrel temp, type of ammo and how much ammunition I've got left – and if I let it get too hot, a red warning light tells me to stop.

I usually listen.

We're pinned down by some nasty things Nick assures me aren't human. Nice. I like the supernatural to get involved in my day-to-day life.

And the fact they've picked up assault weapons worries me more than a little.

At least we've managed to kill or lose those damn hellhounds.

Nicholas Sebastien Louis Duchesne. My son. Nick to me.

A strange hybrid, part human, part vampire. Don't ask me how it works, I've no idea. Maybe I'm not that human. And whoever would know hasn't seen fit to fill me in.

Hunting for Nick's vampire mother (and my…whatever), Madeline, hasn't been as straightforward as I'd have liked it to be. But I promised the kid I'd help him find her.

Madeline disappeared sometime in the last two and a half weeks.

I don't normally worry about Madeline, as she's nigh indestructible. Being a vampire, it's much easier for her to heal an injury than for your average human – all she needs to do is drink some blood.

But Nick is nothing, if not persistent. And as I needed his help to get us through that damn House, helping him find her is the least I can do.

The last time anyone heard from Madeline was over a week ago when she checked in with the vampire equivalent of the local council, The Elders. (I don't know much about them, just what Nick's let slip; I get the feeling he's not supposed to tell me anything about them at all.)

Anyway, Madeline was in Edinburgh on a mission for the Elders, looking for someone. All we can guess is that she found *something*.

Nick found her hidey-hole here in the 'burgh, but she hadn't been there for a while. Even I could tell that.

I think that's when the hellhounds found us.

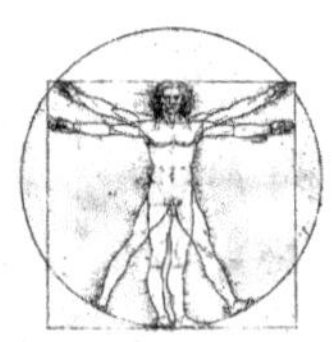

I'M WAITING FOR MY MAN...

Skeet pushed the drooping fringe of her spiky blonde hair back from her eyes and shook her head.

The meeting with Tony Shonin hadn't gone well.

"What the hell do you mean we have to wait?" Tony demanded. He was hissing at her in the crowded confines of a coffee shop off Regent Street. His Thai tan looked out of place in grey old London.

Skeet hadn't wanted to meet him anywhere more private.

"I mean, you ain't gonna find him in London, Tony," Skeet replied. "He's gone up north on a job."

Tony sat back. The Sato twins were with him, uncomfortable in their warm clothes. They looked totally out of their element. Probably had never been anywhere this cold.

"That wasn't the deal, Skeet." His eyes were cold, dead. No, the deal with his boss was to get her Jaared so she could kill him. Skeet wasn't ready to let that happen. And the worst of it was, Tony's boss was Jaared's daughter.

Skeet held her hands palms out. "I ain't shittin' you, Ton, he's off bonding with his kid in Scotland." *Hunting for that bitch.* "I can't help it if youse can't lift him now."

Those icy eyes stared at her a few beats longer. "If you're lying to me, Skeet, I'll do more than kill you, you know that."

Nodding, Skeet picked up her coffee. "I know, Tony. I ain't lyin'."

Sipping the last of his coffee, Tony looked away from her for the first time. Skeet nearly sighed in relief, the snap she'd glanded hyped her senses, but didn't calm her down.

"Okay, Skeet, here's the situation: you let us know when he's back and we'll take care of things from there." Tony reached across the small table and patted her cheek with a hand like a slab of corned beef. “No need to get your pretty blonde head in a tizz.” The smile accompanying the pat almost made her scream.

Gritting her teeth, Skeet smiled. “No worries, Ton, we’ll get the bastard!”

Tony stood up. “For your sake, we’d better, kid – the boss don’t like time-wasters.” He nodded at the Satos. “And I think they’d like to get back to the islands; this cold weather’s not good for them.”

Skeet nodded again. “I know how they feel.”

“Be in touch, Skeet,” Tony threw over his shoulder. “I’d hate anything to happen to that pretty face of yours.”

“You betcha, Tony,” Skeet replied, stomach flip-flopping.

Skeet pulled a flask from her boot top and surreptitiously added it to her lukewarm coffee. The whisky hit her nostrils before the cup reached her lips. She shuddered and tossed the drink back.

Dammit Jaared, of all the times to go off with your scary kid.

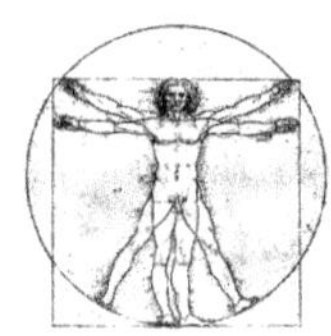

Jonesing for Your Touch

Jonesy's stomach lurched as he dropped out of the data cloud into the canyon of Central's normal processes.

The Grid flew by, glimpses of stray data nodes just registering in the corner of his eye.

Always night in the Grid, the only light comes from the construct's datasets and drone functions.

It was difficult to move through Central's architecture slowly, so Jonesy only had a sense of massive city sprawl, artificial intelligences more organic than planned creations – and no one had a street map.

This is hopeless.

Shaking his head, Jonesy jacked out and sat up with a sigh. His eyesight took a moment to adjust to reality, the Grid ghosting over the dull paint of the walls in his flat.

He rubbed his eyes and wished the throbbing at the base of his skull would slow down. He glanded some *chill* and it subsided to a dull thud.

"Call Sen," he said to his voda. There was a 'click' and it went straight to voicemail.

"...Sen. I'm currently unavailable, but if your enquiry is urgent you can reach the duty controller by saying 'connect me' after the tone."

Jonesy sighed. He hadn't reached Sen in days, hadn't really spoken to him since the quick meeting with an analyst at Company House. He stood up and went to the bathroom.

That was the problem with this kind of bug checking, it left little time for amenities like going to the toilet. He knew a guy once, had a whole setup out of a spacesuit built into a chair so he didn't have to leave it; took care of all his biological needs. One day the chair broke down and the guy starved to death in a pool of his own shit and piss.

Jonesy shuddered at the memory.

When he returned from the head, Jonesy took a pull on the energy drink in the clip next to his work chair. His thoughts returned to the task at hand.

It felt like a pointless exercise. He was never going to spot a single incursion in Central's matrix. Even multiples wouldn't be that obvious, unless the intruder left some kind of glaring signature behind him.

He jacked in again and initiated the intricate one-time codes that let him access Central. He didn't really understand how it worked – that kind of security wasn't really Jonesy's area.

Unsure what to do next, Jonesy cruised over the vast amalgamation of processes and data that made up Central's 'mind'. Occasional details leapt out at him, but nothing out of the ordinary.

Damn.

Jonesy was about to jack out again when he thought of something he hadn't tried yet. With a mental shrug, he initiated a filter programme he'd been tinkering with. Designed to help him find bugs, it would hide a lot of the normal functions of the matrix. Hopefully, the intruder wouldn't be considered 'normal'.

The filter immediately cancelled a lot of the visual information he was getting sent directly into his brain, leaving him in near darkness. The only things left were current activities – things Central was 'thinking' about at the moment.

Shit. It all looked normal.

Out of the corner of his mind's eye, Jonesy saw a sudden outgoing data spur light up like a geyser.

"Ka-*ching*!" he shouted in the quiet of his apartment. "Got ya!

He mapped the spur and slipped up to it with a stealth programme a mate of his in Specials, the tame hacker quadrant, had given him. With a flick of his ghostly wrist, a tracer jumped into the stream of data and disappeared, one end stuck to the edge of the hole whoever it was left in Central's security.

It probably wouldn't last long, but it might allow him to triangulate who and what was accessing Central. All he could do for now.

* * *

Back in the real world, Jonesy told his voda to ring Sen again. There was the burr of the electronic ring then *"This is Commander Jaared Sen. I'm currently unavailable…"*

"Code B-two-theta," Jonesy intoned. "Message for Commander Sen: I've got something for you, Commander – I think I've got a lead on what or whom is messing with Central." He looked at the voda again, shook his head. "Call me."

Tossing the voda onto a cushion, he took another long pull from the energy drink in the holder by his chair and sat down again. "Now, let's see where that goes…" he muttered.

With a single mental flip of the switch he was back in the Grid.

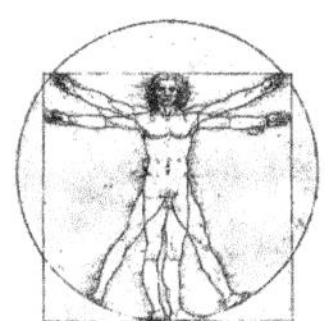

Hunting in the Capital

The figure in the shadows of a chimneybreast watched the duo below dispatch a number of the crawling things. For non-natural creatures, them seemed awfully easy to kill with traditional ammo. He shook his head. Amateurs.

Of course, they could be drawing their pursuers somewhere, but he couldn't see anything ahead of them that looked like a good place to trap them.

Clutching his favourite shotgun, Marybell, the stocky man sniffed the air and frowned. That was bad – one of them was a nightwalker.

He sniffed again. Wait...they were family. Yep, he could just smell a hint of the man on the vampire. Unusual.

The hunter glanced at the area around them; they were making a lot of noise in *his* town. But no one seemed interested, which was more interesting. They were being left alone on purpose or worse, something was cloaking their passage.

"I don' like either of those options, d'ya *ken*?" he muttered to no one. "Wha' the fook are thaes up tae?"

Following the pair for the last couple of days hadn't been difficult, even with his other duties. Besides this annoyance, the rest of the 'Athens of the North' was pretty quiet. *Concentrating on these two?* While hidden, they did seem to be attracting a great deal of attention in certain circles.

More importantly, the question that really needed answering was "Who are yeh?" he asked the air, his brow furrowed.

He rose from a crouch, Marybell slung across his back and went back to following the duo, his passage silent on the slippery roof tiles. Keeping to the rooftops, he shadowed them down the edge of the canal before it became impossible. He slipped to the edge of the roof and dropped to the rooftop below with hardly a sound.

Within seconds he was on the canal path behind them, checking for anything that might hinder his passage.

Nothing. Not even a fox or a stray cat.

He'd best keep an eye on these two – no knowing what kind of mischief they might get up to. And that wasn't good for his town.

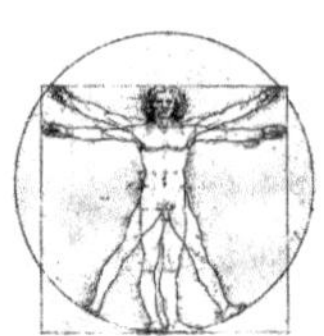

SUPE'S WITH GUNS, WHAT'LL THEY THINK OF NEXT?

My skullphone rings just as another burst of flechettes hits the concrete above my head.

"Yeah?" I shout, forgetting for the moment I don't have to speak out loud.

"...seen Tony...fuckin' Sato Twins..."

Another round explodes nearby.

"Sorry kid, can't hear you very well – I'll have to call you back," I shout, raising the MP5 and squeezing the trigger.

When she told me about it, Skeet's bombshell caused a lot less damage than it should have. Maybe.

It was hardly a surprise. Central's always monitoring at least three unassociated head cases with a hard-on for my death. I've made a lot of enemies over the years.

"You're not surprised?" Skeet asks as we walk back from Wolf's shop.

I shrug. "I get death threats on a daily basis, although some are more realistic than others." I take her hand. "I'm not surprised Tony Shonin's taken a more direct route. Who'd you say the woman was again?"

"Miz Watson."

I don't know her. Maybe Central can pin her down. "And they're offering you how much for a *meeting?*"

Skeet names a sum which even I find hard to believe.

"That sounds like more than a meeting," I reply. "I also can't think of anyone who needs to see me that badly."

"Yeah, it feels more like a hit than someone just wantin' to talk to you."

Central has been digging. A file ref flashes up on my HUD crackling with red warning tags. A quick précis follows.

Of course Watson isn't her real name.

"Ah, Rachel Stone. I haven't heard that name in years…"

Skeet glances sideways at me. "Girlfriend? Ex-wife? What?"

I shake my head. It's more complicated than that. "She's my daughter."

"Daughter? How many kids you got, Jaared?" Skeet's dropped my hand now. Not surprisingly.

I shrug again, light a cigarette, exhale smoke and gaze into the distance, not seeing the view. "Only the two I know about. And you've met them both."

It was obvious from her expression she didn't believe me. "All those years a'sowin' your wild oats, it doesn't seem very likely," she mutters.

"Well, it's true. I don't know if there are any others." I take another drag on the cigarette. The smoke does little to soothe me.

Rachel's mother, Tessa Stone, was a beauty I met in India, daughter of a shipping tycoon with interests all over the world. I didn't know she was pregnant when she left India for Singapore; all I knew was she went very suddenly.

"I only found out about Rachel when Stone, her grandfather, contacted me about Tessa's death," I tell Skeet. "I was in China at that point and didn't even get to see her."

That was before the war and before I lost my eyes.

And no, I'm not surprised she wants to kill me.

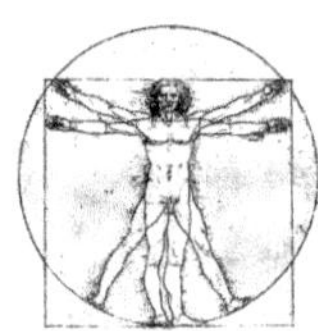

DAMN, I HATE SURPRISES

Skeet put her voda down, worried.

"Dammit, Jaared, I wish to hell you'd let me go with you..." she muttered into her beer. After seeing Tony and the Sato twins and with her flask empty, she'd ended up in the George, wanting something stronger than caffeine.

What was worse was hanging around waiting for him to call.

It was raining again when she left the pub, a little worse for wear. Some of the old gang had been in, Juicy Ramirez, the bookie-cum-antiques trader, Paulie Leftfoot, a small-time hood with a penchant for knives and a few others who's faces blurred together in her tired mind.

And that bastard Sen hadn't called back.

"Asshole!" Skeet shouted up at the wet sky, rain collecting quickly in the corners of her eyes. "Dammit, Jaared." She dropped her eyes back to the pavement, wiping them with the back of a wet hand. Her hair was losing its spikiness in the drizzle.

Skeet was pulling her hood up when her voda went.

"Yeah?"

"Hey kiddo," he replies. "Sorry about that – nearly got capped by a couple of...what were they, Nick?" There was indistinct muttering in the background. "Oh yeah, some kind of 'shifter."

She closes her eyes, relieved and annoyed at the same time. "Glad ya didn't get killed – that what you want me to say?"

Silence. Then, "Skeet, I'm sorry, I didn't mean to worry you, I was just a little busy."

Damn him, she can hear he means it. She tries to make light of it. "Shit, I wasn't worried, old man, just wondered if I was gonna get paid by Tony or not!"

He chuckles and she can sense the relief. "What'd he want, anyway?"

"Wants to know where yo' ass is now – he wants a meetin'. Seems like he's got a bug up his ass about it, too."

"He'll have to wait – we don't have a clear line on where Madeline ended up."

Meanin' I have to wait, too.

Skeet sighs. "Whatever Jaared."

Silence again. "Hey Skeet, don't be like that..."

"Like what, Jaared?" *Worried? Jealous that you're off trying to rescue the mother of your son? Without me?*

"It was your idea to stay in London to keep Shonin off my back..." He goes quiet for a few seconds. "I have an idea: do you know where he and the twins are staying?"

"Hotel Bristol, Victoria."

Jaared's snort comes through the voda. "A bit cheap and touristy. Nevermind. Leave him a message you've got business in Brighton and will be back on Friday."

"And?"

"Come to Edinburgh."

There it is. "Don't know, Jaared..."

"I could use your help here, kid – and you'll get to use that arsenal you've got stashed in the back bedroom."

Skeet smiles in spite of herself. "All right, then – I'll be up in the afternoon. The midday fast train'll have me there by 3.30." *Not that she'd been checking the timetable or anything.*

"Okay, someone'll meet you at the station. Wear a pink carnation." She can hear the smile in his voice.

"What?" She had no idea what he meant.

"Nevermind, guess that was before your time. See you tomorrow kid," he says. "Gotta go, not sure how safe we are here."

"Right. G'night Jaared."

"Good night, Skeet."

And that was that.

Shonin and the twins wouldn't be happy, but she doubted Tony'd have her traced in a couple of days; England was not his neighbourhood anymore. Besides, she liked to spread that sort of thing around.

Suddenly smiling, Skeet hailed a cab and gave Jaared's address. She had things to pack. What did one wear to kill things in the capital city of Scotland? She'd probably just rely on her leathers like she usually did.

Leaning back on the cab's seat, she was surprised how much the thought of seeing Jaared had changed her mood.

"Lovesick cow," she muttered to herself.

"Sorry luv?" the cabbie asked, glancing in the mirror.

"Nothin', just talkin' to myself," she replied. Now, which guns to pack?

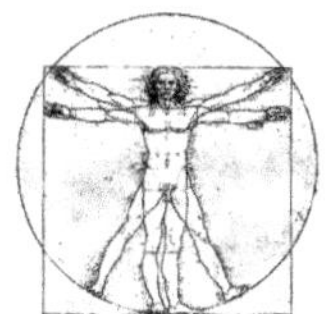

Roamin' and Ramblin' Blues

Jonesy unjacked and just lay there for a moment. After a good six hours tracing the incursion into Central's mainframe, he was still nowhere. He glanced toward his single window, realising it was light out.

A sharp pain from his bowels reminded him he hadn't moved in six hours. With a lurch, he freed himself from the recliner and found his legs were stiff. He staggered the short distance to the toilet, pulled his sweats down and flopped heavily onto the seat. The pain was suddenly excruciating and he doubled over as his bowels emptied.

"Shit!" The violence of it shocked him. "Jesus H. Christ!"

The spasm didn't last long, as he hadn't eaten anything since…pizza? Last night? He glanced at the voda clenched in his hand – over twelve hours ago.

Shaking, he tidied himself up and struggled to get upright and tug the sweat pants up at the same time. He nearly fell over again in the process, sitting down heavily on the toilet. Something cracked beneath him, but at least it didn't give way.

"Crap!" What the hell was wrong with him, anyway?

When he felt he could move again, he carefully pulled himself up with the edge of the door – one of the benefits of living alone was you didn't have to close the door when you used the toilet.

Leaning on walls and bits of furniture, Jonesy managed to get back to his pit and pick up his voda. He almost swooned when he leant over, but managed to hold onto the back of his chair until the dizziness passed.

Retracing his steps, he found his way to his sleeping cubby and collapsed onto the futon there, just managing to pull the duvet over his head before he passed out.

* * *

His voda chimed loudly again.

Jonesy groaned. "Go away."

The chime of the voda became more insistent. Damn. It could only be Sen. Great, just what he needed when he felt this awful.

Sitting up, he ignored the voda a few more seconds. The cubby was dark, the only light trickling down his short hall from the streetlight outside his building.

Sighing, he picked up the voda. NOW AND SEN, the display informed him as it chimed again.

"Jonesy."

"You rang, Mr Jones?" Sen's voice was quiet on the line. Jonsey shivered. Gulp.

"Yeh-yeh-yes, Commander," he almost stuttered. "I think I've got a line on that incursion…Well, I know where it is, anyway – I just haven't found the source yet."

Silence. "Good." There was another silence. "Got to go, but let me know if you make any progress on the 'who'. And Mr Jones, I don't have to stress how urgent this is, do I?"

Jonesy's stomach lurched. Damn. "I– no Sir," he replied. "I'll get back to it."

"Good." There was a 'click' and the line was dead.

"Your welcome," Jonesy muttered.

His head feeling very delicate, Jonesy threw the duvet off and fumbled on the shelf above his bed. Not there.

Using the wall for support, he pulled himself upright and managed to stagger into the shower cubicle where he kept essential supplies.

"Time for the big guns." He found the small bottle on the shelf and a strip of Imodium tabs. He dry swallowed two of the diarrhoea tablets and looked blearily at the small bottle. He knew it was the only way if he was going to find Sen's hacker. The come down would be bad.

"One pill makes you larger…" he half-sang as he twisted the lid. He shook two minute red pills out of the bottle and gazed at them a moment. "…one pill makes you small…"

With another sigh, he tossed them into his mouth and swallowed.

" 'Red or blue', that's the question," he said to his reflection in the mirror as a wave of adrenaline swept through his body, his face almost rippling with the sensation. His fingers and toes tingled and he suddenly felt amazing. “Boy howdy!”

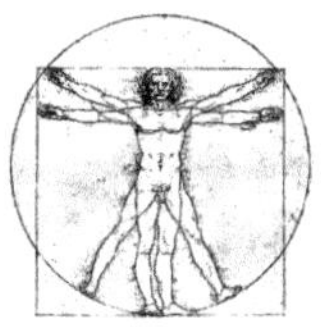

Fasten your seatbelts, we're about to hit some turbulence

I hang up with Jonesy, pleased he's making progress. Something I learned a long time ago – find the right people to do the work and you don't have to do it yourself.

"Good boy, Jonesy," I say under my breath. It reminds me of that adage about having a dog and wagging the tail yourself.

One of the things I just realised I hate are fighting creatures that won't die when you try very hard to kill them. At least we managed to lose the last of the horrible green things with too many joints and oozing sores. And the stench...

Nick and I are taking a breather in what seems to be an abandoned garage in posh Morningside. I say, 'seems to be' because you never know with wealthy people.

At least there's a dilapidated Chesterfield sofa to slouch on while I check my guns, count my ammo and assess my wounds. My HUD seems to think I only have a couple of scratches. The repair nanites are doing their best to fix the wounds, but I ache all over.

It's almost dawn, so Nick won't be much use again until nightfall. At least it's winter, so the nights are longer than the day. And it's cold, too.

We're lucky the things trying to capture or kill us don't seem to like daylight very much. But then, they'd kind of stick out in your average Edinburgh street, even during the Festival. Just as well, as there's little chance I could carry him around while trying to get away.

It was almost 'follow the wreckage' when we started tracking Madeline. Her hidey-hole had been a rented flat in the New Town – good choice with a transient population of students sharing massive rooms in mansion flats.

The first place we found that seemed to correlate with her disappearance was a posh restaurant in nearby George Street. It had been totally gutted and burned. The official story was a gas leak. Hah! At least she avoided the Oxford Bar, my favourite pub in this part of town.

A cheap Italian in Castle Street had its windows blown out and something went through the back and front of a department store on Princes Street, then through a shop selling tourist tat, you know, those tartan berets with a red-haired wig dangling down and just about tartan everything.

We lost her trail shortly after that and I suppose it doesn't really matter which way she went. She was still missing.

The last place we found any trace – Nick found her dark glasses in a close running up to the Royal Mile called Mylnes Court on the edge of the University. A part that ran under student accommodation had been partially demolished, leaving the way out onto the Lawnmarket inaccessible. Just as well a warren of alleys and passages runs all around the area.

Something with black, brackish blood (at least it was by the time we got there) had been crushed under the rubble, then removed. Good girl!

That was where the trail ended. Something decided we weren't welcome at that point and we've been fighting running battles since. Down Victoria Street, into the Grassmarket, tried to turn into the Cowgate and use the close walls and tunnels for cover, but we got pushed up Candlemaker Row.

And no, I didn't destroy Greyfriar's Bobby; you know, the one that old film's about – the one where the little dog stays on his master's grave in the churchyard for years. Some kind of bright blue fire took his statue out. Wasn't me.

"Father?"

"Mmmm-hmmm?" I'm watching through the garage window as a neighbour does something mundane: taking out the trash. I'm tired, but not exhausted yet. I gland some *snap* to kick my system into alertness.

Nightfall is nearly on us and no sign of pursuit. Yet.

Nick's silent for a moment and I turn away from the window.

"Yes?"

His eyes seem to burn in the dimness of the dusty garage. "I–I just want to say thank you…for helping me find my mother…"

I wave him away and look back out of the window. "I don't think life would be the same without her around." I notice something moving in the undergrowth. "Besides, you're my son – all you have to do is ask…"

Yep, not a cat or fox.

"Looks like we've got company – you ready?" I whisper.

He's at my side, peering into the shadows. "More hellhounds."

Bugger. "Great, let's go out the other way and hope they don't have us surrounded." With a 'click', I disengage the clip block from the MP5. Damn it, running low. Then a thought hits me. I call up a map on my HUD. "How do they like water?"

Nick smiles. "They don't – nearby?" Definitely a chip off the old block.

"Yep, canal about three hundred metres from here…"

The smile sharpens. "After you, sir." He bows slightly.

I smile back. "C'mon, then, we can't sit around here all day." I open the door.

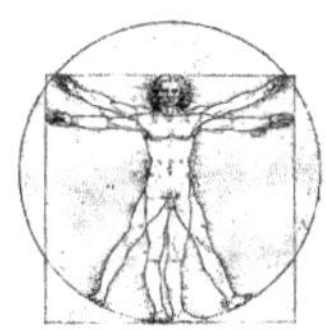

'BOUT TIME I KILLED ME SOMETHIN'...

Skeet stepped out of Waverly Station into the ass-end of a cold and dull Edinburgh day. "At least it ain't raining," she muttered.

One of the ancient black cabs, converted to electric, rolled up. "Yeh Skeet?" the cabbie asked. Older bloke, veins standing out on his reddish nose, two beady eyes under a colourless flat cap.

Hoisting her heavy kit bag, Skeet nodded. "Yep, that's me."

He nodded once. "Guy named Sen ast' me to pick yeh up."

Wary, Skeet checked his memory. "Short guy? Thick beard? Eyes like saucers?"

The cabbie shook his head. "Nah, tall guy, long hair, t'ousand yard stare – scared the bejessus out of me."

That was Jaared. "Okay, where am I going?"

"Said to take you to the *The Waiting Room...*"

"Hah! I'll bet."

" S'a pub, d'ya ken?"

Well, that didn't sound like a terrible idea after her journey. "Alright, you drive, I'll sit," Skeet said, pulling the door of the cab open.

Fifteen minutes later with darkness pushing on the windows, she was seated in a corner of the bar, nursing a pint of McEwans 80 shilling when her voda went. "Speak to me."

There was a husky laugh. "You make it to The Waiting Room, then?" Jaared asked.

"Yep, just having me a pint and waiting for yeh to turn up."

"Okay, we'll have to make it quick as I don't think we'll have time for dinner."

"Got company?"

"Yessiree, bob," he replied. "We'll be with you in about ten, assuming we can shake these assholes long enough to…" a burst of automatic fire cut through the rest of his sentence. "…See what I mean? See you shortly." *Click.*

Skeet smiled her not so nice smile (that bore an uncanny resemblance to a shark's grin) and drank a bit more of her pint.

Glancing around, she didn't see anyone who'd obviously complain about her hardware.

Adjusting her jumpsuit for combat, pulling the ankle straps tight, activating the bullet absorption liner and pulling the zip up to her neck took just a few seconds.

Skeet lifted the kitbag onto the chair, and pulled her twin Sigs and holsters out of the bag. It was a matter of moments to belt them on her hips, butts forward for drawing across her body.

"Hey, you can't do that in here," said a voice from a few tables over.

Skeet gave him the eye. "I think yeh'll find I can."

The drunk started to his feet. "No, I mean, you'd be better off doing that in the back room, Ms Skeet."

Ah. "Sen told you I was coming?"

He nodded, looking less drunk by the second. "I'm supposed t'keep an eye on yer until he picks ya up."

Skeet returned the nod. "Fine. Show me the way." Picking up her kit bag, she followed Sen's contact to a room behind the bar. Small, it had a single table and chairs. And a door that closed.

Stepping into the room, Skeet said, "Thanks for that, mate…"

The feel of cold steel behind her left ear stopped her.

"I ain't yer mate, bitch," the wino hissed in her ear. "We're going to kill you and Sen and the brat, just you watch…"

You're too trusting, kid, came Jaared's voice in her head. Shaking it slightly she couldn't help replying to her unwanted companion. "We'll see who's the bitch."

"Whaddya mean–" he started as she dropped her stance slightly, her body pivoting, right arm pushing the gun arm away from her as he fired. Not even close.

Carrying the sweep through and catching his wrist with her hand, the other hand struck once, the humerus made a sharp 'crack'. He screamed and dropped the gun.

Pulling him forward by the same wrist, Skeet spun him and smashed his face into the wall. The panelling cracked, as did his skull. He dropped to the floor.

No one came to investigate the shot. Funny that.

Leaving the body in the room, Skeet finished her prep, loading various pockets and sheaths as she went. The last thing to come out of the bag was her trusty Mossberg 590; she jammed shells into the magazine until it was full. She draped a bandolier of shells across her chest, clipping it in place and snugging it up so it didn't catch or flap about. Everything else, including the kit bag, compacted down to a small pack slung on her back and she was ready to go.

Skeet was just finishing her prep when she heard her name.

"Skeet?"

Pulling a Sig from its holster, she cautiously peeked around the doorframe. "Who wants to know?" she called, although she had a pretty good idea.

A laugh. "It's me – we've got about a minute before they catch up."

And it was. She picked up the Mossberg and left the room.

Jaared gestured around the empty pub. "What the hell'd you do? Where is everyone?"

Skeet shrugged. "Had an asshole stick a gun in my ear and he didn't really like the results."

He laughed again, the MP5 in his hand casually pointed at the ground. "That's my girl!" He gestured for the door. "Time to go."

Skeet nodded, but paused to kiss him, soundly, before she exited the pub.

Softer this time, "That's definitely my girl."

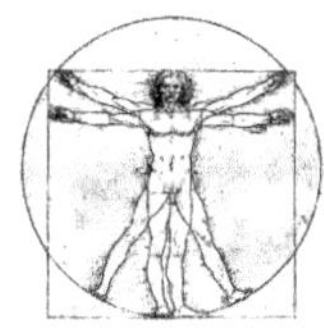

INTERMISSION

There is a scrape in the doorway. He can tell it's Squires. Bad news, no doubt.

Without turning, he continues to stare out over Princes Street Gardens and into the new part of Edinburgh. "Well?"

The stocky figure hesitates, clearing his throat. "We...uh...lost the girl."

He sighs. Incompetence. The Council would not be pleased. They needed the boy and his father for a very specific purpose.

The longer the pair remained at large, the more damage they would do to the situation.

It didn't help they'd already managed to kill two of his prized hellhounds, Zeus and Argus, as well as a good portion of his staff.

Brooding, he bites his lip, savouring the taste of iron. He was human, albeit a very old human.

"Can Limes find their scent?"

Another hesitation. "Limes is dead, sir."

The anger bursts out before he can check it. "Damn the man! He's inhuman!"

"It-it was a hellhound that killed Limes, sir. I warned him about getting in their way–"

"Very well." He screws his anger down and takes a deep breath, shuddering at the effort of controlling his rage. Berserkers normally burned out quickly, but he hadn't got this old without some measure of control. "Use Pluto and Nyx – but only to track them. I don't want to hear you've lost my remaining hellhounds."

"Understood sir." The figure withdraws from the room with all haste.

Another sigh. He turns to the desk and draws the old-fashioned phone to him. Time to update the Council.

The connection is almost immediate to the Chairman. “You have information.”

“The subject and his abomination have managed to elude us so far,” he says calmly. Anger or any other emotion could get him killed and replaced.

Silence. “We expected more from you, Chambers.”

“I know, sir. And I have to say he is proving more difficult to acquire than I had previously thought…”

“Excuses are not acceptable!” A pause. “As your predecessor found to his cost.”

“Yes, sir, I understand.”

Another moment goes by. “We are sending you someone to help – he has had dealings with Jaared Sen before and bears a grudge, I think.”

“Wh-who, sir?”

“The Elders promise me he’s the best they have – but he can be capricious.” A heavy sigh comes down the dedicated line. “Use him to find Sen and the boy, then eliminate him before he does any damage.”

“Uh, very good, sir. When can we expect him?”

“He should be with you this evening.”

“How will I know him, sir?”

“Don’t worry, he will find you.”

“Very good, sir,” he repeats again. There’s a click and the hum of a dead line.

“Absa-bloody-fucking-brilliant,” he mutters. The thing could be as dangerous as Sen. If the Elders were sending him, he was probably some kind of vampire. Well, there were worse ways to find another vampire…

“I’m getting too old for this.”

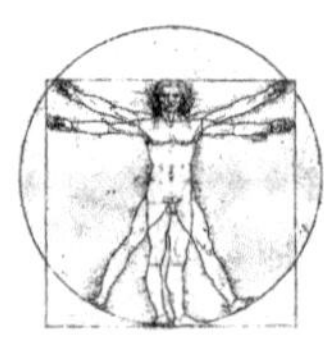

Hunger is a bitch

Madeline slumped against the wall of her dungeon in considerable pain. While it took some effort to injure her, it could be done. Her keeper, the rock giant – she still didn't know his name – had started beating her methodically a couple of days before. He had an uncanny ability to know when to stop and when to start before she had time to recover enough.

If only she could feed.

Thirst clawed at her throat but more than thirst; it was an aching hunger nearly as difficult to bear as the pain. She was nearly blind with it all, her vision reduced to a narrow tunnel with black edges.

She'd been hearing scuttling in the corner of her cell but hadn't been able to reach whatever it was. A rat, she thought.

An idea clawed its way through her brain. Madeline quickly nipped one of her fingers, her sluggish blood trickling from the cut. She wiped the smear on her palm as the cut worked to close itself and placed her hand palm up on the floor.

Stillness had never been difficult, but she closed her eyes to shut out everything but the noises from the corner.

For a long time there was nothing. Then Madeline heard it: the scrape of a claw on the stone of the cellar. Relaxing every muscle, she did her best impression of a stone.

Another stray sound. It had to be closer.

The depth of the silence was almost too much to bear. It must have gone back into whatever run it had behind the walls.

Then came a delicate touch on her hand. She nearly flinched in anticipation. *Still, be still,* she warned herself. The waiting was almost as much torture as the giant's hands.

Another touch, then a warm tongue lapped at the blood on her palm.

Madeline's fingers closed like a vice and she had it.

It *was* a rat, about fifteen inches long, but she didn't stop to examine it, the thud, thud, thud of its tiny heart enough to drive her crazy – well, crazier.

She thrust the squealing, squirming body into her mouth and sank her fangs into its flesh. The hot blood gushed into her mouth as she sucked greedily at it. The blood was gone too quickly, but she felt a flush as it hit her system, weak as she was.

Nearly tossing the carcass away in disgust, another scratch in the corner brought her short and she grinned in the darkness.

Well, there never was just *one* rat.

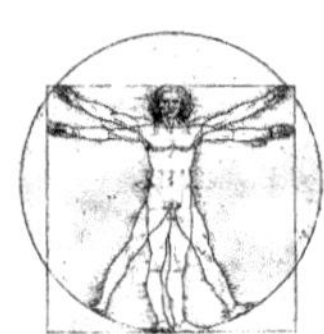

SHE HIT THEM WITH HER TEN CENT PISTOL...

Having Skeet with us in Edinburgh exhilarates and terrifies me at the same time. But I can't deny it improves my morale, regardless of the added danger.

"It's good to see you, kid."

Skeet smiles at me. "Was getting tired of London anyway – too much hassle."

That worries me. "Tony? I can always get him detained..."

She makes a shushing gesture. "You can't be involved, can yeh? He doesn't know you're aware of him. An' I wouldn't put it past him to have a mole with access to Central."

Thinking of Jonesy, I had to agree. "So long as he doesn't come up here and get involved in...whatever this is."

Skeet shakes her head. "I don't think he'll even notice I've gone for a couple a days." She shrugs. " 'Sides, he might help shake your tail – could always get one o' them monsters to munch on him and the Twins."

I smile at the image. "Worse things could happen to him, you're right."

"What do we do now?" she asks, taking my arm.

"Nick lets us know how close the chase is and we evade them until dawn, hopefully finding a bolt hole before the sun rises."

"That's the plan?" Skeet looks at me incredulously.

I have to smile again. "Don't worry, we only have to do this for about another twenty-four hours, then we'll let ourselves get caught."

More head shaking. "You're crazy. Why run, then?"

"We don't want them to think we've given in too easily, now do we?"

"Yes, but..." her hand grips my arm. "Why d'you want to get caught at all?"

"Because we don't know why they have Madeline – or why they want us alive so badly." I stop, having caught enough of a hint of Nick to know he's waiting just around the corner. "It's the only way we can get answers to those questions. Besides, you won't get caught, just me. Then I'll let you two know when to come and rescue me."

Skeet doesn't look convinced. "Me an' Nick? It's not exactly a cakewalk if they've got as many troops as you think." She stopped. "An' he doesn't exactly like me..."

"Don't worry, we'll take care of the troops, well, most of them." I pull her along with me. I can't tell her everything at this point, partly because I'm still making it up.

"Well, I do worry."

"It'll be fine, just trust me." I remember something. "Oh, and Nick..."

Nick steps out from behind the wall, his blood red eyes serious. "We've got about two minutes before they arrive." The left sleeve of his jacket is missing.

I can feel Skeet's shock.

"Yeah, one of the beasties got his arm. Luckily, he can grow a new one."

Nick actually grins. "It doesn't hurt, anymore." He goes serious again. "We should go now."

I nod. "I know, I can feel the hellhounds they're using. I think they found another pair. Odd things, hellhounds." I motion Skeet ahead of me on the path beside the wall. "Time to get off the main road."

She follows Nick down the path to the canal. "What in the name of fuck 're 'hellhounds'?"

Nick piped up over his shoulder. "Think of the biggest dog you've ever seen and double it. They're the size of a small horse."

"Their flesh burns on contact and the ones we've seen can fly."

"Shee-it." Skeet's silent for a moment, thinking about hellhounds, no doubt. "And you two killed a pair of 'em?"

"We think so."

"How?"

Good question. "Nick managed to drop a house on one and the other one didn't like the grappler I led it into."

"Or the canal we pushed it into," Nick added. He's becoming positively verbose hanging around with me. It feels like he's almost sniggering.

"Yes, water seems to dampen their spirits."

"Fuck."

"But that's not all we've seen: I think I've counted at least four other kinds of supernatural creature in pursuit of us so far."

"Like?"

We're on the canal towpath now, the cement boards thudding under our feet. It doesn't matter if the things following us can hear us at this point – they've got hellhounds to track us with.

"Well, something big that can crush things with its bare hands – Nick thinks it's part stone giant – a couple of things with lots of legs and a bad smell, about this high," I say, lifting one hand about four feet off the ground. "They don't let those things near us until we're almost surrounded because of the stench."

"There's also something shaped like a bear – probably a Berserker," Nick puts in.

"What's the fourth?"

I consider how much to tell her because it scares the shit out of me. "We don't know what it is. We only caught a glimpse one time when they nearly had us cornered." I concentrate on the towpath for a few seconds. "It's just a black shape, really. And when I say 'black', I mean it sucks the light out of the area around it."

"Its aura is very cold," Nick adds.

I nod to myself. "Yes and it almost feels like it's draining the life out of you." I'm not going to talk about the despair it generates; Nick and I haven't even discussed that between ourselves. "We just know we don't want to meet it again, if we can avoid it."

There's the sound of a footstep behind us.

"They're coming," Skeet says.

I unsling the MP5 and check the micro grenade launcher fitted under the barrel. "Yep, and right on time."

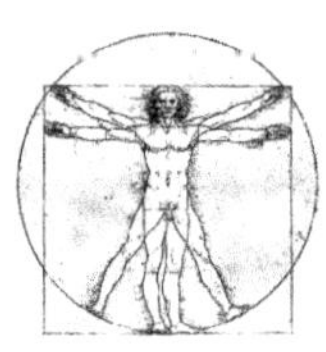

Noise and confusion

The first bang startled Skeet. Then she realised Jaared had turned toward the path behind and launched a micro-grenade. The towpath made sense when she saw the monstrosity behind them. It had to be one of the hellhounds and took up most of the space between the wall and the water. That meant it was unable to get out of the way of their guns.

Its skin was a glowing, flaming red, like it had been burned down to the muscle. She could almost see flames flickering around the head, tiny upright ears pointed in their direction. It seemed to be all muscle from what she could see.

Swearing, she pulled the Mossberg off her shoulder and aimed toward the beast. "Down!" she shouted at Jaared, who dropped obligingly. The boom of the shotgun echoed off the walls.

For a moment, she wondered if the shrapnel load she'd fired into the hellhound had any effect.

On impact, it stopped suddenly, shaking its head and it was obvious one of the slivers of metal had found its left eye. Flame poured out of the injured orb, little flames sprouting on the skin where the deadly needles had punctured the flesh. It roared in pain and started advancing, rage in its remaining eye.

"Oh good, you've made it mad," Jaared said from beside her. The beast was getting close enough they could feel heat coming off it.

Skeet gritted her teeth and glanded some *chill*. "Just watch."

She pumped the shotgun and aimed lower. Her next booming shot hit it in the legs and chest. Continuing to pump and shoot, she targeted the blind side of the animal – the side facing the canal.

Instinctively, the hound moved toward its blind side to try and protect itself, bringing it closer to the water. Water it couldn't see.

In the meantime, Jaared had worked out what she was doing and began chewing up the towpath with mini-grenades. God knows what people in the surrounding houses thought was going on.

Something moved behind the hound – no, it was on the back of the animal; it was trying to unfurl the black wings jutting from its shoulder blades, but the shotgun seemed to be distracting it.

Three more shots from the Mossberg and the animal was teetering on the edge of the canal.

"Nick! Can you help out here?" Jaared called over his shoulder without letting up on the barrage.

There was a sharp report and it looked like the hound's right shoulder was hit by a wrecking ball, the whole shoulder turning concave and pushing the animal over into the canal. With a hiss, it sank from sight, the fiery light dimming in the water.

"Can't swim," Nick observed behind her, a sniper rifle held loosely in one hand.

Skeet lowered her shotgun and turned toward father and son. "What the hell was that?"

Jaared was grinning; it looked like Nick was doing everything he could not to smile.

"Special rounds Adams had prepared for us," Jaared explained. "Something like holy water and belladonna. Hell, I don't know, but they work."

Skeet nodded. "I can see."

"We don't have very many, which is why we save them for special occasions."

"Uh-huh."

Nick caught Jaared's eye. "Time to go."

Jaared nodded. "Yep, I can feel them getting closer. Lead the way."

He gestured to Nick who started running. Skeet glanced at Jaared and followed the kid. Damn he was fast!

She almost missed the turn off the towpath, having lost sight of him. She was also distracted by the sight of something with too many legs skittering toward her. Its head was angular with two tiny, multi-faceted eyes, its neck bending in an unnatural way. She must have been downwind too, because it stank.

Nick's remaining hand shot out and pulled her into the narrow slot between two damp stone walls. "Follow me."

"No problem," Skeet muttered, glancing up as the light disappeared for a moment, then reappeared. "Hope you know where this goes."

Nick didn't bother to answer. The dampness in the air caught in the back of her throat. Mould, mushrooms, dead things.

Jaared entered the passage at a run and was right behind her. "Ready when you are, Nick."

"They haven't followed us yet," Nick threw back over his shoulder.

The sounds of her breath and their running feet were too loud for her to hear anything else. Skeet hoped Nick's hearing was better than hers.

"Nick, I think there's two in here now," Jaared said.

"I can hear them."

A loud crunching sound came from behind them and the passageway thrummed as something heavy hit the floor. Keening filled the thick air, a 'sound' stabbing through her head.

Then silence.

"What was that?" Skeet said out loud.

"Shh…" Nick breathed ahead of her, just above a whisper.

She could feel it then. Something was ahead of them in the narrow conduit. The light dimmed, like something huge passing overhead.

Then the chill set in.

The already cold air turned icy, her breath a cloud in front of her. She ran into Nick's back, stopped short. Quickly she put her hand behind her and caught Jaared in the chest before he did the same.

Despair washed over her with the freezing atmosphere. Skeet wanted to fall to her knees, but Jaared held her up. "Steady…be ready…to move."

"What the fuck's that?" she gasped.

Time slowed. A dark figure stood in the passage ahead of them as feelings of hopelessness permeated her body.

Jaared pushed past her and removed something from his belt. With an overhand throw worthy of a baseball player, he threw what looked like a rock at the thing.

A flash of bright incandescence filled the narrow corridor, leaving afterimages on her retinas.

With a piercing howl, the creature vanished and the raw emotions flooding over her snapped off.

"Run!" Jaared yelled.

So she did, following Nicholas to the end of the passage and out into a quiet suburban street.

"Left!"

Zagging left, the weight of the Mossberg comforting in her hands, Skeet followed Nick's back past quiet and well-appointed houses. No traffic either. Odd.

But nothing seemed to be following them, either.

At the end of the street, Nick went right and so did she.

Jaared was at her side, not even breathing hard. Not bad for a hundred-and-seventy-year-old.

"I don't like this," he muttered. "We can't have lost them so easily."

Nick dropped back so they were running down the quiet streets three abreast. Not good, tactically, but useful for communicating. "I think they are regrouping…I can't sense much more than a presence behind us."

"Great. How far we running?" Skeet asked, starting to feel the pace.

"Not far now – we've got another surprise set up for them near the school."

"A school? Great. Hope everyone's gone home for the day."

"Don't worry, school's out." He smiled. "Another twenty-four hours and we go to the plan."

Somehow she wasn't reassured. A scrape behind her caught her ear. Sounded like claws on asphalt.

"That sound like claws to you?"

Jaared glanced behind them and she followed his gaze. A dim glow was visible in the distance.

"Yep, looks like another hellhound," Jaared confirmed.

Great.

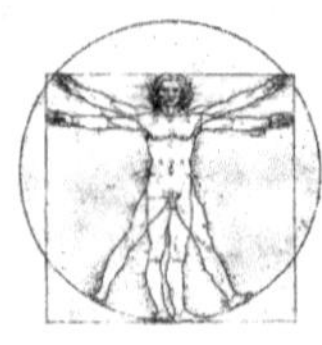

Me and Mrs, Mrs Jones...

Jonesy woke up with a snort. His shoebox flat was dark, but that could easily be down to forgetting to open the blinds.

He groped for his voda and it obligingly lit up, displaying the time. *08.53.*

Morning, then. Groaning, he rolled over, his t-shirt and sweatpants sticking to him with all the secretions of sleep.

Finding the edge of his futon, he sat up and placed his head in his hands until the throbbing ceased. That was the thing about those pills, the comedown was a bitch.

With no idea how long he sat there, he slid his bottom until he was perched on the edge of the pad. Aching in every joint, he slowly found his knees, then pushed himself off the floor with his hands, staggering as he did so. He stutter-walked to the shower cube, stripping off the damp clothes on the way.

The icy needles of spray shocked him further awake.

"Shit!"

They also reminded him he had a 9.30 appointment with the Inspector General.

"I'd really rather have a face peel with no anaesthetic followed by a lemon juice facial," he muttered to himself.

Finishing his abbreviated shower, he stumbled through the apartment looking for (relatively) clean clothes to put on.

He pulled on his usual black jeans, topping them off with a vintage black Red Dwarf t-shirt with the Jupiter Mining Corporation logo in it.

"Probably just as well the one that says 'Smeg Head' is in the wash."

The IG didn't have much of a sense of humour.

It was all Sen's fault.

He'd reported Jonesy's initial finding to the IG, so now the IG wanted to hear it from the horses…well, Jonesy's, mouth.

Cursing again, he pushed the tab to tighten up his black Reeboks. He paused to run some gel through his hair, making sure the top stuck up before pulling the rest back into a loose tail at his neck and clipping it with a silver faux-alligator clip to hold it together. For a long moment he debated taking another of the wonder pills, before deciding he couldn't afford the downtime.

Jonesy took a last look around the flat and grabbed his courier bag, slamming his tablet into it on the way to the door and sprinted for the stairs.

Jonesy's modified-for-hydrogen-cells Harley Davidson Sportster got him from the wrong side of Clapham into the City in twenty minutes.

The motorcycle actually had the soundtrack of an original Flathead, which was clever enough to sound like he was accelerating or slowing down. It must have been convincing, as he'd been stopped more than once by concerned officers who were under the impression he could afford the fines for using petrol.

Hell, he couldn't even afford the petrol.

Jonesy slotted the bike into a parking cubby under Company House. He'd bought the bike with his first – and only – success money; he'd written a routine the Company liked, which they bought and then offered him a job.

He stopped to wipe a bit of road dirt off the petrol tank with a rag before remembering he was almost late for his meeting with the IG. Stuffing the rag into the gap under the seat, he turned and ran to the lift.

Well, almost ran because as he turned, he collided with another person.

"Ooofff," they said.

"Sorry, sorry," he muttered as he checked his bag before continuing his dash for the elevator.

"Yeah, I'm fine," a voice said.

"Good."

"That was sarcasm." He just about registered that the person behind the voice was female.

Jonesy looked back over his shoulder. "Oh. No, really, I'm sorry." He stopped. "Bella?"

The petite woman with jet-black hair stared back at him through large black-framed glasses. "Jonesy? What the fuck? When did you start working for the Company?"

He grinned with one side of his face. "Since they offered me a job in cybercrimes. You?"

Bella adjusted her glasses and frowned. "Well, since I finished Uni – I'm an analyst working with the legal department."

Jonesy nodded. "Oh yeah, you studied law, didn't you?" His voda pinged. "Shit. Look, I've got to go see the IG – fancy meeting up for a beer later?"

"The IG? My, you do travel in rarefied company." Hesitation. "Yeah, what the hell. I've got nowhere to be." She walked toward him pulling her voda out of her bag before bumping it against the one in his hand. "Call me about one and we'll get some lunch."

A grin creeping onto his face, Jonesy couldn't help it. "You look good, Bella." His voda pinged again. "Shit."

"That seems to be your favourite word," she drawled. "Go on, you'll be late – or rather, lat*er*. And you don't want to keep the IG waiting."

"No, right – call you later." Jonesy rushed for the lift again.

"Later!"

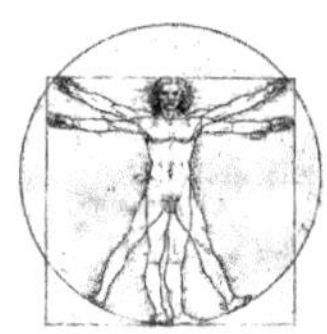

YOU JUST CAN'T GET THE STAFF

My skullphone goes as we settle down for the day. It's Adams.

"Make it quick, Adams," I snap, running on fumes.

"Yes, boss. Good morning boss, how're you?"

"Adams..."

He can hear the threat in my voice, obviously. "Sorry, sorry. I think I know what that thing is you've come into contact with. I had to look through the library's grimoires. I thought it might be in the *Corpus hermeticum*, but it wasn't, then I looked in Agrippa's *Three Books of Occult Philosophy,* but no luck there either. So I tried the *Book of Simon the Magician...*"

"Adams! I don't care where you found it, just tell me what you found!"

It sounds like he drops his flimsy notes. "Uh, sure boss, sure." More scrabbling. "Right. I think it's a Sin Eater."

"And?"

"Uh, right. Originally intended to take on the sins of a person or a household by eating and drinking – usually over the dead body of the person whose sins were being absolved."

Weird. "How does that apply to now?"

"Well, the ritual was presumed to die out in the early twentieth century, but I found some annotations on the *Book of Simon*...nevermind...suggesting one or more of the creatures who performed this ritual transformed somehow. That sucking sensation is their attempt to remove the 'sin' from anyone in their vicinity."

"That's great Adams, but how do we kill it? Those blessed rune stones seem to have some effect, but it keeps coming back; we're down to three."

"Kill it...let's see..." I can hear him breathing heavily. "Uh, it doesn't say...wait, *peruro*...consume...waste...inflame...got it! You'll have to burn it with holy fire!"

I grind my teeth. So bright, yet so dumb. "Yeah? And where do I get this from?"

"Oh. It doesn't say."

"Adams, send me some more blessed stones and call me back when you have something I can use." I terminate the connection.

When I turn around, Skeet's smiling at me from her station by the window of the warehouse we chose for our daylight hours. "Adams?"

"How could you tell?" I'm still grumpy from the call.

"Yeh get a particular tone to yer voice when you're speaking to him." The smile broadens. "I've never heard ya use it with anyone else!"

I guess it's true. "Adams has a particular talent in being able to wind me up."

"So I noticed."

"He thinks that thing's a 'sin eater', but his only advice for killing it was to burn it with 'holy fire', whatever that means." I push a crate against a wall and settle on it, leaning back against the bricks. "You okay with the first watch?"

Skeet nods. "Yep. You catch some shuteye – I think you kin use it."

"Thanks." Suddenly I feel all of my one hundred and seventy years. I close my eyes and the world fades around me.

I lost my eyes in the Korean conflict. Truman called it a 'police action', although I don't exactly know who were the police and who were the bad guys. I guess we were the cops.

The day I lost my eyes, I was part of a Special Forces advance party on patrol near Pyongyang in the northern part of the country. It's north and west of Seoul. Or it was before the North Koreans started that stupid atomic exchange.

Air support was dropping cluster bombs on northern troops, hoping to demoralise them before our main troops advanced. I could have told them it wasn't going to work, but they didn't ask me.

Special Forces were a fledgling group then – we didn't officially exist – and the members weren't necessarily the cream of the U.S. military machine. But we were pretty good at what we did.

Our mission was to scout out the enemy positions and report back for targeted air-strikes before the main force moved up; we didn't have a lot of time.

"Keats, take point," the Lieutenant orders. 'Keats' is me in another incarnation – I had a thing for the poets at one point.

I move up to the front and start moving slowly through the undergrowth.

We haven't heard an explosion for a while and that worries me. I can hear rustling and skittering in the bushes around me, probably lizards or mice. Something that lives in the jungle, anyway.

In the next fifteen minutes, we probably move fifty yards toward the enemy through thick ground cover. The quiet is beginning to annoy me. It's definitely unnerving my mates.

"Why's it so quiet? Kesler hisses at me. I don't even look at him; he wants to draw enemy fire, that's fine with me.

Parting the brush in front of me, I realise there's a Communist patrol just ahead, obviously pulled out of their foxholes in the lull. They're milling around. No discipline.

I raise my hand behind me and the patrol stops, their total silence impressive, even to me. Weapons are already at hand, so no futzing about cocking anything or making unnecessary noise. I feel, rather than hear, the six others move into position flanking me. I push my M3 through the gap in front of me and sight on the one I think is the leader. One of the benefits of working with the same crew for the best part of a year was I can tell when my boys are ready.

The report from my rifle is almost after the target's head explodes. Within a couple of seconds, the entire troop is down, no resistance offered.

No one moves. I can't see any other combatants and lack of return fire suggests we're done here.

I step forward into the open and move my rifle from side to side, covering possible targets.

The rest of my squad joins me. Mick raises a zippo to his cigarette next to me. With a single swipe, I knock it out of his mouth before he gets it lit. "You wanna get us killed?" I hiss.

Mick glares back. "Ain't no gooks 'round here, Keats," he said in a low voice.

"Don't have to be – they can smell burning tobacco, moron."

"Surprised they can't smell his body odour," Sylvester the goofball added.

I smile. "Yeah, he's getting a bit ripe..."

Mick's glare didn't go away as he moved away from me toward the edge of the clearing.

I turned to Sylvester. "Come on, we need to check for any liv–"

My words were cut off by the whistle of a cluster bomb. Headed our way.

"Incoming!" I shouted, or tried to shout.

Flash. Bang. Nothing.

I woke up in a field hospital three weeks later with massive head trauma and both my eyes gone.

I walked out of the field hospital after six weeks and disappeared into the jungle.

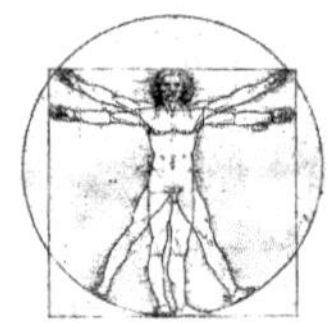

CNN: Today, mudslides buried the village of Moalboal in Cebu, the Philippines. A lone survivor has been found so far, tending his flock on the hills nearby.

No, I ain't sightseeing, I'm here to kill things

Sitting on the edge of a dusty workbench, Skeet watched Jaared for a few moments before looking back through the grimy window. *Poor thing, all exhausticated from being chased by zombies and werewolves.* She smiled to herself and glanded some *snap* to stay sharp.

Last thing she needed to do was fall asleep on the job. Although that wasn't likely as cold as it was in the abandoned warehouse. Even with the portable gas heater Jaared had scrounged up somewhere. She pulled her leather jacket tighter around her and activated its passive warming circuit.

Nick had disappeared into the internal part of the depot once they'd established it was deserted – and unused. Probably didn't want them to know where he was sleeping. Well, not exactly, anyway.

So this is Edinburgh. Her visit had, so far, been lots of boredom punctuated with monsters and gunfire and adrenalin punching attacks.

"Huh."

Jaared stirred at her exhalation, but didn't surface entirely.

The view out of the dirty glass was the sort of disuse that seemed only possible in places like London or Edinburgh. Cracked concrete, straggly weeds, broken glass, a rusted out car probably abandoned when gas became more expensive than gold. She corrected herself mentally – not 'gas', 'petrol'.

Nothing was moving, so she pulled her pack over and dug around for the gun cleaning kit. Might as well do something useful.

Skeet stripped the Sig Sauer 229s down and cleaned them thoroughly before unloading and reloading the spare magazines and reloading the two she'd used running away from whatever those smelly, crawly things had been.

The night had been a nightmare, running from one location to the next, trying to keep one step ahead of the *things* following them and ostensibly trying to kill them. She'd used up all the shells in her bandolier and set about refilling it, then counting her remaining ammo. Not good, only about forty rounds of shotgun ammo left.

As Skeet broke down the Mossberg and started cleaning it, she hoped Jaared's plan was going to work.

Once the guns were clean and ready for action, Skeet used her voda to access local news.

Bizarrely, the running battle they'd conducted over the last 12 hours, through the edges of the leafy suburb of Morningside, was missing from the headlines. There wasn't even a mention of it on 'the news in brief' section. She checked local chatter on the 'boards and still nothing. Strange.

All that noise and no one mentioned it? Someone didn't want their little 'disagreement' on the news.

Skeet shivered in her leathers and blew on her cold hands. She gazed out the window at the grey day and the ruins of the yard and thought about her part in the plan for tonight, before checking the maps on her voda.

A girl scout is always prepared.

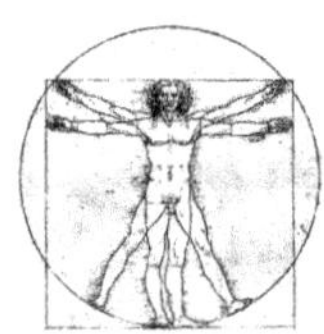

Never walk in dead men's shoes

Madeline opened her eyes and then blinked against the brightness. It was a warm summer day, sun beating down on her from the deep blue sky. She blinked again. Sunlight?

When she looked down, all she saw were gardens: large, extensive formal gardens. Something was familiar about it, but she couldn't think what.

"My lady, would you like a goblet of wine?"

Madeline turned and caught sight of the building behind her. It was the Palace. She smiled. I remember now.

"Of course, Louis, I would very much enjoy a goblet of that vintage you have been saving for today," she replied.

"I am only too pleased to give you your every desire," Louis XIV said, as he handed her the crystal goblet full of a burgundy vintage from his own vineyards.

Madeline put the goblet to her lips and tasted the wine. It was rich and tasted of sun and the deep soil of the region. "Lovely, your majesty. A fine vintage."

Louis smiled and sipped from his own goblet. "I am glad you like it. Will you be my guest for dinner this night? I am entertaining the Viscount of Montpelier and could use the companionship..."

"May I ask why, m'lord?"

Louis looked away, the smile lingering on his features. "He is a very dull man and I do not wish to be left alone with him!"

Madeline smiled. "Of course, m'lord. I live to serve," she replied with a bow.

Louis looked back with a sparkle in his eye. "I will not be mocked, Lady Madeline," he retorted with mock severity. "I inflict dire punishments on those who mock me," he finished, taking her hand and pulling her close.

"Really, highness, and what form do these 'punishments' take?" Madeline whispered as his face drew closer.

"You are about to find out, strumpet," he hissed. He pulled her close against him and kissed her on the lips, his hip thrust between hers. Madeline whimpered, suddenly wanting little else than to take the King to bed.

"Your highness," a voice said from across the garden.

Louis groaned, his thoughts obviously moving in tandem with her own. He released her and stepped back a half pace. "What is it, Lavasseur?"

"You are expected at the Bishop's chateau to discuss the disbursement of the assizes, m'Lord." The skinny clerk in his dark suit and grey wig stood formally awaiting the King's instruction.

Louis smiled thinly, obviously unimpressed with the task. "Tell the Bishop I will see him tomorrow once the Viscount of Montpelier has departed."

"Very good sir," the functionary replied.

"Now where was I?" the King asked in a hushed tone. "Oh yes, I remember now..."

Madeline's laugh was stifled by the King's lips.

Madeline came to her senses to see only the dimness of the dungeon. Dreams among the night folk were rare, their sleep more hibernation than actual rest.

Of course she remembered that day, the sun, the King, Versailles. And the Viscount of Montpelier.

Yes, she would never forget meeting that man – it was the day she met Le Boucher, her maker.

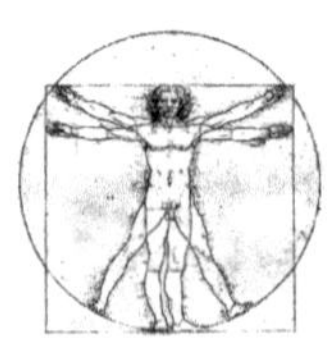

Man, I'm sooooo wasted!

The Inspector General was staring out across the Thames into Bermondsey when Jonesy arrived.

"You're late, Mr Jones."

"Yeah, sorry, sir – I-uh-I haven't been very well," Jonesy stuttered. The huge office seemed to take up most of the top level of Company House, with windowed walls on three sides. Plush carpets laid over solid wood flooring and expensive furniture gave it a classic feel. All it was missing was dark wood panelling on the...oh wait, it was on the fourth wall. Jonesy sighed, thinking of his tiny shoebox flat. The outer office where the IG's pleasant-if-firm secretary greeted those seeking an audience was at least twice the size of his flat. Sigh.

"Yet your location at the intended time of this meeting was in the underground car park." He consulted a large antique watch. "What could have taken you fifteen minutes?"

Jonesy decided not to tell him about the emergency stop he'd had to make in the toilet on the way up. "I'm sorry, sir..."

The IG waved him away, but didn't turn around. View was obviously too good. "Save it for someone who 'gives a shit', Mr Jones. Where are you on tracing this incursion?"

As it didn't seem to matter, Jonesy slumped into one of the uncomfortable chairs in front of the battleship-sized desk. Teak, if he didn't miss his guess.

"I've found a...I guess you'd call it a 'hole' in one of the subroutines that controls the maintenance schedule for the whole of Company House – it obviously allows access to the whole of Central via a Thompson-Didack protocol..." He stopped as the hand waved at him again.

"You lost me at subroutines, Mr Jones." The IG finally turned around, his piercingly blue eyes raking Jonesy's skin as they took in his dishevelled appearance. "More importantly, have you determined the 'who' behind the incursion?"

Jonesy shook his head. "Sen will be looking into that, sir."

"Have you plugged this 'hole'?"

"No sir. I *am* monitoring it for further activity, but it's been pretty quiet of late." He consulted his tablet. "I'm waiting for Commander Sen's instructions before I authorise the team to close the access."

The steely eyes that had faced down adversaries for more than thirty years bored through his until Jonesy was certain they'd pierced the back of his skull. "I'm afraid Commander Sen is otherwise indisposed at the moment – leave of absence. John Tolliver will be picking up in his absence. Once he's identified the culprit or culprits, close the hole."

"But Commander Sen..."

Hand raised, the IG turned back to the view. "That's my order, Mr Jones. And Mr Jones?"

"Yes?"

"Next time, I expect you to be suitably attired – regardless of your aptitude for computers, sloppy 'geek' wear is not acceptable in my office."

"Yes sir."

"Dismissed."

Jonesy grabbed his tablet off the chair and stuffed it into his bag before bolting from the room.

He waited until he was on his bike to try Sen again. The Commander wasn't going to like this.

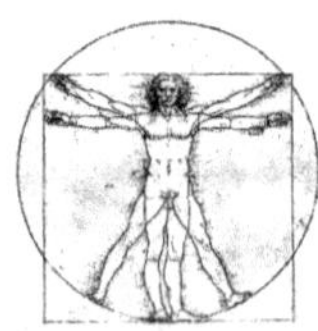

Now that's what I call a Renaissance man

The Artist opened his notebook and leaned back in his chair. The cool night air stung his throat as he rubbed his eyes. Fragrant smoke from a wall censer drifted across the room, punctuating the smell of the garden beyond his terrace.

The calculations had to be right. Whatever was causing the eruptions seemed too well placed to be merely the result of natural phenomena. He leant over the table and began adding to his notes.

"Master?"

He spoke without turning around. "What is it?"

"Your dinner is ready in the dining room."

"I'll be along shortly." He went to open his journal again. "Wait – bring me wine."

"Yes sir."

There was a chuckle from the darkness just beyond his terrace. "Ah, wine. It has been some time since I drank a good wine."

The Artist didn't look up from his notes. "You only have to ask." He waved at the other chair. "Please. Join me."

His servant appeared with wine and two goblets. A good thing they were used to his eccentric ways.

When the owner of the voice sat in the other chair, the Artist didn't look up or acknowledge him, writing precisely in his journal in his usual style, mirror writing from right to left.

His guest cleared his throat after taking a long pull at his wine. "Well? Have you got it?"

The scratching of the quill pen continued unabated, the question unanswered.

Slamming the goblet on the tablet with enough force to rattle the inkpot and slop some of the remaining wine on the table, his guest lost patience. "I asked you a polite question, my friend – have you got the item I have paid you well for?"

Still without looking up from his notes, the Artist waved at a package on the sideboard. "It is over there." Finally he put the pen down and looked up at his guest. "I do wish you had more patience to appreciate the finer qualities of life, Monsieur."

"I am patient, my friend – it is my Master and the Council who are not patient." He picked up the parcel wrapped in brown paper and hefted it.

"I wouldn't shake it too much, Monsieur," the Artist counselled. "You might not like the result and the Council would need a new lackey." He gestured at the other chair. "Come, Trevanian, finish your wine and I will tell you how it should be used."

Trevanian Le Coq, Steward for the Council of Seven Kings, looked at the old man and contemplated just leaving. He disliked the Artist but couldn't quite put his finger on why. In the end it was easier to just sit down and finish his wine.

"Very well, tell me how to use the serum," he said after sipping from his goblet again.

The Artist steepled his fingers for a moment, obviously contemplating something. Or he was looking at Trevanian in a such a way as to make him blush. Eventually he picked up his wine and took a long pull at the red liquid.

"It should be administered at every full moon, at the height of the moon."

Trevanian nodded. "In what quantities?"

"A small spoon mixed in a goblet of wine, but I must warn you: do not exceed this amount or you may have other problems." The Artist took another sip of wine. "I cannot tell you what these may be, but from what I have read, it will not be pleasant."

"In what way?"

"It could destroy the world."

Shaken, Trevanian sipped his wine before carefully placing it on the table in front of him. "Are you certain?"

The Artist smiled, but there was little humour in it. "Of that, I am certain."

Picking up the package carefully, Trevanian decided it was time to go. "Thank you – I will convey your instructions to the Keeper."

"There is the small matter of my payment."

Trevanian nodded. "The estate is yours and you will receive one thousand francs per month, as agreed."

The Artist inclined his head. "Good night, Trevanian."

"G-good night," he stuttered.

By the time he'd left the terrace, the Artist was scribbling in his journal again.

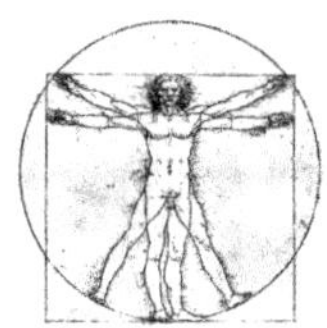

THE PHONE ALWAYS RINGS WHEN I'M TRYING TO SLEEP

I manage an hour and a half, maybe two hour's sleep before my phone goes. Ow. My neck hurts from the uncomfortable angle of the wall I've been resting against.

"Sen." I open my eyes to the grey half-light of the warehouse. Skeet's not by the window, or her guns, probably doing a perimeter sweep.

The sound of rushing air fills my ears. "Commander?"

"Yes Jonesy – what have you got for me?"

"The IG's pissed at me."

I smile. "That's a condition I'm familiar with Jonesy. What's he want?"

"He wants Contractor Tolliver to take over finding the people who put the trap door in – as you're 'indisposed' – and then he wants me to close it."

Shit. "Did you tell him about the possible second hole?" I find my cigarettes and extract one from the pack before lighting it with my Zippo.

"No, I didn't get to it."

"Jonesy!"

"I know, I know – he didn't want to hear it!"

From first-hand experience I recognise, all too well, the IG's way of working. I call up the orders logged in Central on my HUD and amend them slightly. I can't cross the IG, but I can make sure he doesn't do something too stupid.

"Okay, let Tolliver find the hacker and his mates and get your team to close the hole. In the meantime, I've amended your order docket to include you looking for more back doors."

"Right."

"The last thing we need is the IG celebrating closure of one hole while there's more operating under our noses." My eyes wander around the warehouse. "Two things Jonesy: be careful and keep me updated."

"Got it, Commander. Will do."

I can still hear wind in the background. "Where's that wind coming from?"

"Sorry Commander, I'm driving at the moment – motorcycle."

"Ah. I haven't been on one of those in years…Later Jonesy."

"Okay, bye Commander."

Skeet wanders back in, the Mossberg casually held in both hands. "Work?"

"Yep. I do sometimes wonder what they'd do without me." I toss the cigarette on the floor and step on it.

Smiling, she glances out the window at the forecourt again before wandering over to sit on the crate next to me. She leans the Mossberg against the brick, but within reach. "You okay?"

I nod. "Yeah, bit of a crick in my neck, though."

"Here, turn that way."

I swivel on the crate so my back is toward her. Her long fingers pull my jacket down far enough to expose my shoulders. Those fingers start kneading my shoulder muscles.

"Mmmm…that's good," I say, "Don't stop."

"Okay, big boy." Her thumbs follow the muscles up into my neck and I groan as she finds a knot.

There's a noise outside.

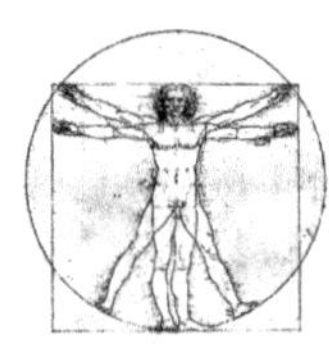

AIN'T IT A BITCH

The shotgun almost leapt into Skeet's hands. In two long strides, she was at the window.

A large grey panel van had pulled onto the forecourt. It was so old and rust-riddled if you hadn't seen the place before hand you'd almost think it had been abandoned there, too.

"What is it?" Jaared asked softly, shrugging his leather coat back up, then checking his Glock.

"Grey van, looks like one occupant." She couldn't see anyone in the passenger seat, but it didn't mean there weren't more in the back.

"Human?"

"Near as I can tell."

"Sounds like Finn." He was beside her in a second, peering through the grimy glass. "Yep, that's his heartbeat."

"I hate it when you do that," Skeet said testily. "Who's Finn?"

Jaared chuckled. "Sorry, habit of ninety years of blindness." He walked over to the barricaded priest's door set into the larger garage door and slipped the cross brace out of the brackets. "Finn's a friend – and you two's ticket out of here."

Skeet watched a thin, stooped old man climb down out of the van and approach the door. "He's at the door."

"I know."

Three short raps sounded on the wood, followed by two longer knocks.

Jaared slipped the latch and pulled the door open wide enough to admit 'Finn'. He was younger than she'd thought, although he seemed to walk with a perpetual stoop. Deep-set eyes under a shock of greying hair scanned the room for a few seconds.

"Sen."

"Finn." Jaared gestured to the room. "Welcome to our humble abode."

Finn emitted a single 'huff' in answer before his eyes locked on Skeet. "Who's the broad?"

"That's Skeet – and I'd be careful what you call her, she's heavily armed." Jaared smiled. "Skeet, this is Finn. If all goes according to plan, I think you'll be firm friends."

From her spot by the window, Skeet smiled her alligator grin. "Pleased t'meetcha." She glanced back out the window, but nothing seemed to have changed.

"When we moving out?" Finn rasped as he lit a cigarillo. A spasm of coughing made him contract further, until he was almost bent double. When he stopped coughing, his face puce, he straightened up and took a drag on the cigarillo.

"Those things'll kill you." Jaared lit a cigarette of his own with a deft flick of his lighter. "We won't be moving until sundown." He glanced at Skeet before looking back at Finn. "One of our party has 'special needs'."

Finn nodded, smoke ringing his head. "Fucking vamps. Can't stand 'em." His vehemence startled Skeet.

Jaared tsked. "Careful now, Finn, one would almost think you were a racist." He blew a perfect smoke ring. "Besides, I'm paying you enough that you should be able to ignore those tendencies for a few days."

Skeet had taken an instant dislike to the man. She also noted Jaared didn't tell Finn Nick was his son – guess that wasn't common knowledge. It wasn't down to her to enlighten the man.

"You 'spect me to hang around until sundown?" Finn demanded. "I got things to do, Sen."

Jaared put an arm around his bony shoulders and leaned closer. "Listen Finn: you came recommended to me." He shrugged. "If you can't do the work, say so now and I'll get Vaughn in on the job."

"Vaughn? That sheep-shagger? He can't piss in a straight line!"

Shrugging again, Jaared's smile had turned very sharp. "Well, needs must, you know." He walked away from Finn, winking at Skeet once his back was to the irascible man. He sat back down on the crate.

Skeet gave the old guy credit, he didn't back down immediately; showed some backbone. After a few more puffs of the cigarillo, he dropped it to the concrete and ground it to pulp under one toe. He gave a heavy sigh. "Alright, Sen, alright." His mouth set in what looked like a permanent frown. "Just wish you'da told me there was vamps involved."

Jaared's expression remained neutral. "And would you have turned down the job, Finn?"

"I'da thought about it, maybe…"

"But you can't afford to turn down work just now with Jimmy Hay breathing down your neck for last month's vig, now can you?"

Flustered, the old man tried to bluster. "What the hell's Jimmy Hay to you?"

Jaared shook his head. "Nothing, but I know you owe him a lot of money. What happened? Lose on the horses?"

It looked like this would push Finn away. "Feck off, Sen. Don't need your money…"

"Yes, you do." Jaared got that unfocused look that said he was accessing Central. "Looks like your wife's cancer treatment is going to be a lot more expensive than you thought."

Open-mouthed, Finn gaped at Jaared. Skeet could almost seem him crumple in the washed-out light from the window. Never play poker with someone who holds all the cards.

""Okay, Sen, okay." He fumbled another cigarillo out of his pocket and lit it with shaking hands. "I'll do it, but that don't mean I gotta like it."

"You won't even know he's there."

"So we wait, then?"

"Actually, I need you to go get a couple of things for me." Jaared stood up again. "Oh, and some more cigarettes, as well."

"Whaddya need?"

Jaared handed him a list scribbled on what looked like the back of a fag packet. "Just a few small items. I'm sure a man with your connections can source them for me."

Finn scanned the list before looking back at Jaared. "You gotta be kidding me, Sen – what the hell's 'belladonna'?"

Jaared chuckled. "Ask your pharmacist friend, Finn." He put an arm around Finn. "I'm sure he can supply it for me."

Not looking reassured, Finn stuffed the list in a pocket. "Right. Need me for anything else?"

"No. I expect you to be back by sundown." Jaared took another cigarette from his pack. "Or else I'll have to call Jimmy Hay."

At this, Finn's jaw locked together. Skeet could hear his teeth grinding together. Without a word, he stomped over to the door and let himself out.

Skeet followed him, re-locking the door behind him and slipping the cross-brace back into the brackets.

Once the van had pulled off, Skeet returned to the crate and sat down next to Jaared.

"You pushed him pretty hard."

Jaared turned away from the distance he was staring into and smiled. "If I hadn't, I couldn't guarantee he wouldn't sell you and Nick out first opportunity he got."

"So, you were just looking out for us? Not enjoying it?" For some reason this mattered to Skeet.

"Oh, I enjoyed it a bit, but it was way too easy to punch his buttons."

Hmpf. "Right." She looked away from him a moment before she felt her gaze drawn back to him. "What do you want us to do, anyway?"

"Well, Nick knows the plan, but it can't hurt you knowing the details as well."

So he told her.

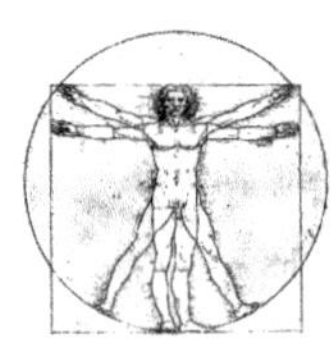

ARE YOU THE HUNTER OR THE HUNTED?

It hadn't been difficult for him to follow them to the warehouse.

But why daes nae one else see them? he asked himself. *They're burning a path through Edinburgh like a turd on a hot plate.*

They could handle themselves, that much was obvious, with the help of some blessed items. He was particularly interested in those rounds they used on the hellhounds.

The girl was an interesting addition to this little soiree – and she looked pretty good in leather, too.

Shaking his head, he sniffed at the breeze coming off the Firth. Something was coming, but he couldn't tell what. It was big.

As the trio seemed to have settled in for the day, he decided to do the same, settling down on the roof across the way. He trusted his wards to wake him should anything 'interesting' happen.

He was awakened from a doze about mid-afternoon by a shot on the warehouse forecourt.

A courier in a motorcycle helmet was lying on the ground next to an electric motorbike. He shook his head – they just weren't the same without a petrol engine.

The man in black came out of the warehouse fast and dragged the prone figure into the shadows of the door. For some reason, he returned for the bike.

Glancing both ways down the narrow street, he saw no one, nor could he sense anyone watching. Just a precaution, then.

"What are yeh doin' now?" One eye on the warehouse entrance, he checked his weapons and ran a rag through the barrel of his shotgun. He hadn't used it recently, but it paid to be prepared. No point in checking the double Rugers on his hips, but he did anyway.

It was only a matter of minutes before a tight cluster of figures slipped down the alley, trying to use the walls of the buildings as shelter. They were hard to see in the dim light.

"Company, ya brazen feckers," he muttered.

The ones he was watching obviously knew, as he saw them leave the warehouse a few moments later by the back, heading down another branch of the canal. The entry team wasn't going to find them very quickly.

Enough glow from a nearby building illuminated one of the figures bent down to the ground, apparently sniffing.

Tracker. Shite.

He fumbled in the pouch at his waist and pulled out a heavy ball wrapped in cloth. Unsure why he was helping the trio, he overhanded it towards the crouching figure.

It landed just in front of its face and exploded.

The tracker howled when the powder hit its face, clawing at its eyes.

One pain-in-the-arse down, three to go. He unlimbered a hollow tube from his back and with three well-placed darts, took care of the rest.

Wha' the hell am I doin'?

He reslung the blowpipe and moved along the roof to the junction with the next building, following the unlikely trio.

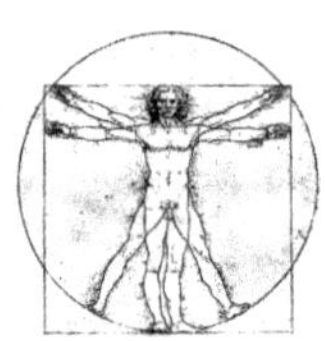

Oh, is that what it's for?

As sundown nears, I check my weapons again.

Adams phones. "Commander, the courier should be with you shortly."

"What?"

"I said, the courier with your stuff should be with you any moment," he replies.

"How do you know where we are? I was planning on collecting the package somewhere more public, that's all."

"The Company is tracking you all the time – I can probably pinpoint your location to about three feet." There's a pause and even over the skullphone I can hear him scratching. "Didn't you know that?"

I knew that, of course I knew that. "Why are you scratching, Adams? It sounds like you're using sandpaper."

"Got to close to a bug Rab was trying an exorcism charm on and it exploded on me."

That's an image I don't need in my head. "Thanks for that – I *will* have nightmares now."

Skeet hisses, "There's a bike outside."

I nod. "Yeah, apparently Adams sent us a courier. Got to go, Adams. Thanks for the kit."

"No problem Commander. Anything else, let me know."

I reholster my Glock, go to the doors and peer through the dirty glass carefully. A figure stands next to a bike in a helmet unstrapping a package from the rack.

"I don't like a courier knowing where we are," Skeet says behind me.

Reminding her Central always knows where I am probably isn't a good thing. "Leave it to me." I open the door a crack. "Leave the package on the ground."

"I can't do that – needs your thumbprint," the figure in the helmet calls.

I shake my head, consulting Central. There's a flash in my HUD. "I'll give you verbal authorisation: code Beta-one-one-three-six-oh-gamma."

The helmet nods. "Okay, roger that." He puts the package on the ground about ten feet from the door. I say 'he' but it could be anything under that helmet.

"Fine, now go."

There's just the slightest hesitation before a large handgun appears in his hand. "I don't think so, Commander."

The Glock in my hand fires one shot and the courier's on the ground. I look around for signs of backup and throw open the door. "Cover me!"

I can hear Skeet follow me out the door as I scramble over to the body on the ground. Nothing. I put the gun and what I hope is Adam's package on the courier's back and drag him toward the door.

"He dead?" Skeet asks.

"No, stun round. Get him inside while I get the bike."

I race back to the bike and wheel it up the drive and through the door Skeet's opened for me. It slams behind me with a 'clang'.

I prop the bike up on its stand and turn around. The stunned courier is lying on the concrete, face up. Skeet walks over to the body and, after releasing a chin strap, slips the helmet off.

"Huh. It's a girl."

Sure enough, long dark hair flows out of the helmet around an elfin face. The eyes stare glassily at nothing, after effects of the stunner. I pick up the pistol. "Hmmm, Makarov – that's got to be an antique."

"What the hell's she doing with a museum piece like that?"

"Good question. Shall we find out?" I pull a small leather wallet out of my belt pouch. Three ampoules glitter in the dim light. I select one and inject a five mil dose into her neck.

With a gasp, she sits straight up and for a second I think Skeet's going to shoot her. "Wha' the fuck?!" Interesting. Edinburgh accent. It comes out 'fook'.

I hold up a hand. "Stun round. If I wanted you dead, we wouldn't be having this conversation." I motion to Skeet. "And if you don't tell us who sent you, she will shoot you in the head."

The girl's eyes swivel to Skeet. "Fook you!"

I sigh. "Okay, we'll do this the hard way." I select another ampoule from my kit. "Ten mils of truthtell should do it." She flinches away as I lean over with the injection nozzle pointed at her.

"Get away from me!"

I shrug. "Two choices: tell us what we want to know or she shoots you." I smile. "You obviously know who I am, so shooting you is always an option."

She blanches, so yes, she knows me. "I was told to shoot her," she nods at Skeet. "Then tie you up and wait for the recovery team."

"And?"

"And what?"

"Who hired you?"

Now she shakes her head. "No idea – big white guy in a bar offered me three hundred to bring that package and the rest yeh know."

I consider her for a moment before selecting the final vial. "Fine. When's the recovery team arrive?"

She checks the old watch on her wrist. "Any time – didn't think I'd have to wait this long, yeh ken?"

Skeet steps over to the window and rubs at the grime. Shakes her head.

I nod and press the ampoule against her neck. She jumps and then collapses. A sedative. "Probably time to go," I say out loud.

"Yes, Jaared, there's a group of four men coming down the lane." Nick's voice behind me doesn't startle me. I'd felt him arrive while the girl was protesting.

"Good thing this place has a back door," Skeet says. "What about Finn? He's bringing stuff we need…"

"We'll have to hook up later – if he's not the one that set us up, of course." I open the package and bizarrely, it's the supplies Adams sent us. "Here, take these." I hand her a few of the blessed shells and some kind of charm on a necklace. Might help, who knows?

Nick's at my side now and shakes his head at the ward. "Messes with my head." He takes a handful of the blessed bullets for his handgun.

I put the rest of the supplies in my pouch and slip the ward over my neck. There's a tingling then it just goes warm on my skin. I clip a bead mic to my throat and hand them to the others. "So we can keep it as quiet as possible."

"Time to go, boss," Skeet says from the door. "I can see one, figure the rest of them aren't far behind."

Yes, time to go. I need to call Jonesy and see what he knows about my positioning system.

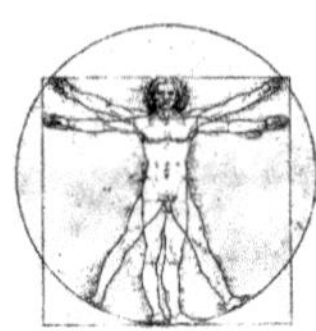

WASTING TIME IN BRISBANE

Jonesy's voda rang just as he opened the pizza box. Siciliana, nice. He closed the box and picked up the phone.

It's Sen. "Commander – I was going to ring you..."

"No time, Jonesy." It sounded like he was running, judging from the footfalls and slight breathiness of his voice. "What do you know about the tracker Central has on me?"

"I helped with the upgrades about six months ago – it keeps track of you via a modified GPS system and updates every ten seconds."

He flinched at what sounded like gunfire. He lifted the box lid again and pulled out a piece of pizza.

"Right. Can anyone besides Central access my location?"

Jonesy shrugged. "With clearance, yeah, but after the recent incursion, I can't promise your location's not compromised." He took a bite of pizza and chewed. "Why?"

"No time to explain – can you turn it off?"

"What? Central?"

"No, Mr Jones, just my location monitor."

"Oh, right." He thought about it a moment. "It's probably a violation of some kind..."

"Don't worry about that right now...can you do it?"

Jonesy nodded again. "I think so. But what about..."

"Just do it, dammit, Jonesy – I don't have time to argue." More gunfire. "I'll also put in a report that I asked you to do it, to cover your ass. Now, gotta go, I'm a bit busy just now."

And the connection cut out.

"Bye, Commander."

Jonesy contemplated the slice of pizza in his hand for a few seconds, took another bite of cheese, ham and mushroom, then jacked in.

With some retro punk blasting in his headphones, it was a matter of a few minutes searching to locate the location subroutine in the Grid. Finding Sen's part was a bit trickier and took him a good half an hour to turn off.

He could almost hear the warning klaxons in the background. A big danger sign appeared in front of his eyes, but he wiped it away with a modified version of the Commander's clearance.

"It's his idea, anyway," he muttered, his voice loud in the headphones.

Jonesy tidied up, camouflaging the change to the system as best he could with a bit of code borrowed from an accounting subroutine. No one would see it and it shouldn't affect the performance of the other trackers.

"There," he breathed, jacking back out to find the cold pizza beside him.

He shrugged and picked up another slice.

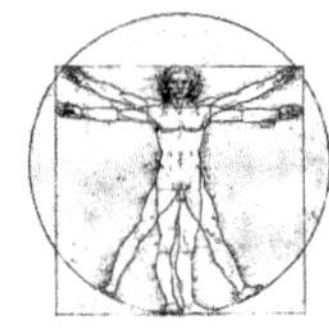

I AM A PASSENGER, AND I RIDE

Lucien stepped down from the door of the private plane onto the tarmac. The wind off the Firth was cold.

The welcoming committee, two women, got out of the limo which had parked near the plane.

He sniffed. Human. Just as well as he'd already fed on the plane, otherwise they might not have made it to their destination.

One opened the door for him. Neither spoke.

Strictly speaking, he didn't need the car as he could, quite easily, get to where he was going without it. It was a luxury he had become accustomed to, like the private jet.

A man he assumed to be his contact was sitting in the back seat.

"Hello," Lucien purred as he slid easily into the limo. The driver closed the door behind him.

The man nodded. "I'm Chambers." He didn't offer his hand, which suited Lucien fine.

"Lucien de Foret." The man smelled musky, overly male. Probably some kind of shifter, but not a wolf...more like bear...

Silence fell over the occupants of the car. They were entering the outskirts of the city before Chambers spoke again.

"You know what you're supposed to do?"

The impertinence. Any other day he would have killed this little man, shifter or not.

Lucien tipped his head slightly, but didn't bother answering. It was simple: find Sen and his brat.

"You're to keep them alive."

"Of course."

"I can't give you his exact location – we lost track of him a little while ago. He was in Morningside last we knew."

Lucien didn't reply. Incompetence didn't deserve a response.

He ignored the little man for the rest of the ride, watching the passing scenery and thinking about his prey. He'd met Sen before, when he was working for Jacob Euonymus, although the man couldn't pick him out of a crowd, at least by sight. Lucien had killed the man's partner, so who knew? Sen had incapacitated him enough that he couldn't stop the man executing Euonymus.

Lucien had underestimated the man that time – something he wouldn't do again.

Wait...he smelled something familiar. His senses were hyperactive at the beginning of any hunt. This was no different.

"Stop the car," he hissed.

Chambers looked at him oddly. "Pull over, Peters."

The driver pulled the limo over at the first opportunity.

Lucien leapt out.

"Wait – where are you going?" Chambers called after him.

"To find Sen and the boy and bring them to you," Lucien spat. "My job."

"How will you know..."

"I'll find you, Chambers. Do not worry about that."

And with that he followed the scent he'd picked up in the car, disappearing into the dimness.

Chambers watched him vanish before nodding at Peters. "Go. He'll find us when he's got Sen."

Without a word, Peters pulled the car back into traffic.

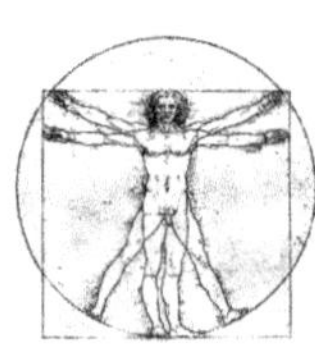

DON'T FOLLOW ME - I DON'T KNOW WHERE WE'RE GOING!

Skeet followed Jaared and Nick out the back door, the Mossberg in her hands. The darkness behind the warehouse was nearly complete. With one finger, she flipped her goggles to night vision and the darkness resolved into clearer walls, a tree and a path down to the canal. Jaared was darker blob in front of her, his coverall diffusing his heat signature to well below human warmth.

"Keep to the left path – we're looking for a gap in the fence about twenty metres down."

No response from Nick and Skeet didn't reply either. Unless absolutely necessary, they weren't going to be talking that much. Odd, there didn't seem to be any pursuit behind them.

The expected gap appeared before them and Nick scouted it quickly. *"All clear,"* he said before he ducked through to the other side.

There was gunfire, but it lasted only seconds. One of the benefits of superhuman speed or strength. Hard to tell from what she could hear.

"Really all clear, now."

Christ, the kid cracked a joke. Proximity to Jaared must be wearing down the dead-seriousness Nick had most of the time.

Jaared ducked through the fence with Skeet right on his heels, a last sweep of the towpath behind them not revealing anything more dangerous than a heron standing at the canal's edge, one eye staring at her from across the water.

For a second, Skeet had the strange idea it was watching her.

Shaking it off, she turned back to the gap and followed Jaared.

* * *

Hours later, they settled down for the day in an abandoned shop just off Lothian Road. The night had been relatively quiet, a handful of encounters with more of the smelly things and one sighting of a hellhound. Pretty tame, all in all.

Still, Skeet and Jaared collapsed on the floor behind the dusty counter, out of sight through the large glass windows. Nick had taken himself to a tiny storeroom behind them for his daytime repose.

Skeet felt grubby after two days without a shower. The water was still on in the sink behind the counter. She sponged her exposed skin as best she could with a handful of dusty paper towels. It wasn't a hot shower in a proper hotel room at the Sheraton that was just around the corner from the shop, but it would have to do.

That done, she field stripped her Sigs and cleaned them thoroughly. She did the same for the shotgun then reloaded as best she could. "Damn, ammo's running low."

"Hmmm?" from beside her.

"Nothin', go back to sleep."

Jaared rolled over on his side and was asleep again in seconds.

Sigh. Skeet placed the gun to her side with her pistols in their harness just beyond. She settled back on the cardboard they'd placed on the floor for some padding. Chances were good they'd be fine – not likely anyone would come for them during the day; they hadn't so far.

This plan stuck in her throat. She didn't like being separated from Jaared, even if it got them what they wanted. And they still didn't know what they were dealing with.

Well, he'd survived this long…she sighed again and closed her eyes. Sleep wasn't far away.

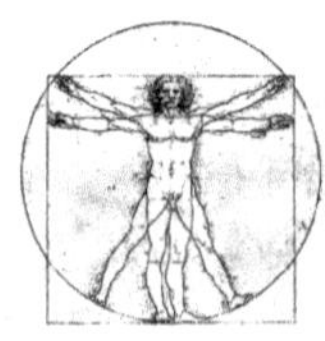

Madeline rested her head on the stone behind her. There was a ridge that seemed to poke a hole in her skull. Being over three hundred and fifty years old didn't make sitting in the same place for days any more comfortable.

She rearranged herself and flexed her mind. It was weak, the rat blood wasn't sufficient to give her powers the strength they normally had. Still, she had to try.

At first she felt nothing. The stone was cool beneath her. A mist seemed to fill her head. The more she pushed against it with her will, the more solid it became.

Ah, she thought, relaxing. Madeline willed herself to become as mist and it vanished. She could see a corridor, lined in stone. A silver-clad door was on her left, leading down into her dungeon. That didn't help – she knew where she was. No guard, though. Useful. But with that silver on the door, it might as well have been made of stone.

She turned her attention to the corridor and drifted along it. More doors, not all silver, some just wood or steel. Another staircase at the end led upward and she followed it up to a solid wooden door. Her mind flowed through the door like so much water and entered the ground floor level of the house. Madeline had already decided it was a house, built into the side of a hill, judging from the raw stone jutting from the wall of her dungeon.

The door opened into a well-appointed hallway, painted the historic green old houses tend to favour, not quite minty and not quite turquoise. A large mirror opposite the door to the lower level flashed her reflection for a moment. Did she imagine that?

A large guard stood next to the door – the rock giant she'd encountered before. They weren't known for their psychic abilities, so she was likely safe.

Further down the corridor an open door allowed her into a large room that was part study, part library. She was distracted by the twilight view across the gardens of Princes Street, with a partial view to her left, of Edinburgh's famous Castle.

"...I told you *not* to waste my hellhounds!"

Madeline's attention snapped to the two people in the room: one seated behind the desk, one standing in front of it.

"W-we didn't have a choice, s-s-sir," whined the obvious lackey. "They were getting away..."

"And they got away anyway!" The man behind the desk stood. "Do I have to do everything myself, Reynolds?"

"It-it's 'Squires', sir," the stocky man replied.

"I don't give a good god damn what your fucking name is! Can you capture Sen or not?" No response. "I didn't bloody think so!" He sat down again and turned his chair toward the view. "Get out. You've got twelve hours to bring Sen to me or I'll put your head on a pike."

Squires turned and bolted from the room.

Madeline knew the man in the chair. Sir George Chambers: a lackey himself, for the Council of the Seven. He must be two hundred years old, if the rumours she'd heard were true.

Backing out the way she had come in, Madeline continued down the hall to what looked to be the front door. One more push...

With a snap she was back in her body sitting on the hard floor.

It was so close! Madeline couldn't teleport out of her cell any more than should break the silver shackles burning her skin or break down the spelled door.

Besides which, if Jaared was captured, the best place for her to help him was here.

She had better concentrate on regaining some of her strength.

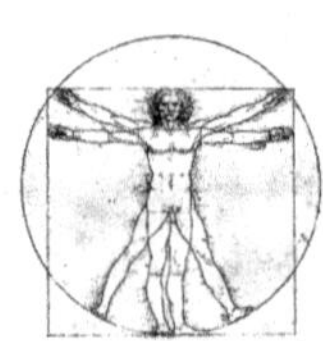

I ALWAYS HATE THE WAITING

I always hate the waiting. I've never been very good at stakeouts or waiting for something to happen. Hence the plan.

Skeet is still asleep on the pad of cardboard we crashed on.

Careful not to wake her, I ease off it and slowly ease my head above the countertop. It's dusk, not long until dark. The clock in my HUD says '14:58'. So precise.

"Where you going?"

I turn back to find Skeet leaning up on one elbow, her other hand resting on the Mossberg.

"What? You're going to shoot me?" I smile.

Skeet smiles back, but hers is a wicked grin. "No, I had something more fun in mind." She reaches up and unclips the collar of her leather jacket, sliding the zip down in what I can only call 'a seductive manner'.

I glance toward the back room where Nick is resting.

What the hell.

"Your wish is my command," I whisper.

I check my Glock one last time, unloading and reloading until I'm sure there's no chance for jamming. The MP5 gets the full treatment as well, clean within an inch of its life. Then I shrug out of my leather coat.

I hand the ammo to Nick. "Hope you two're going to be all right..."

Nick glances at Skeet and then back to me. "You will be in more danger than we will be." He removes the armoured leathers I made him wear and hand them to me in exchange for my coat. Good job we're similar in size. "And we do not even know if this will work."

"I know, but we have to assume there's some kind of scent involved – this may fool them for a while." I shrug on the armour. "I'll be fine."

Skeet nods. " Hope so…what'll they do when they work out yer not with us?" She grins. "We'll keep 'em busy, long as we can."

I smile back. "Don't forget: stick with the plan. You'll meet Finn at the safe house at eight, assuming you can lose your tail. If he gives you any shit, tell him I'll be back to visit him when this is all over."

Nick nods. "Understood. I believe I can keep the – what do you call him? – 'little toe rag' in line." He smiles that scary smile. "I frighten him nearly as much as you."

I smile back. "Yeah, and it's *you* he should be afraid of!"

Skeet puts her arms around me. "You be careful – ya hear?"

I nod, my smile fading. "I will, so long as you promise to do the same."

She nods. "Promise. It'll take more than a few hellhounds to keep me away."

My skullphone goes. It's Jonesy. "Sen."

"C-commander? Your locator is disabled. You wouldn't believe how hard–"

I interrupt the undoubtedly fascinating report on my locator. "Jonesy, still a little busy. Just tell me it can't be reactivated without you knowing."

"It can't be reactivated without my knowing, but…" There's always a 'but'.

"Yes? What?"

"It might get reactivated when Central checks against backup. I can't stop that…"

Great. "How much time do I have before that cycles?"

"Less than twenty-four hours."

Sigh. "It'll have to do." If I haven't got where I'm going by then, the plan won't work anyway. "Listen, can you do one more thing for me?" I explain what I want and he gets it.

"Not a problem. It'll activate when you get where you're going."

"Thanks Jonesy – will speak to you in the next couple of days.

Nick and Skeet have been watching my face. "Bad news?" Skeet asks.

I shake my head. "Time just got shorter – this has to work before this time tomorrow." I heft the MP5 and wave them toward the back door. "Time to go."

Skeet leads the way and we leave the shop, scanning for enemies and more than a little aware that we don't really want to start a fire fight just off a main road.

I give them a wave as they head off to the left and I go right.

"Be careful," I mutter as the incongruous pair disappears around a corner headed toward Tollcross.

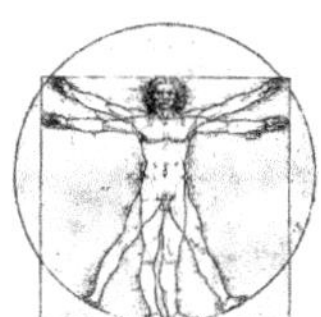

THIS IS JUST GREAT...

Jonesy tossed the voda onto the cushion beside him.

It would be nice if the Commander listened to him just once in a while. Okay, the man had issues, clearly, but he was just so rude.

"Yes sir, keeping my mouth shut, *sir*," he muttered as he contemplated the display in front of him. As a 'civilian' in the Company, Jonesy wasn't really used to being ordered around. Consulted, yes. Ordered, well, it seemed like everyone was ordering him around these days.

He popped the top on another energy drink and slouched back.

And what he'd done was probably against Company policy.

Sen had just better cover his arse.

His mind drifted to more pleasant things: mainly the glimpse he'd had of Bella's cleavage as she leaned over the table in the swanky bar she'd dragged him to for lunch.

"So, how long you been in what was it? Techcrime?" Bella asked, sipping at the white wine and soda she'd ordered.

Jonesy nodded, sipping his very expensive craft ale. "About a year, now."

Magnified by the thick lenses of her glasses, Bella stared at him. "A year?!? How the hell have you avoided me for a year?"

Shrugging, he laughed. "I wasn't 'avoiding' you – I didn't know you worked for the Company." He took another sip and looked away. "Besides, I work from home mostly. I don't even have a cubby at Company House."

Bella was shaking her head. "Okay, I guess that explains it." She paused, thinking about something and gazing at the reflections on her wine glass. "I'm still mad at you, by the way."

"Mad at me?" Jonesy had no idea what she was talking about.

Nodding, she leaned forward, the tops of her breasts appearing briefly in the gap of her top before disappearing again. “You were supposed to take me to that club behind the Rex – you know the one.”

Distracted by the view, he was slow on the uptake. “Club? When?”

“You don’t even remember.”

A vague recollection of a drunken promise to go clubbing niggled at the back of his head. But no, not really. Jonesy didn’t say that. “Sure I do.”

“Then what happened? Why didn’t you call me?”

“Call you?” Everything he said seemed to be coming out as questions.

“Forget it.” She stood up. “This was a bad idea.”

“Wait!” He glanced around, realising his voice had sounded loud, even in the noisy bar.

Bella stopped., half turning. “Why? You obviously aren’t that interested in me – I don’t think you ever were!”

He grabbed her hand before she could leave. “Wait, Bella – sit down and I’ll tell you why I didn’t call.”

The look she gave him would have turned lesser mortals to stone. But he’d been dealing with Commander Sen for weeks now, he could take it. She sat down on the edge of her seat and looked at her glass for a moment before picking it up and taking a large swig.

“Well? Speak!” she commanded.

Jonesy took a sip of his beer. “Look…the reason…” He grimaced, then blurted out: “I didn’t think you liked me!”

Bella sat there, a stunned look on her face. “Why?”

Taking more beer for courage, he glanced at her and then away. “You were horrible to me all the time – taking the piss out of my clothes, calling me ‘geek boy’…”

“Well, you are a ‘geek boy’,” Bella said, deadpan. “Aren’t you?”

Jonesy shrugged. “I guess…but it didn’t feel very good at the time.”

Bella didn’t say anything and Jonesy was afraid to look at her. After another drink of his beer, he glanced up at her face and she seemed to be going through some kind of contortions.

“What?”

She gave in and burst out laughing. “You berk – I said things like that ‘cause I liked you!” Her laughter faded, but the smile remained, her eyes twinkled behind her glasses. “I still kinda like you…”

Jonesy smiled back, swearing inwardly – *I'll never understand women.* "I kinda like you, too." He picked up a menu, feeling awkward. "Do you want some food, then?"

Bella picked up the other menu. "All right, *geek boy,* let's order some food."

The energy drink bubbled in his stomach and he belched, releasing the gas. He belched. "Dammit Bella, why didn't you say so?" he murmured. All that time…wasted.

He shrugged again. It didn't matter because they had a date tomorrow.

Jonesy flipped back into the Grid.

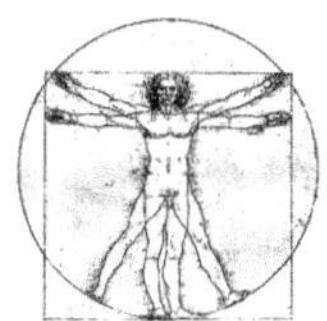

Sightseeing's for Tourists

Skeet followed Nick as they headed for the Grassmarket. It was cold and dark in the streets and still relatively quiet in the not quite time to go home period of the afternoon.

Glancing over her shoulder, she sees no signs they're being followed. "What if they don't find us?"

Nick shrugged. "Then we'll have to find them."

"You can do that?"

"They have a...*distinctive* odour." He glanced at her for a second. "You can't smell them?"

Skeet shook her head. "Nope. Guess I just don't have the nose for hellbeasts."

The boy smiled. He seemed so grown up most of the time, Skeet often forgot he was little more than a teenager, even if he was a fast-growing one.

"Come on then. Let's go huntin'."

Nick turned and led the way on towards the Cowgate.

Whatever it was found them in one of the tunnels under bridges the Cowgate runs through. This one had a pub on one side and a mass of stone above their heads.

Skeet pulled Nick into a side road beside the pub, unslinging her Mossberg. Lights from the pub flickered as people walked past. Great.

"Just what we need...an audience," she grumbled.

Nick gestured across the road where there seemed to be a continuation of the road they were on. "There are less people that way."

Skeet nodded and glanced quickly around the corner. Nothing visible. With no further ado, she checked for traffic and darted across the road. Nick was right behind her.

A weird warbling sound filled the air, followed by the sound of feet. Lots of feet.

"Shit!" The road climbed up out of the cleft of the road.

"Just run," Nick advised, keeping pace with her easily. He pulled something from a pocket. It looked like one of the things Adams had sent them. Jaared called them 'holy hand grenades'. Some kind of joke. But they worked.

Concentrating on running with the shotgun in both hands, Skeet felt herself pulling ahead, just in time to see an approaching wall.

"Shit fuck! It's a dead end!" she shouted over her shoulder. Then she spotted the archway. "Wait, I see something." Skeet dashed into the opening, praying it went through. She could see lighter air the other side. "This way!"

"Right behind you."

The cry of the creatures behind them sounded again. She sensed more than heard Nick stop and throw the explosive toward the sounds.

"Run!"

And they did. The explosion didn't make a sound; Skeet couldn't hear anything as a wave of energy swept through their heads.

A last howl and she could suddenly feel an absence of pursuit. Not that it'd last long. There were always more.

Their feet took them through a car park and out the other side, turning right up the hill toward lights and civilisation. They couldn't stay there long, but they could at least make it interesting for their pursuers.

It only took them a few minutes to realise they were being followed.

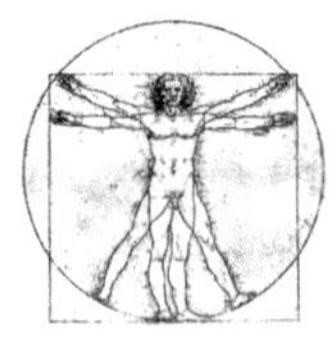

I pull Nick's coat tighter around me against the cold wind after checking my Glock and the MP5 for the umpteenth time.

It's not clear where I'm headed. I think it's probably the Old Town. I guess that makes sense.

I dismiss the HUD – don't need the distraction.

I head up towards the Castle, the most prominent man-made feature in Edinburgh. I've not been here for years, but it still feels the same. Cold, smells of breweries and a small town feel that London has never had for me.

As I head uphill, I lose sight of Prince's Street. The lights of the lower part of Edinburgh, looking over the park called The Meadows towards Morningside, appear, twinkling in the dimness of an early winter's evening.

I round the bottom of the Castle mound passing St Columba's church on the right. There's another church, decommissioned as so many are in this city, on the left. I look both ways down the Royal Mile.

A twinge in the back of my head tells me someone – or some thing – is following me. I'm not going to spot them with streetlights gleaming down at me, particularly if they're above me.

I shrug to myself, settle the MP5 in my armpit and turn right. Now, just have to hope Jonesy's little trick will work.

I feel the blow coming before I sense anything else. I gland some *jolt* and manage to avoid the worst of it, but it still sends me spinning toward the open stone staircase. I grab the metal railing just in time to arrest my fall.

It pulls free of the stonework with a shriek.

I let it go and pray it altered my trajectory enough to avoid those steps. The MP5 clatters on the pavement beneath me. I roll, willing my senses to pick up something. Anything.

The next blow catches me in the kidney, sending me sprawling and excruciating pain pours through my back before I manage to shut the worst of it out.

Nothing. No heartbeat, no breath sounds, barely the sound of their passage through the air.

The MP5 comes loose as I continue my roll. Not the best defensive posture, rolling around on the ground. I roll up against an iron bollard. Shit.

A slight hiss tells me another blow is coming and I move my head to the side just in time. Whatever it is hits the bollard. A sharp intake of breath suggests that it hurt.

I manage to get upright just in time to catch a blow to the chin. Without thinking about it, I flip backwards into the street, most of the punch losing impact.

There's the blare of horns and blinding headlights as a black cab swerves to avoid me. Dammit. I've lost him again.

The next blow catches my temple and I see lots of points of light. Another blow to the kidneys sends me reeling and the agony returns. I gland some more *jolt*, hoping it'll help me counteract the pain. No luck.

A sharp kick to the back of my leg and I'm on the ground again, eyes screwed shut against the pain. *Okay, that's enough.*

I lie on the ground, waiting for more, but thinking they need me alive.

"Jaared Sen," a voice says mere inches from my face. I've got nothing again and open my eyes. A face I don't recognise is above me, inverted. "Allow me to introduce myself: Lucien de Foret, at your service."

"Do-do I know you?" Something about him seems familiar.

He smiles. "We met once, perhaps you remember. It was at Jacob Euonymus' house." He watches my face. "No? I killed your little friend…what was it? Fulbright?"

Ah. "That was you?" I never knew who it was I had incapacitated. He hadn't stuck around after I subdued him.

"Yes, that was me. I used to…'freelance'? I think that's the word, for the highest bidder."

I nod, the pain receding slightly as I get my breath back. "Now you work for the Council." Not a question.

His eyes narrow above mine. "I work for no one."

My turn to smile. "That's why you're doing their dirty work, then? Just another dog in their kennels..."

The blow is so obvious, my long-dead grandmother could avoid it. And just like that, I'm back on my feet.

"Ah, ah, ah, not very nice. What? Did I upset your feelings? A big, ole' ugly vampire like you – and I do mean ugly..."

He blurs and I lose him again. Damn, he's fast.

My left arm is suddenly locked up behind me. "There you are – I thought I was going to have to find you after all that."

The pressure on the arm increases and I wonder if he's going to dislocate it.

"They just want you alive," he hisses in my ear. "They didn't say anything about you being intact."

I huff a short laugh against the pain.

"Now, where's the brat?"

"Brat? What're...oh, you mean Nicholas." I shake my head. "He's gone. Back to London."

The pressure increases. "I seriously doubt that, little man. Now tell me."

"I already did," I grate out, glanding something to dull my aches, but not too much.

He puts his lips next to my ear. "Do not worry, I'll find the bastard soon enough."

"Oh, please. You only found me because I was coming to find whoever's holding your leash." Grimacing, I shift slightly, trying to ease the tension in my shoulder. No luck. "Now why don't you shut up like a good little dog and take me to your master."

He picks me up and we're airborne.

I catch a glimpse of the massive car park in front of Edinburgh Castle. All the houses up here are old.

Lucien de Foret drops us into a cul-de-sac shaped like a large courtyard. Something tells me this is the place. I can't detect any signs of life. Even non-human life. Nothing.

I close my eyes, listening, activating the senses I used to rely on before I regained my sight.

One of the houses in front of me is humming. I can almost see it glowing in my mind's eye. Something powerful is in there.

Do I really want to go in there? The pressure on my arm increases. It's not up to me. I sigh and open my eyes. Besides, I don't have a choice if I want to find Madeline.

I can't reach any of my weapons, the Glock pinned in place by the creature behind me.

The door of the vibrating house is painted a deep red the colour of dried blood.

"A bit cliché, don't you think?" I ask the vampire behind me.

He shrugs. "I have no opinion about such things."

There's a massive bronze knocker in the centre of the door in the shape of a demon's head, a large ring dangling from its mouth. The eyes are so realistic, I almost expect them to blink at me.

De Foret lifts the ring and lets it fall back again with a deep 'thud'. I gland some *snap* and my senses burn with the new infusion of drugs.

After a long ten count, the door opens. A tall, cadaverous man stands in the doorway.

"Ah, Commander Sen, this is a surprise." The voice matches his looks, grating across his vocal chords like he's not used to speaking. At least not regularly. "Please, come in."

The long hall beyond is empty. A light shows under the large door at the end.

The gaunt man frisks me, removing my weapons and my utility pack. He finds most of the items I have on me. Damn.

"Thanks for your cooperation," he grates. I can't tell if he's being sarcastic or not.

De Foret guides me past the butler and leads me down the hall.

I don't resist. I want to be here, after all.

The door opens easily and silently on its hinges.

"Commander Sen," says the seated man behind a desk the size of a small aircraft carrier. Dark hair, cut short, a sharp mouth like a slash across his olive-coloured face. I can't tell how tall he is, but I'd guess average height. Not fat, not too thin. He's holding a large brandy snifter which he raises to his lips and takes a sip. "Thank you, Lucien."

De Foret guides me by the arm into the otherwise empty room. Bookcases line two walls, large windows behind him on the other two.

"Nice room," I say before being forced into a seat in one of the leather wingback chairs in front of the desk.

He smiles, black eyes glittering in the dim light. "Thank you." He sips from his snifter. "That'll be all Lucien." Then, when the door closes behind me. "I have waited so long to meet you."

"Wish I could say the same. You have me at a disadvantage: who're you?" I'm tired and in no mood for pussyfooting around.

Sip of brandy. "You may call me 'Chambers'."

"Is that your name?"

It's his turn to shrug. "It's as good a name as any, and one I have grown used to." He stands and places the glass on the leather top of the desk before stepping over to a sideboard covered in bottles and glasses. "Would you like a drink, Commander?"

"Whisky, no water." I settle back in the chair. "And make it a good one."

"Tsk, Commander, we're not barbarians, whatever you may think of us." He pours some amber liquid into a heavy tumbler. In two steps he's beside my chair, extending the glass to me. He puts the bottle on the table beside me.

"Thanks." I take the whisky and sip. "Very nice."

Chambers reseats himself behind the desk and picks up the snifter.. "You have caused me a great deal of trouble, Commander."

"I do my best – particularly when someone's trying to kill me."

A shake of the head. "No one has tried to kill you, Commander, I merely wished to converse with you." He waves at the room with the hand holding his brandy. "As we are doing now."

I sip my whisky again. "So…talk."

"I'm guessing I have something you want, Commander, or you would not have left London for the cold North." When I say nothing, he continues. "The Lady Madeline has been a most cooperative guest…although lack of nourishment may have something to do with that…"

The whisky burns, but in a good way. He's trying to get a rise out of me. I'm afraid I'm too old and tired to be taken in so easily. "Good, I would hate to hear that she had come to any harm." I stare at him for a long count. "I would have trouble explaining that to our son."

"Oh yes, where is your son and that irritating bitch you've involved in our affairs?" His eyes glitter again, with a flare of something red in the depths.

I pour myself more whisky. As I said, I'm where I want to be, I'm tired and he's not going to kill me – there's not much point in sobriety. "They're safe. Probably killing more of your minions, if I'm not mistaken."

Chambers is silent for longer than I expect, although I don't squirm. When he finally speaks, what he has to say is not surprising.

"You are lucky we need the boy alive, otherwise I would have him killed." He waved his free hand. "My people will have to settle for eating your bitch instead." He looks over my head at the three beings that have entered the room behind me. A man and two identical women; I can hear normal heartbeats, so I doubt there's anything special about them. No sign of Lucien de Foret, though. Obviously his work is done. Nevermind.

I finish my whisky and stand up. "Thanks for the drink, I guess I'm going now."

"Take him to the Lady Madeline."

Just where I wanted to go. I turn towards the hall and the two women and a man standing around my chair. "Come on then, lead the way."

After the trio relieve me of the Glock, the MP5 and just about everything else they can find, including my leather coat, we go back down the entry hall, stopping outside a door I had passed earlier. I must be slipping as I didn't feel Madeline's presence before. I can now, but maybe that's because the door's open.

One of the women precedes me down the dimly lit stairs.

"Nice, this place has it's own dungeon."

The remaining woman prods me with a nasty looking dagger.

"Okay, okay, I'm going." I take the steps at a normal pace. No point in upsetting them just yet.

The first woman is waiting outside an open door which even I can tell is clad in silver. "Nice. Bet this place has been in Architectural Digest a time or two." No response. Chatty lot.

I take a last glance around before stepping into the room beyond.

With a long, silver-tipped spear, the man follows me in and watches Madeline warily. One of the twins points at another set of chains. I'm obviously not going to get the keys to the cell.

I slip down the wall not far from Madeline and the woman clicks the shackles in place on my wrists, pulling my arms above my head. My abused shoulder protests.

"Oh good, I could use a bit of physio." Still nothing.

The door slams behind them and locks engage.

Madeline looks like she's in a coma. Great. I had hoped she would at least be mobile.

Then she opens her eyes. "You fool." Her immobility was, at least partially, an act.

"Good to see you, too, Madeline."

"I do not need rescuing," she hisses.

"Could have fooled me," I say, walking over to her and sit next to her, my back against the stone.

Those eyes stare at me before a smile turns up the corners of her mouth. "Why am I not surprised? And I suppose you brought Nicholas, too?"

I nod. "And Skeet. Nothing like having the whole gang in one place for a rescue attempt."

The smile fades slightly at the mention of Skeet. "This is a 'rescue attempt'?"

"I'm exactly where I wanted to be." I wave around the room. "My backup just hasn't arrived yet."

She hushes me. "They may be listening."

I grin, my confidence growing with the success (so far) of my plan. "I wouldn't expect anything less." I pull my shirt away from my throat. "Now, do you want some or not?"

Madeline regards me silently. She's never been able to tell when I'm joking, a product, I suspect, of her age and being a vampire. "Are you sure?"

"Of course. We'll need your strength when we make our break."

A last glance, then her teeth are in the vein on my neck.

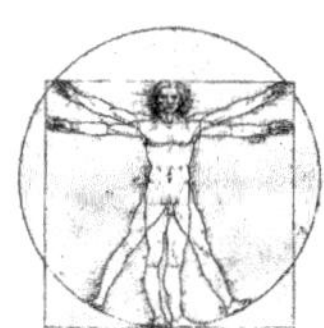

Problems, problems...

Whatever he was chasing, it wasn't good.

The thing banked left, jigged right, then left again. It was hard to tell if it was human or some kind of construct. These days software surpasses humans in a lot of things.

Then it did something no human would do: it slammed on the virtual brakes and flipped past his head. It was so close, he did that actual ducking thing a lot of gamers do.

He had a momentary impression of blue-black steel feathers and it was gone.

"Dammit."

This was only supposed to be a level 8 incursion, meaning it was probably some bored kid trying his hand at cracking Central. The problem had escalated so much in the last ten years that there was no 'central' computer – hadn't been for a long time – just lots of distributed units and decoys. Jonesy had yet to meet anyone without the appropriate clearances who knew where anything actually resided in Central.

The memory of those 'feathers' told Jonesy it was something more than a level 8.

He flagged it up on his status screen and received an automated notification from the hunter-killers. Automated seek and destroy programmes, the 'hunter-killers' usually didn't get involved unless it was something like this. Something Jonesy couldn't catch himself.

Of course, if there wasn't something odd about this one, he wouldn't have been 'here' at all.

A momentary impression of sleek, matte black and ultra-fast triangular-shaped-things went past his head. The intruder imploded and winked out with a deep black version of the white dot you used to get on old CRT televisions.

With a sigh, he logged the kill and flipped out of the system.

Greeted with the grey walls of his flat, he almost put himself back into the Grid. Then he remembered what he'd been avoiding thinking about all day. Bella. Their date was tonight!

"Shit, shit, shit, shit, shit, shit..." he muttered as he levered himself out of the chair and headed for the shower.

Half an hour later, clean, face depilitated and gel rubbed through his spiky hair, Jonesy glared at his two good shirts: one had a stain down the front, the other looked limp but clean.

Jonsey sniffed it. Not overly pongy. He was going to have to spend some money on clothes. It wasn't like he had an expensive lifestyle. The bike was his only indulgence.

Opting for the limp one, Jonesy shrugged his way into it and turned to look at his (small) collection of cologne. It consisted of an ancient bottle of Brut given to him by his grandmother and a tiny bottle of *Chanel pour Homme*. Definitely not the Brut. He spritzed himself under the arms and around his neck, careful not to get carried away.

With a final sigh, he picked up his leather jacket and headed for the door.

Public transport tonight – he didn't want to chance the bike getting left somewhere after he got pissed. Not that he was planning to, of course. But he knew he drank more when he was nervous.

He got to his front door without his voda ringing.

His voda rang.

"Shit! Not now!" he looked at the display. *Unknown caller.* "Huh?" He thumbed it on. "Hello?"

"Is this Mr Jones?" The voice was flat, almost monotone.

"Yes, but I can't..."

"You are in a lot of trouble, Mr Jones. We know what you did for Sen and we are not happy."

Great. "Who are you? What do you want?"

"Who we are is not your concern." There is a hiss of static on the line. "– Sen's location."

"Sorry? You're breaking up..."

"GIVE US SEN'S LOCATION AND WE WILL NOT KILL YOU."

Jonesy dropped the voda on the floor and looked at it for a moment. He could hear more static, bending in strange patterns, reminding him of an ancient dial-up modem connect tone he'd found on the net somewhere.

"Great," he muttered. "Dammit, Sen..."

Leaving the voda where it was, he opened the door and bolted from his apartment.

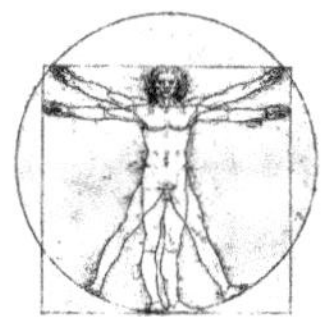

I HATE YOU SO MUCH RIGHT NOW

Dammit Jaared, what have you gotten us into? Skeet thought with an inward groan.

The man in the alley, not pointing a gun at them was a strange sight.

The cold wind coming off the North Sea didn't seem to affect him, even though he was only wearing a hunting vest and matt black leather trousers, which tucked into knee-high Pathfinder boots. All of his exposed skin was covered in black tattoos, strange whorls and symbols whose meaning was not immediately obvious. Caught from the corner of the eye, they seemed to writhe on his skin.

On his face was the most striking tat, however. It was a variation on a Celtic knot, a cross running down from his forehead to his chin and across the cheeks. But where the intertwined loops of the knot should be, there were more of the odd symbols. His shaven skull held more of the marks, leaving very little of his dark brown skin exposed.

His black eyes watched them with the coldness of a predator, glittering in the scattered light from the main road.

"Whaddya want?" Skeet asked. Nothing like the direct approach.

Those eyes continued to stare for a long minute. "Wha' are yeh?" he hissed.

Huh? Skeet glanced at Nick, but the boy didn't look her way, concentrating on their company. "I'm Skeet, and this here's Nick." Her Mossberg lifted slightly. "And you?"

He spat. "I know what he is – I can smell him." Seeming to come to a decision, he dropped the shotgun a few millimetres. "I want to know: why're you in my city? And why do you attract trouble wherever you go?"

Skeet smiled. "Yeh ask a lot of questions." She glanced away, the squirming tattoos on his body making her feel nauseous. Affecting a nonchalance she was far from feeling, she leaned against the dank brick wall beside her. "Yeh want to play twenty questions, we should find someplace less exposed."

The dark eyes watched her a moment longer, flicked to Nick before he let out an audible sigh. "I don' normally associate with night walkers." Skeet thought he was going to spit again. He sighed. "Follow me, I know a spot nearby."

"It better not be a place to kill us," Skeet retorted.

A contemptuous glance over his shoulder before he turned. "If I wanted yeh dead, we wouldn't be havin' this conversation."

The 'spot' turned out to be the back room of a pub called Shinty's that didn't seem to mind folk carrying weapons.

"Beer?" he asked Skeet.

They settled into seats watching the doors.

At her nod, he glanced at Nick, and came back in a few moments with two pints of 80 shilling. "Sorry, they's fresh out of the red stuff."

Nick didn't move, but Skeet could tell by his stillness he was very much on guard.

Skeet picked up her pint and raised it to their host before taking a sip. Good. It had been too long.

"Is this safe?" she asked, gesturing at the room around them. "You know we're being hunted."

The man nodded. "It's warded, if that's what you're askin'. 'Sides, you took care of the last batch." He paused, listening. "Nothing nearby t'ain't human, 'cept him."

"I repeat myself – whaddya want?"

"Daes he no talk?"

"He's shy."

Their host took a long swallow of beer. "I ast yeh before: wha' are yeh?"

Shrugging, Skeet thought about the question, still not sure what he was asking. "We're trying to find his…mother," she answered finally.

A look of disgust crossed the man's face. "Why here?"

Skeet shrugged again. "It's where she was last heard from." Another sip of beer. "And we're pretty sure someone took her."

"Shite. I'm no' getting involved in this," the man said getting up.

"Wait! That's it?"

He nodded. "Yer intae something beyond a mere hunter's ken, if'n they took a vampire – yer on yer own."

Skeet nodded. "Don't blame yeh – I'd do the same." But the word 'hunter' had triggered something in her memory. "Wait – you're a Hunter?"

His chest inflated. "Best damn Hunter in town," he boasted. Then he let out the breath. "Well, only damn Hunter."

"You police the supes, then?"

"Try to – it's usually a damn-sight harder than some t'ink."

"Do you know the Council?"

"Aw shite, thes' who's involved? I def-in-ite-ly don' want nothin' to do with that lot!" He turned to leave again.

"Why are you following us?" Nick asked, speaking for the first time.

"I don't like messes in my town." He didn't turn back, but he didn't leave.

Skeet nodded. "Right, and we're making a mess." She sighed. "Look, yeh don't have to help us, can you just...tell us what we're up against?"

The stocky figure turned back. His dark eyes glinted in the dim light. "Why should I?"

A last shrug. "Yeh want us to leave, help us find what we came for."

He shook his head, the look on his face saying he already regretted not leaving. With a heavy sigh he sat back down and picked up his pint.

"What's yer name?"

He put the pint down and looked her in the eye. "Zeph...Zephaniah Murdock."

Skeet raised her glass to him again. "Cheers, Zeph. How'd you find us?"

His laugh caught them both off guard, Nick stiffening even more, if that was possible. "Yeh t'ain't exactly keepin' a low profile – yeh seem t' be attractin' all sorts. I t'ain't seen a sin eater fer years!" He took another pull of his beer. " 'Sides, things have been a bit quiet since yeh got here."

"It's not the sort of attention we were lookin' for."

This set him off again. "I'll bet. Wha' the hell did yeh do?"

Honesty seemed to be working. "We think they're lookin' for my partner – Nick's father."

"The man in black? He's good – he'd make a good Hunter."

"He already is, just normally he's hunting humans. He's with the Company."

A sour look crossed Zeph's face. "Damn Company…nothin's been the same since they started interferin'." His head shot up and swivelled to the door.

Nick had tensed up as well.

"Dammit, looks like we didn't lose them for long," Zeph muttered, unlimbering the shotgun. "C'mon, I'd just as well leave Shinty's place in one piece."

Smiling that grin of hers, Skeet downed the rest of her pint before checking her Mossberg. "You'll help us, then?"

Zeph smiled back. "Like I gotta choice?"

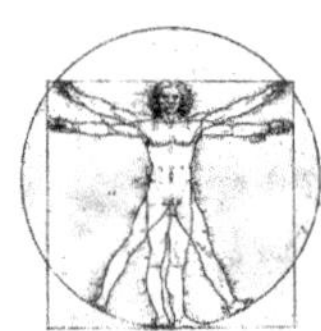

Dungeons and Dragons This Ain't

When I wake up, Madeline is more animated. For her.

I check the clock on my HUD. Guess we've got daylight to wait. "Morning."

"I know."

She should be asleep. "Why aren't you asleep?"

Even in the dim light I can see the disdainful look she gives me. "I do not always sleep during daylight...vampires my age do not require as much...sleep."

I shrug. "I did *not* know that."

She sighs. "Ah, *youngling...*"

"What's that supposed to mean?"

Madeline is quiet, not looking at me again. "Just that: you are very young."

She could have fooled me. After hours on a cold, stone floor, I ached all over. "So you keep telling me."

"What is your plan?" she whispers.

I shake my head. "Not now."

She goes silent again, thinking whatever it is she's thinking.

We don't talk much as the day passes and boredom sets in. My skullphone is still in my head, but there must be some kind of shielding around the dungeon as I can't contact anyone. Not even Central.

I just have to hope Skeet and Nick will be ready. But not yet.

They will be. And Finn better be on his toes or I *will* carry out my threat.

I touch Madeline's shoulder. "Do you need another drink?"

"You need to keep up your strength."

"I'm a fast healer – go on." I can feel her resisting me, but the hunger wins out. The sensation of her teeth in my neck is sensual. I start to drift.

We're interrupted by the sound of the door. For some reason it's like being caught having sex.

Madeline slumps against the wall, feigning lassitude. I wipe blood from my neck and pull my collar up above the wound.

The trio reappear, the man on guard against Madeline as one of the women unlocks my chains and cuffs me with a bar. I can't tell them apart. A light in the bar blinks steadily, indicating there's something in it; probably a charge large enough to blow my hands off, without killing me.

"What, you're letting us go already?"

Stony silence.

"Shit, you guys are just a bundle of laughs." Still nothing. I glance at the woman next to me. "So which one are you? Tweedledee? Or Tweedledum?"

Not even a glance.

"Cat got your tongue? Does ole Chambers remove them so you don't give him any lip? Or are you guys just naturally quiet?" Still nothing.

I chance a look at Madeline and spot the glint of her eyes, watching us and an almost imperceptible shake of the head.

Hiding a smile, I turn back and follow my zombie guards up the steps.

Chambers is looking out that window again, obviously obsessed with his view over the glacial trench known as Princes Street Gardens.

"I'll bet you can see Fife from here."

He turns and looks at me, a thin smile below those dead eyes. "Ah yes, you are very…witty, Commander." He signals the guards who guide me to a chair in front of the desk. They don't unbind my hands.

I sink into the softly stuffed chair. No way I'm getting out of it in a hurry. "What can I say? I've had quite a while to practice my act."

Chambers sits behind the desk. The daylight is fading behind him. "Yes, Commander, we know. Your age is a very poorly kept secret." He picks up a pad from his desk and flicks through some pages. "You've had a number of identities over the two centuries of your existence." He looks back to me, one eyebrow raised. "I *am* surprised the Company has allowed you to operate as freely as you do."

I shrug. "They obviously have their uses for me." I don't tell him that I sometimes wonder what the Company wants from me.

He nods, staring at me over his steepled fingers. "I'm sure." The stare goes on for too long.

"What? Have I got something on my face?"

A shake of the head. "No, Commander, I was simply wondering how much to tell you...and how much you would be able to understand."

"Try me."

Chambers sighs. "How much mythology do you know, Commander?"

"Until recently, not a lot." I shift in the chair, my back beginning to ache again. "We talking Greek? Roman? Something else?"

"I would say...'something else'." He takes a drink from a solid tumbler on his desk. I can smell the whisky from here. Good stuff, too. This time he doesn't offer me one. "Have you ever heard of something called 'The Undoing'?"

I shake my head. "Not that I can recall. Wait– it's a term from old computers!"

His eyes glitter as he decides whether to continue or have me beaten. In the end, he flips open a humidor and takes out a cigar, clips the end and takes out a matchbox.

"I'd offer you a cigar, but I doubt they're your 'thing'." He lights a match before holding the end of the cigar over the flame. Finally, he puffs for a moment before examining the tip to see if he's properly lit.

"Nah, I prefer those fags that make you feel like you've smoked a cigarette. Nothing beats that forty-a-day cough."

Chambers takes a packet of cigarettes (my brand) from a drawer and tosses it to me with the matches. "Knock yourself out."

Feels like I haven't had a cigarette in days. The smoke makes me light-headed from the first drag. One of the zombies puts an ashtray on a table near my elbow before I can flick ash on the antique carpet.

"So, this 'Undoing'...you were about to tell me."

He watches me through the smoke for a moment. "It's the end of the world, Commander." Chambers says it so matter-of-factly I don't question him. Well, for a minute, anyway.

"Really? That's all you got? Some kind of end of the world monster?"

To give him credit, Chambers takes my reaction in stride. He shrugs. "It doesn't make any difference whether you believe me, or not, commander." Looking at me over his whisky glass, he smiles. "But that *is* why you are here."

My turn to shrug. "Why me?" I smoke, letting him think about an answer.

Chambers looks out at his view before answering. "The Undoing is…shall we say…'unstable'. It requires regular treatments to keep it passive."

"If it's so dangerous, why keep it around?"

His eyes snap back to me. "Its demise has been sought for over 4,000 years, Commander. No one has been able to find a way to kill it *without* destroying everything."

"So, why me?" I can get repetitive when I'm bored.

"Your blood, Commander."

"My blood?" What the hell? I stub out my cigarette.

"Yes, your *blood.* If, as we suspect you are a hybrid of human and vampire stock, your blood can be used to create the serum that keeps the *Undoing* from destroying the world."

Holy crap. "Li'l ol me? That's a bit heavy for this time of the morning." I light another fag and think about it.

Chambers lets me think for a few moments.

I think of a question. "So, why all the fuss? Why didn't you just ask me?"

A smile I don't like very much crosses his face. "We doubted you'd be willing to part with *all* of it, Commander."

All…Ah. "I see. Why not just take a pint at a time? Or synthesise it – I mean, in this day and age…"

"Our…expert is adamant that it must be all of *your* blood and all at once. Synthesis misses some vital component – your life-force perhaps – which is not acceptable." He sips from his tumbler. "There's a ritual and various things that have to be done…to you…you see."

I don't like the sound of that very much. "Right. And when does this ritual have to happen?"

"At the winter solstice, to coincide with the new moon."

"Not an eclipse? I'm shocked!" The cigarette tastes bad. "Why are you bothering to tell me all this?"

Squire's smile fades. "I thought it only fair to let you know the 'why' of things, Commander." He stands up and moves to the window. "After all, you don't have a lot of choice in the matter. Or a lot of time."

I stub out my cigarette and slip my hand free of the cuffs to scratch my nose. I slip my hand back inside the loose cuff before he turns around.

One of the disadvantages of those SmartCuffs is the universal unlock code that most law enforcement types (like me) know. Well, that and Central's ability to work on some electronic devices remotely and I seemed to have some access here, probably because of that window.

"Really?" I say, sure that any minute now…

There's a loud 'bang' from down the hall.

Chambers whirls from the window, surprise on his face.

My turn to smile that nasty smile. "Oh, sorry, I forgot to tell you I invited some friends."

It was just as well he'd turned away from the window or he might have had an eyeful of glass fragments as his picture window exploded inwards. I saw it coming and closed my eyes, turning my head to the side. That's one of the disadvantages of being able to see – it wasn't that long ago that I'd have ignored it completely.

A tattooed man I don't know appears in the window, a shotgun with a pistol grip clasped to his chest.

"Commander Sen?"

"Yep, that's me," I say, standing up. The cuffs fall to the floor. "I'm guessing you're with the rescue party."

"Zeph Murdock, at yer service," he replies, moving to slam Squire's hand in the desk drawer where he's undoubtedly got a pistol, or something worse, stashed. A quick thrust from the butt of the shotgun and Chambers is down for the count.

"That's the problem with bad guys, they always seem to have glass jaws."

Murdock grins. "No challenge a'tall." He tosses me a large handgun. My own is in the house somewhere, but it'll do in the meantime.

I smile back. "Thanks. We've got one prisoner to liberate, my guns to find and then get out. Any other plans I need to know about?"

He shakes his tattooed head. "Nah, that about sums it up."

The door isn't even locked. The hall is thick with smoke when we open it, but the now open window behind us creates a cross draft thinning it quickly. The sound of scuffling comes from down the hall.

One of the women guards is lying in the hall, a pool of blood spreading around her. I quickly search her pockets for a key to the dungeon.

Nothing. "Damn." I look toward the entrance. "Skeet, you there?"

"Sure am, old man," comes the reply. "Bit busy now, though."

"Be there in a sec." I motion Murdock past me and stop at the dungeon door. Oh well, old-fashioned force will have to do. I aim the pistol at the lock – angling the gun so it won't ricochet my way – and fire. The lock mechanism fragments and the door swings open. Madeline is on the other side, grimacing in pain as the silver-plated chains she pulled from the wall hang around her wrists, burning her skin.

I tear a strip from my shirt and try to wrap it around her wrists, under the manacles. "We'll find the key in a minute. Sorry."

"I can manage," she hisses. "Go."

Running up to join Murdock by the turn to the front door, I check the hall behind us. Last thing we need is an ambush.

"Thae's two in a cupboard and one I cannae see."

"I'll cover you if you want to take out the cupboard," I suggest. At his nod, I lean over him and fire around the corner. Two blasts later and it's quieter. In fact, the shooting stops.

"You okay Skeet?" I call.

"Fine. Think there's one more..." there's a grunt and a thud, like a body falling over. "Clear!"

At that instant, two hands circle my throat. Dammit, how'd I forget the vampire?

"Don't move, Commander, I'd hate to snap your neck by accident," he whispers in my ear.

I shake my head slightly. "Kill me and the world ends, weren't you listening?"

A dry laugh is all the response I get as the hands tighten. *Damn, this nutjob really doesn't care.* "There's always the abomination that is your son, Commander."

Shit. I can't respond, as his rock-hard hands are now compressing my vocal chords. My fingers desperately search for purchase on his fingers. I can't even loosen his grip enough to get air.

The vice-like hold relaxes before I'm convulsively thrown across the hall. I look up to find out why he's let me go. It's Madeline, her silver chains wrapped around Lucien's throat while her own flesh smokes and bubbles at the contact. The chain seems to be eating its way into his neck, creating more smoke.

With another convulsion, the older vampire – it's the only reason I can think of as to why he's stronger than Madeline – uses the chains against her, effectively throwing her over his head and releasing the chains at the same time. His neck hanging open in flaps of skin, blood pouring from the wounds, he turns back to me.

Somewhere to my right, a pistol fires multiple shots and smoking holes appear in Lucien's clothing and skin. Silver-jacketed bullets, at a guess.

A scream of pain and anger tears from his ruined throat and he's gone.

Shuddering, I take a gasping breath. Murdoch appears and holds out a hand. "Damn vamps," he mutters. "Sorry, Commander…"

I smile at him, pleased I'm still breathing. "Don't worry…I– understand," I rasp.

Madeline is shaking convulsively from prolonged exposure to the silver in her manacles. Murdoch glances at me and pulls a small device from his belt. "Try this."

I recognise it – useful for opening mechanical locks. I totter over to where she's leaning against the wall and make a grab for one of her hands. She swats me away.

"Easy, I'm trying to get those off you." I try again, grabbing her hand firmly. The thimble-shaped device makes quick work of the lock and one of the cuffs falls free. The other come loose shortly after and Madeline breathes a sigh of relief. Her wrists are raw and bloody where the silver burned her flesh.

"Thanks," I say.

She shrugs. "And thank you."

I motion to Murdoch behind me. "He's the one that needs the thanks for this." I hold up the thimble.

Madeline nods. "I know, but I somehow doubt he would appreciate it coming from me."

I gland another hit of *jolt* and feel things stabilise. "C'mon, Mr Murdoch, let's see what's happening around that corner."

We step around the corner and see Nick standing over a body. I nod. Skeet enters behind him, Mossberg ready. "Good work. Let's get what we came for and blow this joint."

"Could' na'gree more," Murdock mutters. He starts searching the bodies.

"If any of those are still breathing, do you think you can you help the vampire down the hall out? Feeding would help her wounds right now."

A look of revulsion crosses his face for a second. "Uh…ifn' it's alright w'yeh, I'd rather not…"

I snap my fingers. "You're a Hunter, right?" I look at Skeet who shrugs. "Okay, don't worry. I'll take care of it. I need to find our host…"

When I get back to Chamber's office, after helping Madeline find a suitable food source, he's gone.

Of course.

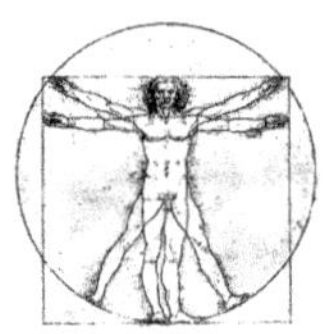

BBC World Service: Flooding on the Danube has reached new heights with water levels reaching a two hundred year high of almost 10 metres in places. Thirteen people are confirmed dead and a further 26 are missing...

I WENT DOWN THE CROSSROADS...

Bella was glaring at him as he tried Sen's number again on her voda. Still nothing. The music from the bar they were sitting in was (thankfully) not too loud for him to think.

"Come on, come on, come on..." he muttered as the connect sounds muttered in his ear.

"What is the problem, Jonesy?" Bella asked. "The Commander's a big boy, he can take care of himself."

The call dropped out again. He resisted the urge to throw Bella's voda across the room and placed it carefully on the table. Four beers on an empty stomach had gone to his head and he closed his eyes to stop the room going in and out of focus.

"It's not *him* I'm worried about, Bells..."

Bella took his hand. "You've been freaked all night and I know it's not *me!*" She said the last bit with a half-smile. "Now spill."

Jonesy took another drink of his beer and let out the breath he'd held all night. Or so it seemed. "I got a call...just before I came out..."

Waving two fingers in the air in a 'get on with it' gesture, Bella interrupted. "Yeah, you covered that part already, demanding to know where he is. Next!"

"Well, they threatened to k-kill me if I didn't tell them where he is." He took another drink. "That's why I left my voda at home."

Bella's mouth was open. "Seriously? And you didn't think to tell me that part?"

"I didn't want to worry you..."

She slapped the back of his head. "Dumfuck! What do you think I've been doing for the last two hours?!?" She slapped him again. "Fuckwit!"

"Ow! What was that for?"

"For not telling me everything!" Bella looked as if she was going to head-slap him again and he ducked. "Gobshite!"

"Okay, I'm sorry!"

Bella glared at him before grabbing her voda and launching herself from the sofa. Jonesy started to follow before an imperious hand waved him off. "Just don't! I'm going to the bog, if that's okay with you!"

Jonesy didn't even have time to reply before she disappeared through the crowd by the bar.

He put his head in his hands and felt like crying. The night had been a disaster. What a geek.

"Mr Jones?"

He looked up to see a nondescript man standing next to his table. He couldn't really describe him, as the man's features seemed to shift and waver, making his head hurt more. He looked down for his beer. *More to drink, what a good idea.* "Yeah? That's me."

"Please remember, Mr Jones, you were warned."

Beer in hand, Jonesy's head shot up. The man's features blurred again as he tried to focus. "Whaddya mean? I've been 'warned'?"

An image appeared in the palm of the man's hand, held in front of Jonesy's eyes. It was Bella – and it looked like she was wearing the same clothes she'd been wearing all evening. "We have Bella Kincaid and will only release her when you tell us where Sen is."

"I already told you, I don't know…"

The slap came without warning. "But you know how to find out, do you not, Mr Jones?"

Uh…shit. "I don't know what you're talking…"

Another slap. "We are monitoring your vitals, Mr Jones and know when you are trying to deceive me." The hand touched his forehead for a moment and a voda number appeared before his eyes then faded. "You have twelve hours to contact us with Sen's location or Ms Kincaid dies."

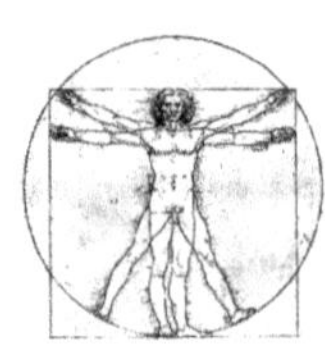

Cleaning up after a party is a pain in the ass

Nick stood next to it and nodded.

Skeet threw open the door, revealing a linen closet.

"Damn, I hate this," she muttered.

"You would hate it more if something ambushed us," Nick retorted.

Waving him away, Skeet lifted the Mossberg and proceeded to the next closed door. "Yeah, yeah." Without waiting, she pulled it open.

She didn't have time to raise the shotgun as the huge dog charged her, teeth bared and a deep growling sound coming from its throat. The clatter of Nick's MP5 in her ear was very loud. The animal fell to the floor of the hall, very dead.

"Okay, that was stupid," Skeet admitted, adrenaline coursing through her veins. She looked Nick in the eye. "Thanks for that."

Nick shrugged. "Don't make a habit of it," he replied.

"Bloody hell, was that a joke?!?" She prodded it with her boot. "Not a hellhound, then?"

No smile. "*I'll* get the next one."

"Knock ye'rself out." Skeet readied herself and the Mossberg as they approached the last door in the hall.

Before Nick reached it, it began to open, on darkness. Already jumpy because of the dog, they both targeted the opening with their guns.

A pale figure with hands raised stood just inside it. "Don't shoot!"

Nick lowered his gun. "It's okay, it's only a girl," he told Skeet.

"Yeah? Suicide bombers are often women and children – I'll keep her covered, if you don't mind."

"She smells of fear, nothing else," he replied. "Come out where we can see you."

The apparition, or so she seemed, dressed in a long, white gown, stepped through the doorway, more light revealing a white-blonde girl with very pale skin and piercing icy-blue eyes. "I am not armed."

"Who're you?" Skeet demanded.

"Lucy Philips. I'm Uncle…Mr Chambers' niece."

Skeet looked at Nick. *What do we do now?*

"Jaared will know what to do with her."

"Right. C'mon, then missy…" Skeet kept her shotgun levelled, if not centred on the girl.

"Anything else we should be aware of down here?" Nick asked the girl.

She shook her head. "No, there was just me."

As they passed the dead dog, the girl uttered a cry, "Prince!" and fell to the floor beside it, hugging the corpse. Her white gown was quickly covered in the animal's blood.

Skeet suddenly felt bad. "C'mon, little girl…sorry 'bout your dog…" she reached down to help the girl up.

Lucy turned back to them and her eyes flashed. Her face began to elongate and a shriek sounded from her open mouth like nothing Skeet had heard before. The girls teeth suddenly sharpened and there seemed to a be a lot more in there than there should be…

The girl launched herself at Skeet, who was caught off guard, again. The forest of teeth clamped on her arm as she dropped the shotgun and reached for one of her Sigs.

There was a 'boom' and a red hole opened in the girl's chest. The teeth released, Skeet's blood dripped as a look of shock replaced the fire in the icy eyes. Free to move, Skeet pulled away.

The fire returned and the creature followed Skeet's arm.

A second boom and the top of its head disappeared in a mist of blood. The eyes finally dulled and the once again frail body slumped to the tiled floor.

Jaared stood a few feet down the hall with Madeline at his side. The hunter, Murdock was just beyond them.

"That was careless," Jaared said in the sudden silence. He made a tutting noise.

"Did ya just 'tut' at me, Sen?" Skeet demanded, fingers clamped over the bite in an attempt to stem the bleeding. "If I had a gun in my hand…" she sank to the floor, blood loss and something else making her faint.

Nick was at her side, a first aid kit pulled from his belt. "Let me look at that, Skeet," he said gently.

"I don't feel so good," she whispered, her eyelids fluttering.

"Banshee poison," Murdock said.

"*That* was a banshee?" Jaared asked. "I had no idea."

"I hain't seen one in years," the Hunter replied.

Skeet's eyes closed, the voices seemed far away. "If'n ya'all want to…go fuck yer'…" her voice trailed off. "Too tired…"

"Skeet, hang on!" Jaared shouted in her ear.

"Don' worry…not…goin'…anywhere…"

Whatever consciousness she had left faded away.

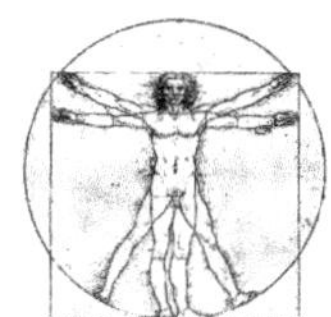

What the hell?

"What do we do now?" I demand as Skeet lapses into unconsciousness.

The look that crosses Madeline's face seems like fear. "We have to remove the poison."

Okay, how bad can it be? I kneel down next to her. "Like a snake's venom?"

"Something like that." She grips my shoulder. "But not you. It would affect you too, if not as quickly." She easily pulls me to one side and lifts Skeet's shredded arm. The blood oozes blackly, but not in the normal way – it seems thicker, almost solid.

A flicker of distaste passes over her face before she clamps her lips over the wound. She sucks quickly and spits onto the black and white tiles before repeating. I catch a glimpse of Murdock's face and he looks as pale as I feel.

Unable to perform the cleansing myself, I can only watch as Madeline works to remove the toxin from Skeet's bloodstream.

She pauses, watching the blood flow from the tooth marks. It is redder and doesn't seem as sluggish. After a few seconds, she resumes sucking and spitting.

"I think that is it – I can no longer taste the venom in her blood." She shudders. "I hate the taste of it, too."

Nick takes Skeet's arm from Madeline and starts dressing the wound.

"I can only imagine." I help Madeline stand up as she seems a little unsteady. It wasn't that long ago she was injured herself. "Thanks."

A wan smile. "It was...how do you say? 'The least I could do'," she replies.

"Are *you* okay?"

"Fine, just the aftereffects of the poison on my system." Her eyes flick to me. "And silver poisoning...and malnutrition..."

Taking the hint, I pull a chair over and let her sit down. "You almost done there, Nick?"

"I think so. Do you want me to give her a stimulant? She has lost quite a bit of blood," he nods at the mess on the floor.

"No, we'll ride out of here." I look around and realise someone's missing. "Where the hell's Finn, anyway?"

Nick shook his head. "He did not turn up at the meeting place." His glance at Murdock held more meaning than the Hunter realised. "If we had not met Murdock, we would have been late."

The Hunter looked a trifle embarrassed. "It t'were nothin'…"

I smile at him, glad for the help, regardless. It takes a matter of moments to summon a car via Central and lift the restriction on the area. "A car's coming."

Murdock speaks up. "I knows a safe place for 'er, Commander."

I nod, local knowledge is always a good thing. "Good – dammit!" Central wants me to stay.

"What is it?" Madeline asks, looking paler than normal.

"I have to stay here and explain the situation to the locals." I check my HUD and see it's not long until dawn. "You two'd better find someplace to hole up as I don't think Murdock here's offering you a room." I smile at the Hunter, knowing how his kind feel about vampires.

He looks chagrined. "Not exactly. Sorry."

Her pallor prompts something else. "Besides, I think you need to feed, as well."

Madeline nods. "That would help." Seeing the look on the Hunter's face, she smiles. "Do not worry, Hunter, I will restrain myself; I have *some* control after 350 years!"

Murdock, sheepish, nods back. "If anyt'ing, in the last 24 hours I've learnt not all blood…*vampires* are created equal." He looked back at me. "Jus' don' 'spect me to invite 'em for a pint…"

I laugh. "Murdock, I think you've been more helpful than you can possibly imagine and I wouldn't expect you to compromise so far as to invite them in."

There's a sound in the hall. "That'll be the car." Murdock helps me pick Skeet's unconscious form, leaving her shotgun to Nick. I carry my unconscious girlfriend to the main entrance and find an Asian man standing nervously in the door.

"Did you call for a car?" he asks, looking at the blood on the floor.

"Yes, can you take my friend here? And him," a nod to Murdock. "To the address he'll give you, please?"

"Does the young lady need a hospital?"

I shake my head. "No, she'll be fine, she's just had a hard night." I pull a credit chit from my pocket (one of Chambers) and hand it to him. "This should cover your expenses."

He glances at the chit and is suddenly more accommodating. He opens the door and helps me get Skeet into the back seat. Murdock climbs in next to her and nods to me.

"I'll call you when I'm done here," I say to Murdock. At his panicked look, I smile. "I know your voda code, don't worry."

The driver bows to me. "I will get them safely to where they are going, sir."

I nod, suddenly tired. "I know you will. Thanks."

He bows again. "My very great pleasure." He procures a card. "And if you have need of my services..."

I tuck the card in a pocket. "I think we'll be leaving very shortly, but I'll keep you in mind."

Nick and Madeline are just inside the door. I hand Nick the pistol and he hands me my Glock and a pouch with the contents of what had been in my pockets in return. "Cheers. We're going back to London tomorrow – shall I see you there?"

Nick nods. "We will also be returning, although I think Mother has business to attend to..." Madeline nods agreement.

"Okay, you'd best clear out." And without a word, they're gone.

The sound of tires on gravel tells me I have company. I turn back to the open door and put on my official face.

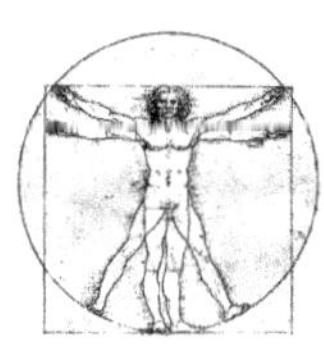

Headaches, pains and bellyaches

Jonesy took another hit of *snap*. The view in front of him wavered and readjusted itself.

He hadn't been to bed in 24 hours and the stimulant wasn't helping much anymore, besides giving him a raging thirst. And he was plugged into the grid trying to find Sen.

The timer he'd placed in his view told him it had been over eight hours since Bella had been taken. *Why the hell wasn't Sen answering his phone?*

"Dammit Sen, pickup your goddamn phone!" he shouted after yet another trip to voicebank. "Fuck it," he muttered. *Why hadn't he just done this to begin with?*

He was already in the location matrix where he'd deleted Sen's location – was it only yesterday? All he had to do was undo the deletion and Sen would light up like a Christmas tree.

Except Sen's module was missing.

"Fuck!"

Nerves jangling from the snap combining with the adrenaline surge as he panicked, he pounded on the arms of his chair with both hands.

In frustration, he tried to stand up while still plugged in. His head hit the retro suspended lamp over his chair with a muffled 'clang' and everything went black.

When he returned to something resembling consciousness, Jonesy had a dull throb to add to his buzzing nerve endings and what felt like an ice pick inserted just behind his left eye.

And he'd disconnected from the grid.

How long had he been out? Hard to tell in his mostly windowless shoebox of a flat. Jonesy found his voda on the floor beside the chair and checked the display: it had only been a few minutes, it looked like.

Jonesy went into his tiny bathroom and relieved himself. He avoided looking into the mirror.

Back in his chair, he sat staring at nothing, into space, trying not to think about Bella.

Where was Sen's location information?

"Did I do that good a number on it that he's invisible?" he muttered. *Unlikely*. It was more likely someone else had done it. But who?

Jonesy suspected Bella's kidnappers were also the ones behind the incursions into Central's systems. Why would they delete Sen? *They wouldn't.*

Something was nagging at Jonesy's shredded mind, but he couldn't focus on it. In desperation, he plugged back into the Grid and went to his 'office'.

His office was a construct in the virtual world where he kept important things and where it was easier to manifest some part of the web.

It looked like a square, Japanese room with rice paper screens for walls, a low table, tatami on the floors, the sound of trickling water just beyond the screens. He opened one of the screen walls and looked down over Tokyo, Mount Fuji rising in the background.

With a sigh, he turned from the view and said, "Wastebasket."

A round bin appeared in one corner of the room. He walked over to it and picked it up. The inside was virtually empty, barring a few scraps of 'paper'. He turned around and emptied the contents on the low table.

"Sort by time." The balls of information unscrambled themselves and flowed into a pattern on the desk, oldest to newest.

A purple post-it caught his eye. It was notes he'd made when removing the Commander's transponder from the grid. The torn envelope it was stuck to was probably more important.

"Gotcha!" He took the envelope and punched back out of his office. It wavered and was replaced by the Grid once more, by the location pod.

The envelope had become a pulsing, brilliantly white crystal. Locating an empty node, he almost slammed the crystal into place where it turned emerald green. Good, it was working.

He jacked out of the grid and slumped in his chair. This called for a coffee, he wasn't thinking straight.

He'd just started the machine when his voda rang. It was Sen.

"What do you want, Jonesy?" the Commander demanded.

"What, no 'hello, how are you, Jonesy?'" he quipped.

"I'm not in the mood, kid – it's been a long night."

He *did* sound tired. No! They had Bella! "What I wanted, *Commander*, was a little help with a problem caused by erasing you from the grid."

Silence. "What kind of problem, Jonesy?"

"They took my girl– my friend last night and demanded I tell them where you were. But I couldn't." He looked at the voda. "I've got about two and a half hours to tell them or they're going to kill her."

"Look, they're not going to kill her. If they did that, they'd have no hold over you." More silence. "Any idea who *they* are?"

Jonesy shook his head. "Not really, but they could be the ones behind the...alterations we've been monitoring." He decided to confess. "And I just made your location info visible again. Sorry."

"Not a problem – I'd have done it earlier. It doesn't matter now anyway." It sounded like Sen was walking, but ambient noise was usually minimal with a skullphone. "Have you got a way to contact them?"

"Yes...but they should know where you are now, anyway..."

"Doesn't matter. Give me the number and call them."

"Really? You want..."

"Jonesy, it doesn't matter if they know where I am! Call them!"

He rattled off the code and the connection went dead.

Jonesy shrugged and hit the dial button for the kidnappers' code. It didn't even ring.

"You have what we want?"

"His location info's live. I'm forwarding it now."

"Thank you for your cooperation, Mr Jones. Bella Kincaid has been released." Then nothing.

"Hello?" he was talking to a dead line.

His voda rang. "Jonesy! What the fuck!"

"Bella? Where the hell are you?"

"No idea. Outside some block of flats...Uh, number 136, looks like."

"You're outside my building! I'm coming down – don't go anywhere!"

"Where the fuck would I go, Jonesy?"

"You swear too much."

"Fuck you. Now get down here."

"Two secs."

He ran down the three flights of stairs and burst through the doors into daylight. Bella was slumped on the steps. It was all he could do to stop himself doing more than just sitting down next to her.

She looked at him through bleary eyes. "You fucktard. What the fuck was that all about? Your precious *Commander?*"

Jonesy had to look away. "Yep. I'm sorr–"

Bella waved it away. "Save it. I want to hear it from him."

"Uh, you just reminded me…C'mon, let's get indoors where it's warmer."

Glaring, Bella stood up from the step and allowed him to take her hand. She looked dead tired, but the glare didn't die down.

He got her into his apartment as quickly as he could.

"Jesus, Jonesy, it smells in here."

"I know, sorry."

"And stop fucking apologising!" She slumped onto the sofa.

"I'll make some coffee…"

"Put a whisky in mine – you wouldn't believe the night I've had. Oh wait, you would."

Smiling in spite of himself, he went into the kitchen cubby and put the coffee on, dialling Sen at the same time.

"Well?"

"Bella's here– in my flat."

"Good. Anything from the kidnappers?"

"Beyond letting her go, no." He picked up two mugs and rinsed them out. "What happens next?"

"For you, nothing. Leave it with me, Jonesy."

"Bella's pretty pissed with you, sir," he ventured.

There was a suggestion Sen was smiling when he replied. "I imagine she is. I'll be in my office first thing tomorrow morning – bring her in for 10.00 and I'll apologise in person."

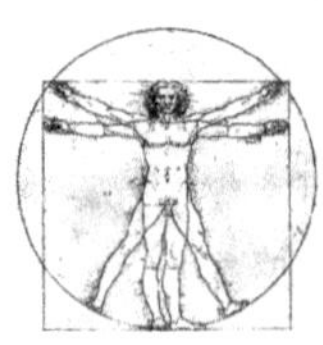

Too old to rock and roll

Skeet groaned and rolled over without opening her eyes. Clean sheets. A bed. Pure luxury!

When she finally opened her eyes, she didn't recognise the room.

"Where the hell am I?" she muttered.

"Murdock's safe house, from what he told me," a voice said.

Her head whipped around to see Jaared sitting in the corner, covered in shadow. "Shit, don't sneak up on me like that, old man."

"I was hardly 'sneaking', unless you call sitting in a chair quietly a form of sneaking."

Skeet ignored that, looking down. She was wearing an over-large t-shirt, but nothing else. "What time is it?"

"Half past two. How're you feeling?"

"Like I got bit by a fuckin'...what was that?" she threw back.

"A banshee, apparently. Luckily Madeline was able to remove the poison from your system before it did permanent damage."

"A banshee, huh?" Skeet rubbed her eyes, then focused. "What's the plan?"

"I need to get back – the train leaves at 4.30, gets me into King's Cross for 7.15."

Skeet stared at him. "You leavin' me here? No way."

Jaared shrugged. "Up to you – if you want to stay and rest, that's fine, too." He looked away. "There is the Tony Shonin situation..."

"Yeah? I can take care of them."

Jaared nodded. "I know, but you could take another day, take it easy."

Skeet shook her head. "Nope, I'm jumping in the shower." She stood up, then sat back down again, woozy. "Fuckin' banshee."

Before she knew it, Jaared was out of the chair and had one arm around her. "Let me help."

A spike of anger tightened her features for a moment. "I ain't an invalid!"

"Shhhh...No, but you were bitten by a 'fuckin' banshee' in the last twelve hours and nearly died. So you'll do me the courtesy of accepting a little help. Okay?"

A wave of tiredness washed over her and she leaned against his solidity, her head on his shoulder. "Sorry...know I can be a bitch..."

"Come on, let's get you in the shower – we've got a train to catch."

Washed, dried and with clean clothes (which she didn't even ask about), Skeet felt almost human as they threw their kit bags into the cab from the night before – complete with their Asian friend – and headed for the station.

A watery, winter Edinburgh day flashed past the windows. "Can't say I'll miss this place," Skeet murmured.

Jaared laughed. "C'mon, it's a lovely place...just not so much when fighting for one's life."

"Too far north." She glanced at the driver behind his partition and said quietly. "And, I can't understand a thing they say."

Shaking his head, Jaared laughed again. "You get used to it." He took her hand. "Never mind, we're going home now."

Skeet liked holding his hand. It felt...normal.

The cab dropped them at Waverly Station in a matter of minutes and they had no problems with security, Jaared's credentials whisking them through (avoiding weapons checks, as well) and onto the train, into the First Class carriage. As it was mostly empty, they had a table and four seats to themselves, their nearest passenger across the aisle.

Promptly at 4.30, the train left the station and began picking up speed. Within a few moments, it had reached its 320 kilometres per hour cruising speed, which would be maintained until it reached the outskirts of London.

After the attendant brought them a drink – real ale for her, Guinness for him – Skeet decided she needed to ask something. "Jaared..."

"Yes, my dear Skeet?"

Skeet, normally unflappable, blushed, so she took a gulp of her drink. He had that effect on her sometimes. "I–I was just wondering what you had in mind for Tony and the Sato twins."

Jaared was quiet for a moment, sipping his Guinness. "I don't have any definite plans, but we'll deal with them." He looked her in the eye. "I'm not worried about them, if that's what you mean.

"I'm not *worried*, either, I jest don't want 'em turnin' up at a bad moment," Skeet replied.

"Well, that's not going to happen – I had them detained this morning, as suspects in an international arms trafficking investigation."

Skeet punched him in the shoulder. "Ya coulda fuckin' told me that to begin with!" She caught the middle-aged man in the suit across the aisle frowning at her. She glared back, but spoke in softer tones. "Thanks, anyway."

Jaared rubbed his shoulder. "I can't keep them long, probably until tomorrow, but it should give us a day or so to work out what to do with them."

Skeet nodded, reassured. Her eyes suddenly felt heavy, a combination of the beer and the aftereffects of banshee venom. "I'm gonna close my eyes," she said, with them already closed.

"No problem, I've got work to do," Jaared replied.

"Wake me up when we get there."

"Of course." She felt his lips on her forehead before she slipped into darkness.

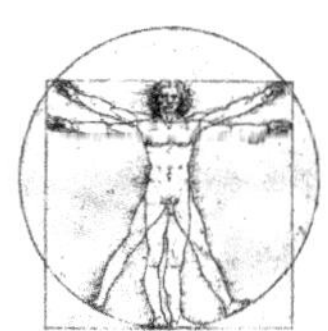

MAKE MINE A LARGE COFFEE

I get Skeet back to my mews house easily enough, although she falls asleep again in the cab.

Once indoors, it is only a matter of moments before she is in bed, snoring softly. I won't be far behind her.

Dickens follows us around, making plaintive 'mrrrwwwph' noises as he does so, reminding us that we'd left him alone for days.

When Skeet's tucked into bed, I pick him up and carry his purring form downstairs to the kitchen. He head-butts me, bony skull connecting solidly under my chin.

I put him down and open a tin of tuna just for him. He tucks in contentedly, purring as he gulps down the fish. I sometimes wish I had his life.

Opening the cabinet in the corner, I get a glass and pour myself a whisky, add water, all the while wondering what to do next. Shrugging to no one, I light a cigarette and go into the living room.

I caught up with a lot of my paperwork on the train, so there isn't anything needing my immediate attention. I sigh and drink my whisky. I know I have to visit the old man, I just don't particularly want to do it.

A quick search of Central throws up nothing new. I purposely keep his entry short and haven't added anything since our first meeting almost twenty years ago.

Okay, he doesn't like me and I haven't particularly warmed to him, either.

I swear I hear something crack as the hulking brute slams me up against the solid wooden panelling.

"Who sent you, Contractor?"

I do my best to shrug, difficult with my coat balled up in the giant's fist. "Someone who obviously doesn't like you."

The other person in the room croaks in what I assume is laughter. "That narrows it down, then." After a pause, the behemoth repeats the slamming, knocking the wind out of me. I struggle to catch my breath.

"H-h-hold on…" I pant. "What…happens if I tell…you?"

Next thing I know, I'm wobbling on my feet.

"Who sent you?"

"What happens?" I gasp.

"When you've told me."

"It was Phelps…Jasper Phelps…"

The giant pushes a leather wing chair into the backs of my knees, which I gratefully collapse into. "Thanks."

"Contractor Sen, I will tell you this only once…"

"That sounds ominous."

"Do not interrupt me again." He leans over to the humidor on the table beside him and I smell the scent of tobacco as he removes a large cigar. I keep my mouth shut. "I value my privacy and do not appreciate being disturbed in this fashion. If you intrude on my valuable time again, Geoff will kill you." I can almost see it as he gestures at the large man behind me again.

Geoff the giant? I ignore that one. "I understand. But…"

He holds his hand up. "No buts, no ifs, no exceptions." For emphasis, there's a snap as he cuts the end of the cigar off.

I nod. "Fine. Just don't blame me when I have to come back, Mr Crowley."

Crowley smiles, I can hear it in his voice. "I'm beginning to like you, Contractor." He flicks a large match holding it under the end of the stogie for a moment. When it starts to smoke, he draws air through it. I sense the heat from it as it begins to burn.

"Very well, Contractor, I will allow you this: bring me something of interest and I will stop Geoff from killing you. Deal?"

I nod again. Best I'm going to get. "Yessir, deal."

Dickens jumps up into my lap, still purring and padding my crotch. I shift him away from anything important and scritch him behind the ears. He soon settles down to warming my lap instead, motorboat purr going strong.

I've only seen the old man three times and once it was a near thing whether Geoff was going to kill me or not.

I stub out the cigarette with a sigh and finish my whisky. The happy cat in my lap allows himself to be stroked, his rumble vibrating through my fingers.

Tiredness etched into my bones, I'm feeling too old for this shit. The last week's been waaayyy too exciting.

Dickens stretches and puts his head on his paws, settling in. His warmth is comforting.

I close my eyes for just a moment…

…and wake with a start. Someone's in the room but the cat is gone.

I stand up, gun in my hand and pointed at the far corner where the shadow is deepest. I can't see anything but two glowing eyes, gold not red, like amber with live flames in their centres.

"What do you want?" I demand, finger tightening on the trigger of the Glock.

I get the feeling the figure is smiling, but can't see anything but those eyes. No reply.

"I said, what do you want?"

You know exactly what I want, Jaared.

"No, no I don't. Show yourself!"

Laughter. The eyes fade leaving only shadow.

"I said, show yourself!" The finger on the trigger tightens and a burst of bullets tears the shadow…

I jerk awake, Dickens solid and warm in my lap. I look into the corner where the eyes had been in my dream and there isn't even a shadow.

It was only a dream.

I pick up a sleepily protesting cat and stand up. It only takes a second to place him on the seat where I'd been sitting. He settles down with little fuss. I stroke him one more time and pick up the empty glass.

"Time for bed." Dickens doesn't answer. Can't say I blame him.

I put the glass on the kitchen counter and head up to bed.

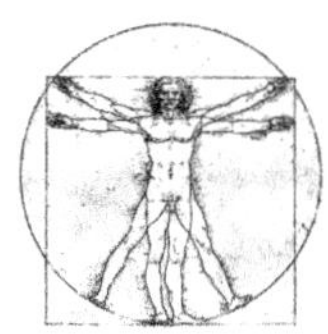

YOUR EMERGENCY IS NOT MY EMERGENCY

Jonesy picked Bella up from her apartment on the way to work.

She'd insisted on going back after a few hours on his couch and he'd called her a cab after she'd refused a ride on his bike. "You can give me a ride tomorrow," she'd leered. Jonesy had, predictably, blushed.

Bella had phoned as soon as she was in her flat to let him know she was fine and to be at her building for 8.30 the following morning. No excuses. "I have to meet your precious Commander, after all," she'd needled him.

"He's not *my* Commander," he protested again.

"So you say – I think you're secret bum-buddies and you're using me as a beard," Bella replied.

Jonesy went red on the other end of the voda, again, unable to think of a suitable reply to that.

"See? Gone all quiet on me. Just proves it..."

"We're...not..." he squeaked, totally mortified and feeling much as he had when talking to girls in high school.

Bella sighed. "I know, dummy, I'm just kidding. Jesus, you need to chill."

So here he was, on the way to work on his bike with Bella clinging to him behind, wearing his spare helmet. It was bright green and had a large dragon head painted across it.

He glanced over his shoulder one more time. "You okay?" he shouted over the (fake) noise of the motorcycle.

"Great! Keep your eyes on the road!" she shouted back.

Jonesy turned his eyes back to the road, grinning as much from having Bella on the back of his Harley as from the joy of riding it.

They made good time, arriving at Company House just before 9.00.

"I'll meet you on the tenth floor..."

Bella rolled her eyes. "Yeah, just before ten, I know." She started to turn away, then changed her mind. She grabbed the front of his shirt and pulled him down to her level before laying a kiss on his lips. Stunned, Jonesy froze. Then his lips took over. It was nice. *Very* nice.

His eyes had closed of their own accord by the time she pulled away. "Been wanting to do that for ages," Bella admitted. "See ya later…stud."

Silly grin plastered on his face, Jonesy watched her walk away. "Later." In a daze, he turned and headed for an empty cubicle he often used.

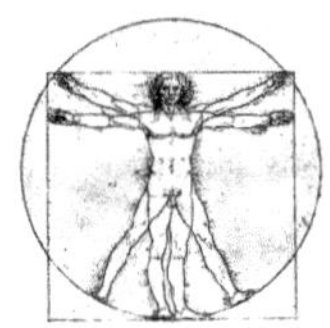

God's Away On Business

Skeet woke tangled in the sheets on Jaared's bed. He was long gone and she had a vague memory of him leaving in the dark. Wouldn't have been the first time.

When she opened her eyes, a darkly furred face was mere inches from hers, staring intently at her and purring. Loudly.

"Fuck, Dickens, that's scary," she gasped. "To what do I owe the pleasure of your company, young man?" she enquired, reaching over to scratch his ears the way he liked.

The cat responded by closing his eyes, enjoying the attention.

"If ya think I'm going to feed ya again, ya've got another thing coming," she muttered. Abandoning him, she got up from the bed and headed for the shower. Her body ached and her head was still fuzzy from whatever had been in that poison. Felt like a hangover with none of the benefits.

Shower started, Skeet found some painkillers in the bathroom cabinet and washed them down with water from the tap. She glared at herself in the mirror, noting the dark circles under her eyes, her spiky hair limp from sleep. "Not exactly looking your best today, darlin'," she murmured. She turned away from her reflection and got into the shower, adjusting it so the needles of spray felt like a sharp massage. The heat felt good.

What seemed like hours later, Skeet dragged herself out of the shower and dried off before pulling on a pair of jeans and a heavy jumper she found in one of Jaared's drawers. She still felt cold, but the sweater was comforting. She went downstairs to the kitchen and poured herself some coffee. Dickens had followed her downstairs, ever hopeful.

"Yer a chancer," Skeet said to him before relenting and adding a few biscuits to his bowl.

He looked at them and then back to her as if to say, "Biscuits? Really?"
"That's all yer gettin' from me, mister," she replied. "Shit, I'm talkin' to the cat." She picked up her coffee and found a note on the counter by her voda.

Tony and the Twins are out.

Call him and set up a meeting. Tell him you've got what he wants. And to bring the Sato twins.

"Jaared, your handwriting sucks," she muttered. Checking the time – Tony wasn't an early riser – she went into the living room and sat down. Feeling slightly vindictive and almost hoping she got his voicemail, she dialled his number.
He answered, all business. "Skeet. I hope you've got good news."
Skeet swallowed and forced herself to be her usual self. "Yep, Ton – want the package? Meet me at the George tonight at seven."
"Why?"
"Because he's going to be there about seven-thirty, that's why." Skeet licked her lips. "And bring the twins."
"You better not be messing me around, Skeet, for your sake." The connection clicked off.
Skeet drank some more of her coffee and dialled Jaared. When he answered, she said, "All set. They'll be at the George at seven."
"Good morning to you, too," he responded.
"Sorry, this mess puts my back up," she said, feeling stretched thin.
"Not a problem. You okay?" The concern in his voice was evident.
She took a drink. "Yeah, fine. I'm not going anywhere today, though."
"Don't blame you. Shall I just see you at the George? What time you want me visible?"
"I tol' him 7.30, so come in about then." She hesitated. "I wouldn't bring backup, least not visible backup."
"Not a problem. This will all be over tonight."
"I hope so." Skeet suddenly needed reassurance.
"Trust me, I've got it covered."
"I love you, Jaared." Damn, she'd said it out loud.
There was a beat of silence. "I love you too, Skeet," he replied.
"Good. Was startin' to wonder."

He laughed. "I'll see you later – got to go."

"Later."

Feeling more herself, Skeet went to the kitchen and poured herself another cup of coffee. She returned to the sofa and pulled the old quilt over her, snuggling down into it. She flicked on the vid, prepared to zone or drowse. Some mindless talk show appeared and she relaxed.

Dickens entered the room, took one look at her on the sofa and jumped up to curl up on the other end, going around twice to make sure of his space before settling in.

Content, almost happy, Skeet drifted off.

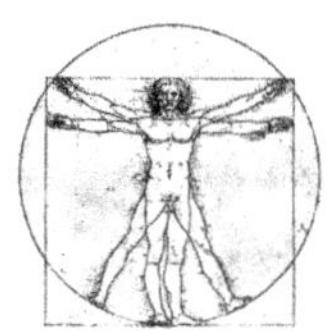

BLOOD MUSIC

Madeline leapt from the warehouse to the garage roof, following her target in the alley below.

She could feel Nicholas nearby, also occupied in the hunt. It was good to be free again and the hunt made her feel more alive than she had in weeks, the scent of blood strong in her nostrils as she gauged the distance to the rooftop of an adjacent factory.

A shriek nearly threw her off her stride, but not enough to make her miss the jump. She landed softly on the skittery asphalt roofing without even skidding. *Happy hunting?* she enquired, touching her son's mind lightly.

No challenge – I thought he was going to open his jugular for me, so eager was he to help me.

Madeline smiled, his confidence cheering her. *I am nearly done myself.*

She could hear her prey below, vainly attempting to force open the door of another building. Edging her head over the parapet of the roof, she saw the girl slump against the locked door, shaking with the effort that running had cost her. Junkies aren't built for endurance.

Finding a drainpipe just over the roof's edge, Madeline gripped it with one iron hand and allowed gravity to pull her mass down its length, the hiss of the iron loud in the stillness of the alley. The junkie spun round, determined to escape. Or at least fight.

"What do you want?" the girl demanded.

Madeline smiled, knowing how disconcerting her teeth were. "Why, your blood. That is all."

Do not play with your food, Mother, her son chided, observing from a nearby rooftop.

I am deadly serious, she replied. "Come now, child, do you think to fight me?"

The girl raised her wasted arms, her hand in claw-shapes, baring broken nails, her lips drawn back in a snarl. "What do you want?" she almost shouted, sounding like "Whaddayawant" it came out so slurred.

Madeline tutted, raising her own hands, the long nails made for rending. "Really?"

The junkie shrieked and dashed toward the opening to the side of the alley. Madeline anticipated her movement and calmly stood blocking her way.

"Leave me alone!"

Madeline shook her head, left hand darting out to pin the girl to the wall by the neck. "I'm sorry, that is not an option."

Her fangs pierced the skin of the junkie's throat like it was paper, the hot fluid flowing into her mouth. The girl had frozen at the same instant, all resistance gone, swooning as her blood was released. There was a hint of burnt chemicals in the blood, one of the problems with drug users, but not wholly unpleasant.

Madeline stopped before draining the girl completely. "I leave you your life, such as it is," she whispered. The limp figure drooped down the wall, too weak to move.

Come, we are not home yet.

"You remind me?" Madeline smiled again, delicately wiping any remaining traces from her lips with her middle finger. *It will be good to be home.*

Yes. Nicholas hesitated. *Although I fear there is still much to do.*

"Agreed." Madeline's eyes blazed. There were too many things happening which couldn't be explained. It was time for answers.

And Lucien de Foret.

Damn the man.

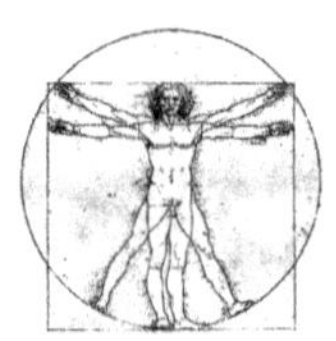

DON'T WASTE MY TIME AND I WON'T WASTE YOURS

I put down the tablet after pressing my thumb on the screen. Another requisition signed off. Oh the joys of senior management.

The backs of my thumbs itch, wanting to do something besides paperwork.

There's a knock at my door. "Come."

Jonesy and a small woman enter.

I stand up and move around my desk. "You must be Bella Kincaid," I say, holding out my hand. "I would like to apologise for any inconvenience you may have had on my account."

She cocks her head to one side, not taking my hand. "Inconvenience? You call kidnapping an 'inconvenience'?" She isn't loud, and that probably is more impressive than shouting.

I drop my hand. "I'm sure it felt much worse to you. Do you need any kind of support? Counselling? Compensation? Someone's head on a pike?"

She stares at me for another moment before laughing out loud. "Yeah, that'll do it, Commander – I want the bastard's head on pike in front of Company House!"

I smile, relieved. "I'll see what I can do, Ms Kincaid." I gesture at the seating area in front of my view. "Please. Would you like coffee? Tea? Something stronger?"

Bella looks shocked for a moment. "It's ten o'clock in the morning!"

I nod. "Yes. And?"

She laughs again. "Just coffee for me, ta."

"Jonesy?"

"Yes, coffee for me, too." He looks uncomfortable for some reason. I can hear his heart beating faster than normal.

"Relax, Jonesy, you're not in trouble here." With a mental nudge, I ask the pool coffee machine for three coffees. It only takes a few moments for the coffee to arrive, and I join them looking at my view.

"Have they used your location information, Commander?" Jonesy obviously can't abide silence.

"Not that I'm aware of." I sip my coffee. "And the number does not connect when I try to access it. Very strange."

"So what was so goddamn urgent?!?"

I smile and sip my coffee. "That's the million dollar question."

Bella's watching me, not really drinking her coffee. Her heartbeat is a normal resting rate, so she's not nervous or upset...curious is more like it.

Well, if she's not going to drink my coffee and sit there staring at me, it's time to wrap it up. I put my cup down and stand up. "I can only apologise again, Ms Kincaid and hope you won't hold this against me."

She and Jonesy also stand, her head cocked to one side again.

"I guess I can see it," she says finally.

"What's that, Ms Kincaid?"

"The reason Jonesy jumps through hoops for you."

That makes me frown. "I wouldn't think I inspire that kind of loyalty..."

"But you do – he's the proof!"

I tilt my head and glance at Jonesy. He's just standing there, watching, a dumfounded look on his face.

I don't know what to say. Jonesy saves me in the end.

"Later, Commander – you be careful," he chides, lamely.

I nod at them both. "I will."

They troop out of my office, Bella with a backward glance at me.

I turn back to the view. Am I really that, I don't know, 'inspirational'? I light one of my black cigarettes and turn the room fans up to high.

Adams, clad in a black *Suicidal Tendancies* t-shirt and stained cammo trousers and smelling like he hasn't had a shower in a few days, drops by, wanting to know how his gadgets worked in Edinburgh.

I sit behind my desk, shuffling paper, ignoring him as best I can, Bella's words echoing in my head. "Adams, they worked fine – thanks."

He tries to catch my eye with his droopy beagle look. "Really? Just 'fine'?" He's disappointed. I often feel like I've kicked a puppy when dealing with Adams.

"Yes, they saved our asses on more than one occasion," I reassure him.

"Great! What happened? I need to put it in my report..."

"Adams, it wasn't an official project, you know that," I say quietly. I can get away with pushing the boundaries sometimes, but it's not a good thing to encourage in one's subordinates.

My skullphone 'brrrrrs', interrupting him. "Yes?" I ask, knowing full well who it is.

"I've got those files for you Commander...when you're ready." The Inspector General doesn't pause for niceties like 'hello'.

Ah, the files on the Council...that could be interesting. "I'll be right up, Sir." There's a click as he hangs up on me. As I say, no pleasantries.

"Gotta go, Adams." I stand up and head for the door. "Thanks again, you got us out of a few tight spots."

"Anytime Commander, all you gotta do is call!"

Shit. Maybe Bella's right.

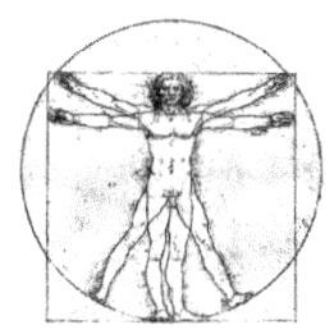

Something never comes, never leads to nothing

Jonesy didn't know what to say to Bella on the way back down in the lift to her floor. He stared awkwardly at the numbers flashing in the little indicator.

"Hey, earth to Mr Jones – anyone in there?" Bella tugged at his sleeve. "Hell-oooooo?"

He couldn't help but smile. "Yep, I'm here, just not sure what to say. Sorry."

Bella thumped him on the arm.

"Ow! What was that for?" He rubbed the impact area, glaring at her.

"What did I say about apologising?" she asked, glaring back.

Jonesy ducked his head. "You're right. Sor–" Another thump interrupted him.

The lift seemed to be taking forever and Bella sighed. "Oh hell," she muttered before grabbing his shirt and pulling him down to her level. "Okay Buster, you asked for it."

"Wh-what?"

"This." Bella kissed him before he had a chance to get away. Startled, it took him a moment to relax into it, by which time, she'd pulled away. More dazed than before, he smiled at her. Bella smiled back.

"My floor. Now I'll see you at 5.30. Sharp."

"5.30?"

"Yes, 5.30 – you're giving me a ride home."

"Oh, right. Yeah."

"Later, Mr Jones."

"Bye."

He stood in the lift after she'd gone, wondering where he was going next. The lift moved and he got out when the doors opened, before realising he had no idea what floor he was on. Jonesy turned back to get in the lift, just as the doors closed. He swore and looked around while punching the button for the lift again. It seemed darker on this floor, like the lights hadn't been replaced in a while.

"You'll need a pass card to get off the floor now," a voice informed him.

Jonesy turned around. There was a skinny guy in a *Suicidal Tendencies* t-shirt and a lab coat standing behind him in the door to one of the darkened rooms. He caught the flicker of what looked like candlelight before the figure came toward him, a pass extended.

"Thanks. I don't know how I got here."

"The lift, of course." The man held out his hand. "I'm Adams, Director, Paranormal Phenomena."

"Jonesy, chief babysitter for Central." Jonsey shook the hand. "'Paranormal Phenomena'? I didn't realise we had ghost hunters on the payroll…"

Adams puffed up his chest. "It's not just ghosts – we deal with possession, poltergeists, multi-dimensional beings, demons and *lots* of monsters."

"Monsters?"

"Yep, you name it, we've probably encountered one somewhere. Or Commander Sen has, anyway," Adams added under his breath.

"You know Sen?" Jonesy's interest was of the piqued variety.

"Yep, I've been helping with his cases recently."

"Really? You do field work?" Jonesy tried very hard to keep the incredulity out of his voice.

"Well, no, I'm not cleared for that, but I supply him with magical items…uh, I'm probably not supposed to say anything about that…" Adams looked sheepish. "Don't tell him, huh?"

Jonesy smiled. "Don't worry, he won't hear it from me."

"Cheers. Oh, I guess you'll be wanting to leave…here you go…" Adams swiped his pass over the reader and the lift doors opened again. "Nice to meet you. Come down any time…wait, no, that's not a good idea. Ring me…"

"Okay, nice meeting you, too," Jonesy said as the lift doors closed between them. "Bit of an odd one. But I like him."

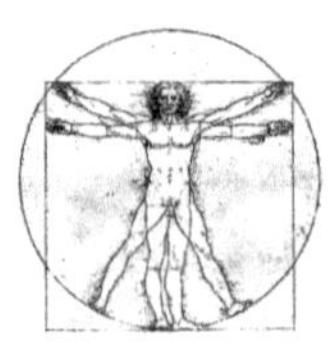

LOOKING FOR A FEW GOOD MEN AND TRUE

The Inspector General stood at his window, looking out across the river toward Sussex and Kent.

"Hazel," he said out loud, knowing full well it would be picked up by his secretary.

"Yes sir?"

"Call my wife and let her know I'll be going to the club this evening. I will be back in the morning."

"Very good sir. Is there anything else?"

"Not at the moment…Hazel, when Sen's been and gone, I'd like to see you, please."

"Yes sir."

He waited. Yes, alone. He sighed. *Hazel isn't going to take it well*, he guessed.

He sighed again. It had been a good job. And one at which he had been exceptional. It was time to spend more time with his wife – whether that was what she wanted or not. There were always the grandchildren. Or golf. Or his roses. He shuddered.

I will need to find something to do, he thought to himself. The view seemed to dim for a moment. *I can't spend the rest of my days chasing a damn ball around or pruning roses that are already stunted.*

He grunted in disgust at the idea and went to his liquor cabinet. He poured a large Armagnac and returned to the view. Besides the job, he would miss this view. It was spectacular.

The Inspector General turned back to his desk, flipped open the grubby folder on his desk and turned to the back. He picked up his Mont Blanc fountain pen, removed the cap and with a flourish, added a line to the back of the last document.

He smiled to himself, capped the pen and flipped the folder closed again and turned back to the view. *I might even miss the old bastard*, he thought, meaning Jaared Sen. *He's got under my skin.*

There was another option, of course. He shook his head, sipping the brandy.

Not an option. He wasn't Japanese and it wasn't like he needed a job; it was more to do with keeping busy. Not sitting down and dying.

Maybe he'd get a dog. That'd annoy his wife. He smiled again, already relishing the arguments and recriminations. Arguing with one's wife was a 'pleasure' not to be dismissed lightly.

The Inspector General threw back the rest of the brandy, knowing Sen would be there at any moment. Shame to do that to the good stuff, but there was more.

He turned away from the view and sat behind his desk.

Good luck Jaared.

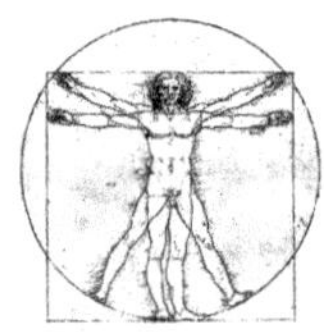

WHAT? DID I HIT A NERVE?

The IG isn't in a good mood. *Nothing new there.* I sigh inwardly.

"Am I disturbing you, Commander?"

I shake my head. "No, sir – not at all. What did you want to see me about, sir?"

He pushes a battered file across the desk. How odd, most filing is electronic these days; even when needed, flimsy only lasts as long as it needs to.

"What's this?"

He frowns again, glances furtively around which we both know is pointless. I'm monitored and so is most of Company House. The idea of having a conversation off the grid is absurd.

"It's the files I promised you – you know the ones I mean..." he said finally.

I know all right – the 'Council of the Seven', whatever that is. I'd made the mistake of asking someone directly and the next moment he'd had some kind if aneurysm and died on the spot.

"Yessir, I know the ones you mean."

He looks away, discomfited or worried, hard to tell. His heart rate's elevated and he's perspiring, too. Definitely nervous. "Sorry about the format, but the contents are passed on from one holder of this post to the next. Not something to be trusted to Central, I'm afraid."

I pick up the dog-eared folder and mentally weigh the contents. It's not very heavy or very thick. I look up to find the IG looking at me, a serious expression on his face.

Finally, "That's all, Commander."

"Yes sir. Thanks for that, sir."

He smiles wryly. "I don't think you'll be thanking me for very long, Commander." He turns away and looks out the window across the river.

The early morning mist has cleared and you can almost see Croydon. "I *am* sorry, Jaared."

What for? I wonder. I take that as my cue and leave his office.

The file is as thin as I had feared. And no, it didn't hold all the answers I was looking for.

"Christ," I said to no one.

From what I was reading, the Council was a very old group, probably tied into most of the ancient secret societies like the Priory of Sion and the Illuminati. According to the file both organisations existed, but the Council had fingers in their pies. The conspiracy theorists would kill for this file. Only problem was the lack of documentable evidence. The file's contents could be dismissed without effort.

I only believed it was true because of my previous exposure to the Council's actions, however slight.

Beyond confirming the existence of the Council of the Seven, the rest of it was primarily speculation on its activities. I've seen more convincing theories on some of the paranoid conspiracy 'sites. There was little evidence of Council involvement – the majority of it was just that, speculation.

A prime example:

> *There is firm evidence to believe the Council instigated the Magna Carta in the person of Geoffrey de Mandeville, Earl of Essex, who was a tool they used on a regular basis with King John. See document MXVIII for further details.*

And of course there was no sign of document MXVIII in the folder.

All three World Wars were apparently at the Council's instigation, as were their resolutions. What was unclear was the origin of the Council and how it had remained so unknown for so long. I could guess, having seen James die right in front of me. Their reach was scary.

A notation at the bottom of the folder in the Inspector General's cramped handwriting stopped me cold.

> *It is recommended that Jaared Sen be conscripted forthwith – his contacts within the supernatural community, organised crime, not to mention*

previous contact with the Priory, make him a natural choice to continue within the Company.

What the hell do I say to that? I take the folder and put it in the case I keep in the cupboard just for such occasions. I can't leave it in the office, now can I?

I am getting ready to leave when my skullphone rings. "Yes?"

"Commander Sen? This is Hennings, from the Company."

I know who Hennings is, he's only the Operations Officer for the Company. Why's he calling me? "Yessir, how can I help you?"

There's an awkward pause. "I'm sorry to drop this on you, Commander, but the Inspector General has resigned with immediate effect."

The IG resigned? Shit. "I just saw him – he didn't mention he was leaving..." *Or did he?*

"I was under the impression he had informed you of his decision, Commander." Another pause. "With immediate effect you're to assume the role of Inspector General, Commander Sen."

Holy crap. "You're joking, right?" But I knew he didn't have much in the way of a sense of humour.

"No Commander, I don't joke about this sort of thing." More silence. "The Inspector General was of the opinion that with your considerable experience, bar your penchant for defying authority, you were the ideal candidate for the role in his absence."

I don't know what to say. "I don't really know what to say..."

"You don't have to say anything, Commander. You've got 48 hours to tie up your current workload. That said, you will be given access to the roles and responsibilities of the IG's office with immediate effect."

He isn't kidding. As I am contemplating this change in my status, a new icon appears in my HUD, simple entitled "Level 12". I don't even think about opening it.

Jesus.

"Any questions Commander? Or rather, 'Inspector General'."

I can't think of anything – I've gone blank. "No sir."

"Feel free to contact my office if you do think of any. And congratulations, Jaared."

"Thank you, sir."
The line goes dead.
Shit.

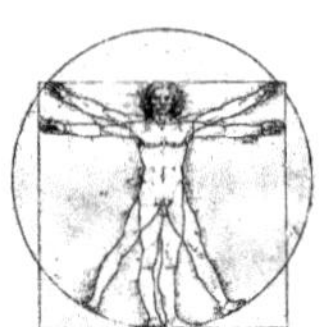

USA Today: A firestorm devastated Henderson, Nevada today, the result of a long-running drought in the area. At this point, the bulk of the town is burning and it is unlikely fire crews will be able to stop it any time soon...

AP: Lightning struck a football stadium in São Paulo, Brazil, instantly electrocuting more than 460 football fans in the middle of a match between São Paulo FC and Atlético Mineiro...at least 70 people are confirmed dead and the resultant fire...

Lying in the bath, thinking

Skeet lay in the bath, trying to relax, but not relishing seeing Tony and the Twins. Regardless of whatever Jaared had up his sleeve.

Her voda rang. It was Jaared. "Heya handsome, I'm in the bath."

"Hey." He sounded distracted.

"Nekked in the bath," she added.

He wasn't listening. "You won't believe what's just happened," he replied.

"More important than me being here with no clothes on?" Skeet was smiling.

"What? Yes, I mean, no…fuck…"

She sat up in the bath. "Okay, jus' tell me what's going on Jaared."

Nothing for a moment. "I've just been made Inspector General."

"Holy crap!"

"Exactly. That's what I said."

"When did this happen?"

"About ten minutes ago. I've been sitting here wondering what the hell I do now."

Skeet frowned. "Guess you ain't got a choice in this?"

"Not really. The IG nominated me as his replacement before he resigned."

"And? What else?"

"In 48 hours, the job's mine. I've got until then to sort out my workload."

"What a bastard, dropping you in it like this…"

Jaared was silent. "It's probably my fault…"

"Your fault? Why would it be your fault?"

"My habit of asking questions people don't want to answer, I think…"

"This is about that bloody Council, ain't it?"

"Looks like it. I may also be tied to them now, I'm not sure."

"Aw, fuckit..." She hit the tap to add more hot water to the bath. "What're you going to do?"

"I guess it's my job now, so I need to sort out a few things."

"Need any help?"

"Probably, but I don't know what – I just needed to tell you..."

"I'm glad you did." She grinned. "Now, sure I can't tempt ya by reminding ya I'm nekked in the bath?"

"You trying to distract me?"

"Well, you're the boss now, ya can probably leave whenever ya want to..."

Jaared laughed. "You're right – hadn't thought of that." He stops. "I would love to take you up on that, but I need to sort some things out around here. I'll see you at the George."

"Okay, old man – don't be late!"

Skeet was sitting at the bar when the Sato Twins came in followed by Tony. She didn't even look in their direction, using the mirror behind the bar to keep an eye on their movements.

"Hello, Skeet," Tony said at her shoulder.

"Tony." No need for niceties, as she didn't like the guy. Skeet didn't even turn her head.

"What, not offering me a drink?"

"I don't drink with scum like you, Tony," Skeet replied, not looking at him.

"Careful, Skeet – you don't want to upset me," Tony said.

Skeet looked him in the eye. "Tony, I couldn't give a flying fuck what ya want – or whether yer upset." Her eyes shifted to the Twins. "And it would be a different story if ya weren't dragging those two hunks a'meat around."

"I'm hurt, Skeet," Tony hissed. "And here I thought we were friends..."

Skeet smirked. "Yeah, right." She sipped her ale and ignored him.

Tony took the stool next to her, but couldn't leave the silence be. "Where is Sen?"

"He'll be here."

"I hope, for your sake, he is." Tony flagged the barman. "Gin and tonic, kind sir." Nothing for the Twins, they were working, of course.

No longer able to see the Twins, Skeet noticed how pale he was looking in the mirror. "Guess the climate's not agreeing with ya, eh, Tony? You need to top up that tan."

"Fuck off, Skeet."

"Oooooooh, hit a nerve? Thought ya preferred the tropics anyway, Ton. What the hell ya doin' in England?"

Tony took his drink from the barman and glanced at her. "I go where I'm paid to go. Even rainy, cold, old England." He sipped at his G&T. "Besides, I speak the lingo, unlike the Twins, here."

Skeet laughed. "Oh, they speak English, Ton, just not necessarily your version of it." The clock behind the bar said 7.20. *Don't be late, Jaared,* she implored him silently. *I'm not sure I can sit here with this prick for much longer.*

Just before half past, Jubal, one of Jaared's contacts/acquaintances/ friends (whatever) came in. A hulking black guy who owned a rare book store near King's Cross, Jubal looked like he'd already been drinking, clothes mussed, glazed look in his eye and a slight stumble in his step. And when he approached the bar next to Skeet, she could smell the beer on him.

"Ah, Mistress Skeet. How are you this fahhhnnn evenin'?" he slurred.

"Good, Jubal – how about you?" Tony nudged her arm, waved at Jubal, meaning, *make him go away.*

Skeet smiled at Tony just as she caught sight of Jaared entering the pub in the corner of her eye. Without giving him away, she turned back to Jubal.

"I'm fahhhhnnn, Mistress Skeet, just fahhhnnn." Jubal grinned from ear to ear.

"You been drinkin' Jubal?"

Jubal's grin got bigger, if that was possible. "I had a big sale today, 18th Century manuscript in primo condition – worth a pretty penny – thought I'd celebrate…"

Skeet could feel Tony getting nervous beside her. And he hadn't noticed Jaared coming up behind him. *God he's thick,* she thought to herself.

"Jubal, you bothering my girl?" Jaared asked from behind them. Tony jumped and spilled his drink, looking around frantically for the Twins.

"Commander! Good to see you, sir! May I have the honour of buying your good friend and yourself a drink in celebration of a timely windfall?"

"What are you on about, Jubal?" Jaared replied with a smile.

"Sold a book today," Skeet interjected, ignoring Tony's increasingly frantic fidgeting beside her.

Jubal frowned. "Not *just* a book, I'll have you know, but an 18th Century First Edition of *Pamela: Or, Virtue Rewarded* by Samuel Richardson. A rare and quite valuable edition, I'll have you know." He swayed, trying to look knowledgeable while attracting the eye of the barman at the same time.

"And where did *you* get it, Jubal?"

"A reputable source, Commander, very reputable..."

Jaared nodded. "I'll bet. And yes, I'll have a Guinness, as you're buying. Skeet?"

Skeet lifted her glass. "Another pint of Ole Scratcher, please."

Jubal got the attention of the barman finally and ordered.

While he was distracted, Jaared turned to Skeet. "Aren't you going to introduce me to your friend?" he murmured. Tony leaned back, still trying to locate the Twins.

Skeet's smile took on the feral quality that scared a lot of people. "Why shore, Jaared, this here's Tony Shonin all the way from Thailand, jes' to meet you."

Jaared nodded, his smile sharpening. "I thought it might be." He leaned toward Tony. "And don't bother looking for the Twins, I'm afraid they're not going to be much help at the moment..."

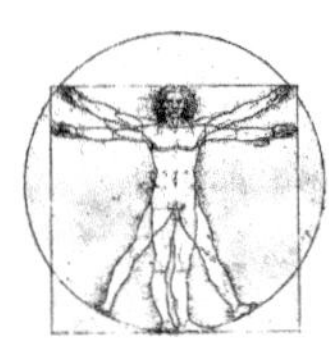

It took all of five seconds.

The fat twin threw a straightforward haymaker which even a blind man could see coming. I step to one side and put two fingers in his solar plexus. He doubles over, trying to vomit and breathe at the same time.

The smaller twin – not entirely sure why they're called 'twins', they're definitely not identical – is a bit more careful. He pulls one of those extendable baton things out and flicks his wrist. Then he adopts a sloppy version of a 'three battles stance' and waves fingers at me to come on.

"Yeah, right," I reply. I take out my Glock and shoot him with a stun round. "I'm not in the mood to fuck about."

I put the Glock away and check that fat twin's not going to run off. He isn't. That done, I call for a car to come pick them up and go into the pub.

To give him credit, Tony Shonin doesn't turn into a jellyfish at the news that the Sato Twins are out of action. He does go a bit paler, though.

Skeet's grin could slice bricks. "What'd you do to the Twins, then?"

I grin back. After the day I've had it was refreshing to do something I didn't really have to think about, like dealing with the Sato Twins. "To be honest, I barely broke a sweat, so I can't really work out what the fuss is all about – they're slabs of meat with a lazy idea of what makes up a martial art." I glance toward Jubal, still occupied. "And no, I didn't kill them – they're currently waiting for a meat wagon out the back."

Skeet cackles. Tony is still silent.

"What's the matter, Tony? Nothing to say after going to all this trouble to meet me? I'm disappointed."

"I-I'm not supposed to talk to you, just bring you back to Ms Watson..."

I shake my head. “Oh dear, I do hate to disappoint my daughter, but that’s not going to happen.”

Tony’s mouth drops open. “Your daughter? What the hell…”

Skeet pokes him. “C’mon, Tony, haven’t you heard a’ rejuv? Shoulda thought you were well acquainted with it, actually.”

This earns her a glare. “So what happens now?” He sound defeated.

I shrug. “You can try and make me go with you – I emphasise the ‘try’ part of that sentence – or you can go with the officer just outside the door.”

His shoulders slump. “Jail, then?”

I shake my head again. “No. Whenever possible, we get rid of troublemakers these days. You and the Twins are going back to Phuket.”

He brightens momentarily, then remembers my daughter will be waiting. And she won’t be happy. “Great.” He gets up, downs his drink and nods at Skeet. “See ya’ Skeet – it’s been fun.”

“I’m not going to be back in Phuket for a while, Tony, so I doubt I’ll see you anytime soon.” Skeet picks up the pint Jubal just put on the bar. “And if I’d had anything to say about it, ye’d be going back in a box…”

Tony blanched even more and wordlessly turned and joined the officer at the door.

I turn back to find Jubal standing there with a pint of Ole Scratcher. “What was that all about, Commander?”

I pick up the Guinness that’s waiting for me. “Families, Jubal. Can’t live with ‘em, can’t shoot ‘em.”

“Hear, hear,” Skeet joined in.

Jubal just laughed. I smiled on the outside, but realised I’d just postponed meeting my daughter to another day.

We stay in the George, have something to eat and a lot more to drink before pouring ourselves in a cab and making our way back to mine. I’m deliberately not thinking about my promotion. Or the file in my case.

We continue, as we have most of the evening, talking about inconsequential things, but happy to do so. I like the easy camaraderie we’ve built up over the years. I just wish it hadn’t only been troubles that brought us back together.

“What’re ya thinking?” Skeet asks as we get out of the cab at the end of the mews.

"Just wondering how things would've worked out if my daughter hadn't got you involved in her schemes." I take Skeet's hand. She resists for a second, before relaxing.

She sighs. "I know. And now I'm wondering why I was scared of Tony and the Twins. Why didn't I just tell you the truth in the first place?"

I light a cigarette one-handed and blow smoke through my nose. "Yep, we could do the 'what if' game all night." I take another drag on the fag and shake my head. "Let's give it a rest and stop dwelling on the past – for tonight, anyway."

Skeet pulls me closer with the hand I'm holding onto. "Sounds good to me, mister." She kisses me. Properly. No fucking about.

"Wow," I say when she lets me breathe again.

"That it?"

I nod, realising the cigarette's burned down to my fingers. "Yep, 'wow' pretty much sums it up." I toss the butt into the gutter.

Smiling, Skeet unlocks the door and pulls me into the house. "C'mon then, let me see if I can improve on 'wow'."

Some time later, I sit in the darkness, listening to Skeet breathe, a lit cigarette in my hand.

I'm the new Inspector General. Crap.

A desk job. Office politics. Managing people. I've never been very good at that sort of thing. "Doesn't play well with others" is likely to be inscribed on my tombstone. I suck in smoke and stare into the dimness.

Is that why no one's tried anything? I've been back on the grid for days now and they could have found me any time they wanted to. I checked, but Central doesn't have any hint I'm being watched or followed, but then I wasn't sure Jonesy had actually found all the incursions that were plaguing us. It didn't prove anything.

I'd guess it's only a matter of time before *something* happens. I need to follow up what Chambers told me in Edinburgh. And I know just the man to talk to.

Too much time on my hands...

Bella met him in the garage where he had left his bike. She was dressed for the ride, thick coat, trousers and gloves and still managed to look good to him.

Jonesy handed her the helmet. "Ready?"

She nodded, slipping the helmet on and draping her bag over the opposite shoulder. He smiled as she didn't seem to be bothered about her hair, unlike other girls he'd given rides to.

He swung the motorcycle off its stand, letting it coast out into the aisle, before throwing his leg over and starting the hydrogen cell motor. The sound effects made it sound like an old-fashioned, petrol-engined Harley – most people couldn't tell the difference, as the old motorcycles didn't make many appearances. No one could afford the fines for burning petrol, or the petrol.

Jonesy nodded to Bella who quickly slipped onto the motorcycle behind him. Her small arms clasped him tightly around the chest, her bag sandwiched in between them. "Ready?" he asked again.

"Go for it big boy!" she shouted over the engine noise.

Grinning, he turned back and gunned it, the big frame leaping forward down the garage to the exit.

Bella's arms tightened convulsively on the first movement and then relaxed slightly as she became accustomed to the movement. Within moments they were on the road and headed for Bella's flat in Waterloo.

Jonesy expertly guided the bike through the traffic, often bypassing slow or stopped lines of cars, the greater agility of the motorcycle paying off in the crowded London streets.

"Whoo-hoo!" Bella shouted in his ear, after they just made a light before it changed. The sound made him grin again, pleased she was enjoying the ride.

When he pulled up in front of the house she owned a part of, she seemed disappointed the journey was already over. Bella took the helmet off and handed it back. "You're coming up for a coffee or something, aren't you?"

"Sure." Jonesy tried to sound like he did this all the time – visiting girls he found attractive in their homes. He failed miserably, shoulders slumped as he followed her up the stairs to her flat at the back of the house.

Now, Jonesy stood in Bella's front room, wondering where the hell to put himself. Socially awkward at the best of times, he was not having a good day.

Bella had disappeared into the kitchen, so he did what he normally would do and started looking at her books. She had hundreds of real paper books, unlike a lot of people. Jonesy only had about twenty and those were collectors editions – he didn't keep physical books in his apartment.

"Finding anything interesting?"

Jonesy turned with a start. "You got a lot of books."

Bella smiled. "Yeah, I like the real thing. There's something about holding a book in your hand that just isn't captured on a voda. A smell, weight...I don't know, maybe it's the act of switching off and doing something that doesn't require electricity." She pulled a book off the shelf. It was a dog-eared and tatty copy of *Pride and Prejudice.* "You also can't bend over the corner to mark your place on an ebook."

Smiling back, Jonesy took the book. It smelled old. " 'Ebooks' – you know no one calls them that anymore, they're just 'books' now."

"I know, but there are still times when it's useful to know which kind you're talking about." She put the book back on the shelf. "Fancy a pizza? I think I have some vintage movies we could put on and talk over..."

Jonesy blushed, once again self-conscious. "Sure, that sounds great." What the hell was he doing? *It's Bella, you dick,* he said to himself. *What could happen?*

Bella finished ordering a pizza – he'd responded to questions, but he couldn't say what she'd asked him – and turned back to him.

"Now, where were we?" She asked, putting her hands behind his head and pulling him closer before kissing him.

Ah, that's what could happen.

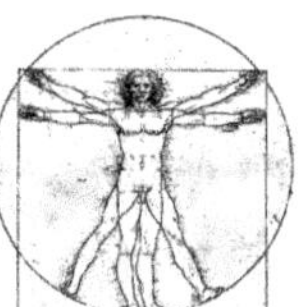

DAMNED INCONVENIENT TRUTHS

Swearing under his breath, Chambers hunkered down next to the desk in his new office, plugging in the leads for the computer interface.

He was annoyed.

He didn't like change at the best of times and the loss of the house in Edinburgh made him grind his teeth in frustration. And not having enough staff didn't help his temper.

The Council wasn't happy with his performance. Sen should be in their control, not running around causing more problems.

And the latest news was even more galling: Sen was only the contact for the Council in the Company – he'd only been promoted to Inspector General!

Sweat trickled down the back of his neck. They were running out of time. If Sen didn't complete the serum, it would all be incidental. It was time to get things back on track.

His voda rang.

"Chambers."

It's Squires. "Boss, we gotta problem!"

"If you're talking about Sen, I know." He sighed, sitting back on his heels, wishing his humidor had made it out of the house in Edinburgh. "Get me an appointment with the new Inspector General as a matter of urgency."

"Sure, boss, but that wasn't the problem I meant – it looks like the estimate's off: we've only got seven days to complete the cycle or all hell's going to break loose!"

"Christ." The serum took a minimum of four days to produce, according to the reports the Council retained from the last cycle 300 years earlier. "Get me in to see Sen. Now."

"Will do, boss." There was a pause. "What do we tell the Council?"

"Leave that to me." The Council probably knew anyway. "When you've got that appointment, have my car ready."

"Of course boss."

There wasn't a moment to lose. He threw the leads down and stood up. There was a cigar in his jacket.

By the time he'd clipped the end and lit it, he was feeling more relaxed, his mind focused on the issue with Sen and the serum. There had to be a solution to the problem as it was very unlikely the Council would condone Sen's death. Not now he was in a position of power.

He stared out the window at St Paul's. At least he had a view to rival the previous one. The pieces of the puzzle would not fit together until…

Then he had it. "Squires, make sure the vampires are at the meeting with Sen tonight – it's important."

"Whatever you say boss."

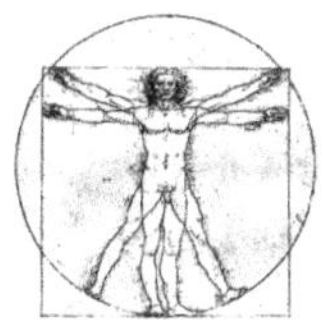

NEEDLES AND HAYSTACKS GOT NOTHING ON ME

I arrive at Company House to find my office stripped clean. I query Central and find a note from facilities informing me that I now reside in the IG's old office. I guess it's only logical as that's me now.

I head up to the top floor. The IG's personal assistant, Heather is waiting for me. Correction: *my* personal assistant.

"Good morning, Heather." I don't know her beyond my brushes with her in the past, might as well start things off civilly. She's sort of average height and weight, dark hair, piercing eyes and I've no idea how old she is. She could be thirty or a hundred, she has that sort of timeless quality about her I can't judge. She's also a formidable character.

"Good morning, Inspector General," she replies formally, tipping her dark head. It sounds like she's always called me that – we both know that's not true.

I shake my head. "That's not going to work. I'm not a peer or royalty or even in the same league as the IG..." This is getting tangled. "Look, just call me 'Jaared', please; I don't think I'll last the day if you call me 'Inspector General' all the time!"

Heather smiles and nods. "I will try, Insp– Jaared."

"See? That wasn't so bad, now was it?" I head for my new office. "I have a few things to sort out, so unless you're bringing me coffee, can you keep me from being disturbed for a while, please?"

"Absolutely. However, you do have an appointment this evening, with a Mr Chambers." She doesn't seem to know the importance of that name, so I guess she's not privy to Council business. Probably just as well.

"I guess *that's* not a surprise," I mutter. "Anything else?"

"His assistant advised me that you need to ensure your son and his mother are there."

Madeline and Nick? What the hell? "Right. Thanks Heather."

"Very good...Jaared."

"See, you're getting the hang of it." I turn back to my office. "I'll have a black coffee when you're ready, Heather. Thanks."

I need to find the old man, pronto. I don't expect he's moved, but you never know. Stranger things have happened.

When Central confirms he's still in St Albans, I call him immediately.

"What do you want?" Always suspicious.

"It's Sen." I sip my coffee.

"I know who it is and I asked you what you want?"

I smile, in spite of myself. "Good to see nothing's changed, old man – still crotchety and paranoid."

"I'm going to hang up now," he replies.

"Wait! I need to talk to you about *The Undoing,*" I blurt out.

There's silence on the line. For a long moment I think he's hung up on me. Then, "I'll be expecting you at eleven." Now there's the click of disconnect.

"Good to talk to you, too, old man," I murmur to no one. "Heather, can you make sure my car's ready shortly? I need to be in St Albans for eleven."

"Very good, sir."

Damned efficient woman. I call Skeet. "You doing anything?"

"Nothing I can't put off. There's only so much daytime telly one person can watch," she replies. "Why?"

"I want you to come with me to St Albans – I need to see a man about this *Undoing* business."

"Right. Where do you want me?"

I leer, then rein myself in. "We'll pick you up in the car."

"Well, that's a turn up: new job has a car and everything, eh?"

"Yep. See you soon."

"Bye."

I turn to the view and wonder for the umpteenth time what the IG was thinking, putting me in charge.

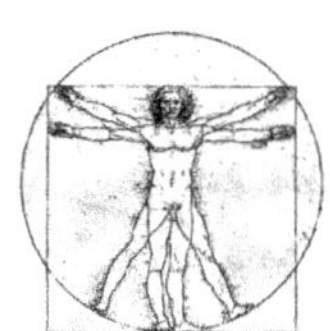

The car that turned up was a heavy beast of a thing – and obviously had a fuel exemption.

"I can smell gas," Skeet said as she got in next to Jaared, the driver closing the door behind her.

"Well, it's a very clean version with lots of additives and performance-enhancing…" Jaared trailed off.

Skeet grinned at him. "Ya don't know what you're talking about, do ya?"

He smiled back. "All I know is this car's armour is too damn heavy for your average electric engine, so the Company pays for the exemptions."

Whistling, Skeet had a good look at the car. Armour wasn't cheap and at a guess this would probably protect them from most light weapons and quite a few of the heavier ones. "So, how's it feel, bein' *IG*?"

Jaared frowned. "No different than yesterday, but I haven't been dragged into any meetings or duties for the role yet. Things'll probably change once that happens."

"Where did ya say we're going?"

"St Albans. Off to see an old guy I know – see if he has any information on this case Chambers was on about."

"What, that guy in Edinburgh?" Skeet hadn't met him, of course.

"Yes, that one. I need to try and verify his story."

Skeet looked at him for a long moment. "You don't believe all that shit he was shovellin', do ya?"

Jaared shrugged. "I don't know, it's getting to the point where I don't know what's possible and what isn't anymore."

"Right. And you need me, why?"

"You're the distraction," he said, grinning. "Crowley has an eye for the ladies and I need to get information out of him quickly."

"Cheers for that," Skeet replied. She snuggled up to him and put her head on his shoulder. "Uh, is this allowed in the IG's car?"

He put his arm around her and nodded. "Whatever I want is allowed in the IG's car." He kissed the top of her head.

Skeet closed her eyes, letting the motion of the car settle her into a doze.

The journey to St Albans from Central London isn't a long one on a normal day and with the exceptions granted by his status, they probably shaved another quarter of an hour off it.

Before she knew it, Jaared was shaking her shoulder gently and saying, "We're here, Skeet. Time to go."

Skeet snapped awake, that clarity that sometimes comes from immediate wakefulness sharpening her senses. They were parked outside a large, if non-descript, house in a leafy street.

The door beside Jaared opened and he got out, holding out a hand for Skeet to join him.

Straightening her leather jacket, she unfolded her long legs and, taking his hand, stepped from the car. "St Albans, huh?"

Jaared nodded. "Yep. Haven't been here in years." Still holding her hand, he preceded her up the walk.

The solid wooden door opened before they reached it, a giant of a man standing just inside it. Glowering in Jaared's direction he waved them in.

They stepped past his bulk into a large entry hall, a carved staircase curling up to the left around a massive crystal chandelier. The door closed behind them, leaving them dimly lit.

"Go through to the parlour," he intoned in a throaty voice.

"You'll be wanting some honey and lemon for that throat," Jaared said to the giant as he steered her toward the only open door ahead and to their right, obviously having been in the house before.

It was a panelled room with a massive stone fireplace. A fire burned away in the grate and Skeet went to warm her hands by it.

"Coffee? Tea? Whisky?" the man's voice came from the doorway.

"Coffee for me, Geoff," Jaared replied.

"And for me, please," Skeet chimed in. *Geoff?!?*

"Esmerelda! Two coffees and the whisky!" he shouted down the hall. "Sit, sit," he motioned them to the sofa. "Mr Crowley will be with you shortly." He smiled for the first time. "Hopefully to let me kill you."

Jaared made calming gestures with his hands. "Now, now, Geoff, let's not be like that. I may have something he wants this time."

"Hummmph," was all he got in reply. The large man left the room without looking back.

"Crowley?" Skeet said to Jaared with one eyebrow raised.

"He's an old…'acquaintance' who almost killed me once." He glanced at the doorway. "Well, Geoff did."

"Geoff? Really? Geoff the…"

Jaared cut her off with a swift shake of his head. "I wouldn't. He's sensitive. And strong."

A tiny woman arrived with a tray on which were a coffee pot, two large china cups and milk and sugar. There was also a whisky decanter of cut crystal and a heavy glass.

The woman didn't look at them as she placed the tray on the low table in front of the sofa. She poured coffee into both cups, glanced briefly at Skeet before adding milk to her cup. She put the jug back on the tray and left the room.

"How'd she…?" Skeet asked Jaared as she moved over and sat down next to him.

He shrugged.

Skeet picked her coffee up and sipped. Good stuff, too.

There was a noise in the hall and a skeletal old man entered the room followed by the giant.

"Commander…no, it's now *Inspector General* Sen, isn't it? I suppose congratulations are in order…" He sat down in the chair on the other side of the table, but nearest to the fire.

Geoff loomed over them all as he daintily lifted the decanter and poured about three fingers of whisky into the glass. He handed the glass to the old man and moved to stand behind his master.

Sipping his whisky, the eye of the old man seemed to glow in the firelight as he studied them. "Aren't you going to introduce me to your companion, Inspector General?"

Jaared smiled, picked up his coffee and turned to Skeet. "Skeet, this is Mr Aberlour Crowley. May I present Skeet, Mr Crowley."

Crowley 'tsked'. "Really, Jaared, I think we can drop the titles now. After all, I'm nearly as old as you are."

Jaared inclined his head.

He turned to Skeet. "Pleased to meet you, Skeet. I'm sure Jaared's told you all about me."

Skeet smiled and shook her head. " 'fraid not…I don't even know why we're here."

Crowley smiled. "That's unfortunate, my dear, because unless Jaared proves…'diverting', you'll get to see Geoff tear his limbs off for wasting my time."

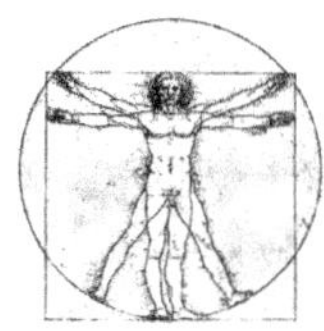

YOUR FRIENDLY, NEIGHBOURHOOD GHOSTBUSTER, THAT'S WHO YOU GONNA CALL...

Jonesy put the coffee on again before pulling a couple of energy bars out of the cupboard and sticking them on the table next to his chair. He was still in a bit of a daze after last night.

He and Bella had spent a great deal of time kissing on her (very comfortable) sofa, but by some unspoken agreement that's as far as it went. They ate the pizza when it arrived and Jonesy left just before midnight to ride his bike back to Clapham. He was picking her up from work again; he had work to do before that point.

When the coffee was ready, he took the large mug and slouched into his chair. He sipped at it, reluctant to flip before he finished it – he knew he'd probably forget it once he was immersed in Central's Grid again. The net had that effect on him.

He finished the coffee, got up to relieve himself before settling back in his chair.

"Time to make the donuts," he muttered to himself and *flipped.*

Jonesy sat high above the plain of data, twinkling lights and flowing datastreams defining the contours of the landscape below him, like a city at night.

Everything still *looked* normal. Nothing seemed to indicate there was anything out of place. It was only his tracking devices and the processes he'd inserted to locate the incursion that said differently. His traps hadn't been disturbed since he'd last been online. Of course, if whoever was creating the incursions was as good as he thought, they might well avoid them.

Jonesy cruised around for a while, tidying up and performing routine maintenance tasks while he waited. He didn't admit he was waiting, to himself, anyway, but it would have been clear to anyone watching him that he was. Waiting.

Once he'd frittered away the morning splitting his time between aimless web surfing and monitoring activity in Central, he flipped out and got up to make himself a sandwich and another coffee.

"Where are you?" he wondered aloud, spreading mayonnaise on the thick bread he got from the baker just down the block. Thick slice of ham, mustard and a bit of green stuff. He cut the slab of sandwich in half and took it back to his chair.

Reading his mail while he ate his lunch, he spotted the announcement of Commander Sen's promotion to Inspector General. "Holy shit! What happened there?" There'd been no gossip the previous IG was going. Well, none that he'd heard. Licking the mustard from his fingers, he put the plate down on the table and picked up the coffee. He called Bella.

"Have you heard? Sen's just been made Inspector General!"

Bella was unsurprised. "Yeah, saw the announcement earlier." She smirked. "I thought you'd have known it was coming, being his best-buddy and all."

Jonesy blushed. Why did he get so defensive about Commander, scratch that, *Inspector General* Sen? "Ha, ha. Very funny. He didn't mention it." *If you can't beat 'em, join 'em, eh?*

"It was all very sudden, apparently," Bella replied in hushed tones. "What's that all about?"

Shrugging, Jonesy picked up his sandwich and coffee, cradling his voda between ear and shoulder, walking carefully to his chair. "Who knows? I never know what's going on anyway."

"True." A beat. "You still picking me up later?" Bella sounded nervous.

A warm feeling surged through his veins. "Of course. Usual time and place?"

"Yes, please. Oh, gotta go – talk to you later."

"*See* you later," Jonesy said. "Bye." The line went dead.

Less than gruntled with his inability to find the incursion and/or the perpetrator, Jonesy picked up his sandwich and flipped back in. He took a bite of his sandwich, half expecting something to happen when he was trying to do two things at once.

Nothing.

He sipped his coffee and took another bite. That's when it happened.

A beam of intense light punched down from the virtual sky, targeting a dull grey spheroid.

The automated defences were already working to beat back the attack and within moments the shaft was dissolved and things had returned to normal.

It was then Jonesy noticed something far more subtle taking place: a tiny, birdlike object was just flying away from another part of Central's primary core. "Shock and awe, huh? Trying to distract me? Me!" he muttered before launching two custom packages streaking towards the "bird".

Both impacted the target which shuddered before disappearing through Central's firewall.

Two windows popped up in front of Jonesy, one displaying telemetry from the probe he'd inserted in the intruder, the other displaying a sample of the data it had tried to steal.

"Shit!" Still jacked in, he dialled Sen.

"Sen here."

"Commander! Sorry, *Inspector General*, we've got a problem!"

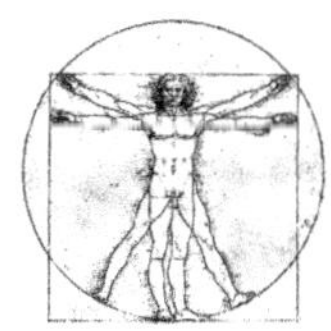

"Really, Crow– Aberlour, threats are hardly necessary. I am fully aware of the terms of our agreement as to what I could expect if I returned." I sip my coffee. Very nice.

It's the first time I've actually *seen* him, since I had my eyes replaced. He's smaller than I thought and looks frailer, too.

Crowley's looking at me with burning eyes. Expectant. "And? What do you have for me that is of interest? I am more than aware of the Council of Seven, so I am wondering what you may have for me to stop Geoff from killing you."

I grimace inwardly. I had hoped he'd be interested in the Council. Oh well. "Have you heard of *The Undoing*, Aberlour?"

That stops Crowley. The smirk falls off his face – if anything he goes paler. He thinks before answering. "I have heard of it, yes." He sips his whisky, obviously buying time. "What about it brings you to me?"

I pause, wondering how much to tell him. Crowley has the power to make things very difficult if he decides not to help me. Again, oh well. "Apparently we're on a deadline – if it doesn't get its serum it's going to destroy us all."

Crowley nods, pulls an old, leather-bound notebook from his pocket. He flips through the pages until he finds what he's looking for. He runs his finger down the page before taking a pencil from the spine and scribbling.

"It certainly looks like it. By my calculations, we have a matter of days." He closes the notebook and returns it to his pocket. "But what do you want of me? Surely the Council has it in hand."

I shake my head. "I don't believe so – they tried to kill me for my blood." I finish my coffee. I gesture at my body. "As you can see, they were unsuccessful."

Now he looks surprised. "You? Really. That *is* interesting."

I put my cup down on the table and the little woman appears again to refill it. Something about her suggests she isn't entirely human. I glance at Skeet and she nods slightly. I hate it when she does that. She smirks. I turn back to Crowley.

"Do you know who made the original serum?"

Crowley smiles that creepy smile again. "Yes." He takes another sip of his whisky while we wait.

"And?" I prompt.

"It won't do you any good."

"Why?"

"He lived over 500 years ago." He chuckled. "I s'pect he's long dead."

"Who was he?"

"He was known only as 'The Artist' to the Council." Something dawns on him at that moment and he gets up without a word and leaves the room, looking distracted.

I look back at Skeet and shrug. We seem reluctant to speak in Crowley's house.

The little old man appears again with a large leather-bound volume in his hand. He's flicking pages as he walks, obviously looking for something. "No, that's not it...what about...no..." he mutters, plopping himself back down in the chair by the fire. "Ahhhh...aha!" Crowley thrusts one finger into the book triumphantly and picks up a voda from the table beside him.

"Fletcher! Crowley, here." He pauses, impatient with the niceties. "Yes, yes. Look I know you're an expert on Leonardo – where did he end up?" Another pause. "France? Yes, yes, I *know* that, but are you sure?" Beat. "Really? And where do those rumours put him?" Another beat. "How recently?" Breath. "Fine. Thanks."

Crowley put the voda back on the table beside him. "I may have been wrong."

"How do you mean?" I ask, not sure what he's talking about.

"I think I have worked out who the Artist was. At least, his locations correspond with what we know of the Council's interactions with him..." He pauses for dramatic effect.

"Oh for god's sake, Crowley, tell us or kill me, whichever!" Patience is not always one of my strong suits.

That creepy grin is back. "You should calm down and not be so hasty," he replies. When he sees the look on my face, he continues. "Oh very well. I get so few visitors..."

"It's not surprising when you threaten to tear their arms off..." I mutter.

"...I believe the Artist was Leonardo da Vinci," he finishes, ignoring me.

"Right. How does that help us?"

He sips his whisky, letting the moment drag out. "I believe he's still your best bet."

Skeet responds first. "Huh? Yeh just said he's dead!"

Now he looks embarrassed. "Well, I may have been wrong on that one. My friend Fletcher thinks he may be one of the long-lived – like us," he says, looking at me.

"Stranger things have happened," I reply. "Where is he?"

Crowley shakes his head. "No idea, but Fletcher thinks the last sighting puts him in London some 40 years after his," he crooks two fingers on either hand, " 'death'."

My turn to shake my head, frustrated. "He could be anywhere. That doesn't help!"

"No, I don't think he left England."

I stand up and Geoff shifts uneasily. I turn from Crowley and start pacing. "What are you basing that on?" I demand when I turn back to the skeletal man in the big chair.

"This." He picks up the voda and flicks his wrist at the wall behind me. A hidden screen appears with an image of a painting. It's modern, liquid and moving figures against a dense, thickly layered background; there's something familiar about it. "This appeared at an exhibition in Manchester a couple of years ago." He pauses for effect again. "Fletcher has analysed it exhaustively and is convinced it's by Leonardo."

"Again, so what?"

Crowley frowns at me. "Besides painting, Leonardo da Vinci was an alchemist, scientist and anatomist, in many ways years ahead of his time when it came to thinking about technology and science." He stands up as well, striding over to me and poking me in the chest. "And think about it: he created the serum for the Council of the Seven Kings when they last had need of it – surely he would be the best person to do the job this time?"

It's hard to refute the logic, particularly when we're running out of time. "If that's the case, how come the Council don't know where he is him now? I would have thought it was in their interests to keep track of him."

Crowley shrugs, stretching his neck like he's tired of looking up at me. "Maybe they do, maybe they don't. They didn't tell you how they were producing the serum, did they?" He smiles at my expression. "I didn't think so. And maybe Leonardo 'killed himself' to escape from the likes of the Council or others who wanted things from him." He turns back to his chair. "You'll never know until you find him."

Skeet spoke up from the sofa. "This is crazy! Yeh want us to pin our chances on a possibly-not-dead 500 year-old alchemist hiding somewheres in England. It's crazy!"

Shrugging a second time, Crowley sat down in his chair and picked his whisky up again. "It's up to you: believe or not. But make your mind up soon. You don't have much time to find him, if he is the Artist." Sip of whisky. "The last location I have suggests he lived in Surrey, somewhere between Kingston and Richmond."

I shake my head. It seems a thin lead.

He looks up, glaring at each of us in turn. "Now get out of here – I'm not going to have you killed today, Jaared."

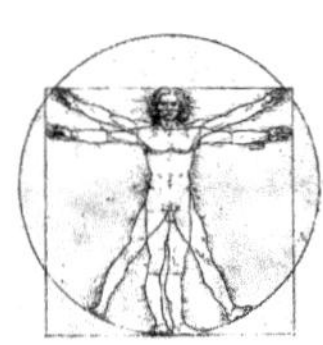

Of all the crazy-assed, ridiculous things to say

Skeet was quiet when they got back in the car, thinking about what Crowley said.

Jaared sat next to her, staring out the window.

She realised it was still a novelty for him, being able to see the passing scenery as they sped back to London. It wasn't that long ago that he'd still been blind, although functioning better than a lot of sighted people. It still wasn't clear whether regaining his sight was a blessing or not.

He still depended on the senses he'd developed over the decades he'd spent blind.

Skeet picked up his hand and squeezed it. "Any ideas?" she asked when he turned toward her.

A quick shake of the head, a rueful grin. "No."

"Me either."

"And everyone telling me we're running out of time isn't helping."

"I know." They lapsed into silence once more. Skeet watched the passing buildings as London went by. And all at once an animated sign for Battersea Dogs Home reminded her of something. "Wait a minute...no, it's stupid..."

"What?"

Skeet turned back to him, doubt etched into her face. "I don't know, maybe it's a stupid idea, but what about that book guy – Wolf – you know, the one who *finds* things."

Jaared's eyes lit up. *Okay, it's worth it to see that happen*, she thought to herself.

"That's not a bad idea at all," he says to himself. His eyes refocused and he leant forward and kissed her. "Hardly stupid and it just might do the trick!"

At that moment something distracted him. He got the faraway look in his eyes again and started talking to himself. *Ah, skullphone.*

"What? Slow down, Jonesy. What do you mean?" His expression darkened. "Are you sure? No, we can't reach them before dusk...No, I'm not going to explain that." He turned back to Skeet. "And you don't know who it is that's behind this?" Another pause. "Okay, let me know what you find out."

"What is it?" she asked when his eyes refocused.

"Someone's been at my personal files on Central – looking for something." His jaw had set, in anger.

"And..." Skeet prompted.

His eyes flicked to hers. "Jonesy thinks they were after details on Nick and Madeline."

"Why would they want that?"

Jaared shrugged. "In light of what we've just been talking about and the fact that Chambers wants them at this meeting, I can only guess they're after the serum, too. Whoever they are."

Skeet sat back, perplexed. "But that means they know about you and Nick..."

Nodding, Jaared went back to looking out the window. "Yep, it sounds like they know a lot more than they should– whoever 'they' are."

They lapsed into silence.

"Okay, why don't I talk to Wolf and you go meet Chambers," she suggested finally.

"That's not until later..."

Skeet took his hand again. "I know, but I'll bet yeh've got other things t'do in the meantime."

Jaared grinned. "Why, Skeet, if I didn't know better, I'd think you were trying to get rid of me," he murmured.

Shaking her head, she smiled and snuggled into his shoulder as she had before. "Now why in tarnation would I wan' ta do that?"

"I don't know, but I have little inclination to go back to the office...to work, anyway."

"I can talk to book boy – you need to pretend you're doing the job, even if you're supposed to help the Council." Skeet glanced out the window and realised they were on Tottenham Court Road. She rapped on the glass partition. "Hey you, let me out anywhere along here, please." She turned back to Jaared. "What's his name, anyway?"

"Uh, let me think..."

"Gregor, Sir," came from the front. "I'll be your driver during the week and it'll be John Swift at the weekends."

"Thanks, Gregor," Jaared replied. "And yes, let Ms Skeet out anywhere you can stop along here."

"Very good, Sir."

Skeet walked down Tottenham Court Road, hands shoved into the pockets of her jeans. It was cold but not unbearable. For a weekday, there seemed to be a lot of people out and about.

A window display caught her eye. "Aw shit, it's Christmas." They had all been so caught up in things for the past few weeks, it hadn't even occurred to her that it was almost Christmas. Oh well, she didn't really have time to think about that.

Hunching slightly into her leathers, she crossed Oxford Street and made for Wolf's bookshop on Charing Cross Road.

The sign in the window of Hopkin's Rareties and Antiquities when she got there said "Back in 5 minutes". The shop was dim and she couldn't see any movement inside.

Skeet turned around and leaned against the wall of the shop and waited. She didn't have anywhere to be, so that was fine.

Wolf appeared only moments later from around the corner, a large coffee cup in his hand.

"Shite!" he swore when he realised who was standing outside the shop. He stopped dead. "What the fuck do you want, Skeet?" He was just over five foot, but well built and seriously muscled. Skeet still thought he looked more like a body-builder than a bookseller.

"Relax, Mr Pocock Woffe, I ain't selling Girl Scout Cookies," Skeet replied. "Cain't I just drop by and say 'hi'?"

Wolf shook his head. "You don't 'just drop by and say hi'." He looked around nervously. "Speaking of tall dark and moody, where is the *Commander*?"

Skeet smiled. "Don't worry, he's not gonna pop out and make you do somethin' you don't wanna. He's busy, which is why I'm here."

"Shite." He moved to the door beside her, pulling a bunch of keys from his pocket. He opened the door and entered the shop. Skeet followed him in. "Whaddya want? I thought I was rid of you only a few weeks ago."

Wolf had been approached about a book long thought vanished by philosopher and scientist Giordano Bruno. The search for it had led Jaared and Wolf's team into a dangerous house from which they had barely escaped.

Skeet shook her head. "Got another job for ya. You heard a Leonardo da Vinci?"

The look Wolf gave her would have disintegrated lesser mortals. "You mean the master painter and Renaissance man who gave us works like the *Mona Lisa* and *The Last Supper*? Nah, never heard of him…"

Ignoring the sarcasm, Skeet walked further into the shop, browsing the titles on the shelves idly as she passed. "Funny that, he was also a scientist and alchemist, apparently."

Wolf shrugged. "Fascinating. What is all this in aid of?"

"You've seen things you can't 'splain, right? Some things you want to ferget?"

"Yeah, you could say that," Wolf replied, thinking of that house again.

"What if I told you we think da Vinci's still alive and living here somewhere?"

Wolf just stared at her. "Fuck. You're not kidding, are you?" When she shook her head. He sighed loudly and headed for the back of the shop, overhead lights popping on in response to their presence. "C'mon, I've got decent whisky in the office."

"Not on my account…" Skeet started, following him.

"Not for you, for me. I think I'm going to need a drink," he replied, throwing a wan smile over his shoulder.

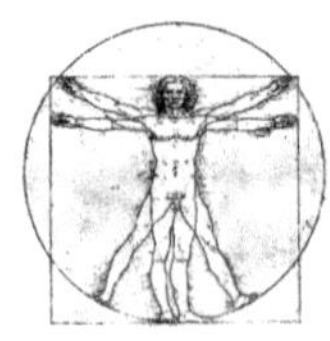

Not you again...

After Skeet left, Wolf sat in his office, finishing the large Balvenie he'd poured himself to hear her story.

"Shite," he said softly to the empty office. "How the hell do I find a 500-year-old genius?"

He phoned Graeme.

"I don't know, how do you find a 500-year-old genius?" Graeme guffawed. Really. He guffawed.

"Thanks. That didn't help."

"Wait," Graeme said, catching his breath. "Send me the photo you've got and I'll ask around."

"*Discreetly,*" Wolf emphasised. "If he's as smart as we think, he'll vanish again if he thinks we're onto him." He tagged the photo Skeet had passed him and forwarded it on to Graeme.

"Thanks." Graeme looked at the photo. "Wait a minute...that looks familiar," he muttered to himself.

"You recognise it?" Wolf asked, ready to be amazed.

Graeme frowned back at him. "Well, not exactly *recognise*, more like deja vu..." He got that far-off look in his eye and concentrated. His eyes popped back after a few seconds. "Nope. I'll call you back."

Wolf nodded. No point rushing him. "When you're ready. I'll be home in about an hour, anyway." He clicked his voda off as Graeme said his goodbyes. He'd have a nosy of his own, see if anything came up.

Finding nothing from a quick check of his usual sources, Wolf headed back to the flat.

Graeme was in the front room of Wolf's Maida Vale apartment when he got home. "Don't you have a home to go to?" Wolf asked him, hanging his bag on the antique hall tree as he passed.

"Yes, but Shirl's got her beau 'round and I thought it'd be more fun ruining your evening."

"Gee, thanks."

"Don't mention it, least I could do after you set me a new riddle." He was nested in the armchair, the vid on the wall on, but soundless, a tablet in his hand as he scrolled through what looked like gallery listings.

"Michael in?" Wolf asked, reluctant to disturb Graeme very much when he was thinking.

Graeme grunted. "Was on his way out to a meeting 'bout that new studio. Said to tell you there's lasagne in the oven."

Wolf grimaced; Michael's cooking was legendary – for it's inedibleness. "Fancy Chinese?"

Smiling, Graeme nodded. "Get some tinnies in, too, woncha?"

"Sure thing. Back in a minute," Wolf turned around and headed back out of the apartment. Sometimes finding things involved ignoring them or pretending you weren't even looking. Besides, Graeme knew more about art and that scene than Wolf. Now, if it had been books…

Stanley Hopkins had taken Wolf in at a bad time. He also taught him everything he knew about rare books. And Graeme Black had been his best friend.

Wolf had finished growing up with a family made up of the two men and Graeme's daughter Shirl, a couple years younger. When Stanley died, he left Wolf his shop, *Hopkin's Rarities and Antiquities.* Wolf had made a go of it, keeping the wolf from the door, as it were, but had continued using his natural talent: finding things. And he'd been pretty successful at that, too.

Then he met Jaared Sen and things got dicey. Or maybe he was fooling himself – maybe they'd always *been* dicey, he was just getting old enough to finally notice.

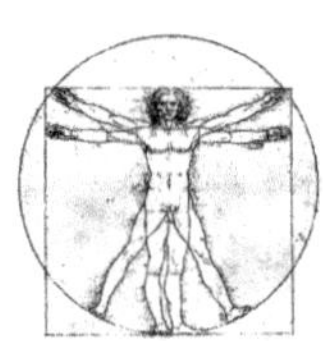

IMPATIENCE IS NOT A VIRTUE AT THE BEST OF TIMES

Heather buzzes me at that instant. "Mr Chambers is here, sir."

'Sir', huh. Well, at least it's not 'Inspector General'. "Send him in."

I stand up and move around the desk to stare out at the view. *My* view now.

Chambers enters behind me. From the speed at which his heart is beating, he's nervous. Good.

"What do you want, Chambers ?" I ask without turning.

"I need to speak to you about that matter we discussed a few days ago…"

When I turn toward him, my Glock is in my hand. Pointed at his head. "And why shouldn't I just terminate you now for kidnapping, criminal damage and generally anti-social behaviour?"

He raises his hands in surrender. "Go ahead, if you feel you must. The Council will only send someone else."

I hate it when they're right. I put the pistol away. I'd hate to have to the office deep cleaned on my first day. "Very well, what do you want?"

"That matter we discussed in Edinburgh has…well, shall we say, become more urgent."

Waving at the sofa, I signal Heather for more coffee. "In what way?"

Chambers sits on the edge of the sofa, his body tense. He obviously believes what he's telling me. I shrug and sit down across from him.

"It appears the original calculations were wrong – we've got less than a week to get the serum created and administered."

Shit. Crowley was right. "Ah." Heather enters with coffee and I wait until she's put it down on the table in front of us. "Thanks Heather."

She smiles and leaves the room.

"You're not exactly inspiring confidence, Chambers. How's the Council feel about that?"

That hits the mark as he winces. "Obviously they're not going to be happy…"

"You mean they don't know we've got less than a week before everything comes to an end?"

Chambers shakes his head. "No, they have not yet been informed."

I pick up my coffee and sip it. "I see."

"Where are the boy and his mother?" Chambers asks nervously.

I stare at him, still not happy about involving Nick and Madeline. "They'll be here any time."

He's nervous, sweating and heart thumping away in his chest. Good.

The door opens and Nick enters the office, followed by Madeline. They both bare their teeth when they see who my guest is.

"Calm down, he's *supposed* to be helping us," I say, standing up. It's unlikely I could stop them – they're both so damn fast – but hopefully the idea of me intervening will make them pause.

The results suggest 'yes'. And 'no'.

Before I can react, Madeline has Chambers by the throat and pinned against the window glass.

"Madeline, please," I say calmly. "Frankly I don't care if you kill him, but I want to know what he knows, first."

She doesn't look at me, which is bad. "You *know* what he did to me," she hisses.

I nod. "Yes. I know. He and the Council have a lot to answer for."

Chambers gurgles. Obviously she's got too tight a grip on him.

"Let him breathe – he's little use to us dead."

Madeline releases him and in a blink she's at the other end of the room.

"Why did you summon us?" Nick demands, stepping forward, glaring at Chambers and me, both.

"I– I have had an idea, if I may." Chambers seems to be having trouble speaking after Madeline's grip on his throat. He takes a drink from his coffee cup, glances at me and continues. "You know our original intent was to use Jaared's blood for the serum…"

"All of it," I interject.

"Yes, yes, all of it," he repeats. Irritable now. "That is no longer an option for a number of reasons…But we may be able to use some of yours and," he looks at Nick, "some of yours."

Nick looks from Chambers to me to Madeline who shrugs like she's wearing a wooden jacket. "My blood? It is not like human blood."

Chambers nods. "We don't think Jaared's is actually human, either, although he seems perfectly capable of dealing with human blood in transfusions or other surgical situations."

I nod. Fine. "What do you want to do with our blood, Chambers? This 'serum' you've been on about?"

He's become a nodding dog, his head seemingly loose on his shoulders. "Yes, that's it precisely."

"And do you know how to make this serum?" I ask.

"We believe so," he replies.

There it is. "Really? You 'believe' so?" I look at the others and back. "If time's as short as you say, Chambers, now is not the time to be experimenting!"

He goes pale and acquires a stammer. "N-n-n-no…I mean y-y-y-yes, we know what we're doing…"

"Uh-huh. Have you got anyone who's done this before?"

He's totally stricken now and I'm not feeling generous. "Wh-wh-well, no. The l-l-l-last person to devise the p-potion is d-dead."

I sigh. It's as I suspected after talking to Crowley. "Let me get this straight: you planned to 'try' a serum no one alive has ever made. Am I following you correctly?"

His eyes bulge, his heart rate is way too high, oh and a blood vessel has started pulsing in his temple. Bound to have a heart attack, I'd say. He still doesn't answer.

"Right. Tell the Council I will get them the serum. *Without you.* Now get out." When he doesn't move, I repeat myself. "Get. Out. NOW."

Chambers gulps, shakes himself and bounds to his feet before running to the door, throwing it open and disappearing down the corridor.

I turn back to Nick and Madeline to find him grinning and her no longer frowning to kill the band. "What?"

Madeline speaks. "That was an unusual compulsion you put on him."

"'Compulsion'?" I ask. "What do you mean?"

"You forced him to obey you merely through your voice – impressive." Madeline leaves her wall and sinks into the sofa. I sit down, too.

"I don't know how I did it – sorry," I reply at last.

"No need to apologise: I would have done far worse to him." Now she smiles. "Do you know how to produce this 'serum', then?"

I shake my head. "No, that's probably beyond me, but I've got people looking for someone who does."

Nick perches on the end of the sofa, near Madeline. He certainly got her looks – it's obvious which block he's a chip from. Two pairs of deep red eyes stare at me.

I shrug. "Sorry for calling you in here on such short notice – I had hoped he had more up his sleeve than that."

Madeline nods. "It is fine, Jaared, we will do our part." She gets up and turns to the door. "Call when you need us."

"Thanks. Hopefully we'll know something soon."

Nick bows and follows his mother.

I turn back to the view and hope Skeet's having more luck than me.

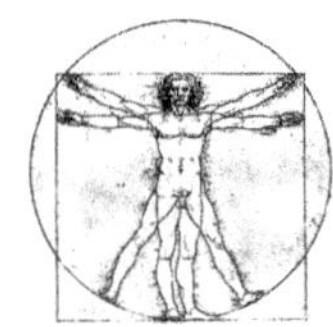

BBC World Service: Tsunamis in the Pacific Ocean have caused new breaches in the Fukushima Daiichi II reactors, which came on line in 2036. The expected fall out is likely to affect most of Japan and good portions of mainland China...

CNN: A freak pothole opened on Route 1 during rush hour traffic last night, creating a hole the size of a baseball diamond in the highway. Some 150 cars are estimated to have plunged into it, killing most of their occupants immediately...

Digging holes in my backyard

Madeleine kicked the door to the chamber open, the heavy slab crashing through the light plaster on the wall.

"This is a surprise," Le Boucher said from the bed, his heavily-furred chest all that was visible above the sheets – thankfully.

The two naked boys, young men really, who were with him snarled at her.

"Get dressed. We need to talk." She turned on her heel. "Leave your companions."

The lights of the city twinkled in the cold darkness as she stalked into the large, stately living room with its view over London.

Standing in front of the large windows, Madeline picked up the bottle of red wine and poured herself a glass – not to drink, more to inhale the rich aromas.

"That's a '64 Petrus." Le Boucher informed her from the door. He slouched into the room, clad only in a thick red robe, before collapsing into a chair with an affected sigh.

Madeleine continued staring out the window. "Very nice." She let that hang.

The Butcher of Leningrad isn't one to sit in companionable silence. "Are you going to tell me why you have interrupted my playtime?"

She ignored him for a minute, taking a sip of the wine. It tasted thin, lifeless, a pale imitation of the lifeblood she needed to survive.

He 'tsk'ed. "That was a mistake – it smells much better than it tastes. Well, to us, at least."

Madeleine nodded. "Agreed." She put the glass down on the window ledge before turning around. "I did not interrupt you're 'playtime' to talk about wine, though."

Le Boucher cocked one bristly eyebrow, his almost black eyes boring through her. "Well?"

"Someone sold me out. In Edinburgh."

This earned her another glare. "You are certain?"

Madeline have him a look that said: *I wouldn't have come to you if I weren't!*

He tipped his head in acknowledgement. "You think one of the Elders?"

"Who else knew I was going?" she snapped.

The mountainous man who had made her a vampire the best part of four centuries before considered the question. The frown crossing his brow suggested he didn't like the results.

He heaved his bulk from the chair, picked up a glass from the sideboard and stalked from the room.

When he returned moments later, the glass contained steaming blood. It wasn't the first, judging by the residue on his lips.

It was Madeline's turn to raise an eyebrow. The smell of the blood was rich in the room.

"Would you like a glass? It is fresh," he offered.

"I would not want to deprive you of your companions," Madeline said with a sardonic smile.

"They have plenty to share," he said, handing her the glass and disappearing again. He returned moments later with a jug. After pouring some into a glass he returned to his chair.

Madeline sat on the sofa, curling her feet up under her. The difference in their sizes would have been more obvious to an observer, his bulk versus her diminutive size.

"Tell me," he commanded.

Madeline sipped the warm blood. "You know they sent me to find Renfield?"

Le Boucher nodded. "Of course. I am an Elder, even if I don't go to all the cocktail parties." He grinned, showing bloody teeth. "And did you?"

Madeline grimaced. "I found him, all right – in pieces scattered down an alleyway." She sipped again. "And it was a trap."

"A trap?"

"Yes. The hellhound that most likely killed him was waiting for me."

"Not to kill you, obviously."

"No – it was sent to herd me to its masters, I would guess. I found myself in a dungeon, partaking of the Council's hospitality."

At this Le Boucher looked up, all conviviality gone. "What did those sheep-fuckers want?" His voice was hoarse, anger evident in his hard stare.

Madeline smiled without warmth. "Not me – they were after Jaared…Commander Sen. They have some task in mind for him."

He nodded. "And they knew enough to set you as bait…You are right – someone knew you would be of use and how to get you where they wanted you." He took a deep drink from his glass, obviously thinking. "Only the other Elders and myself knew of your mission…although I *did* wonder…"

"Wondered what?" she demanded.

Le Boucher glanced up, remembering she was there. "Why you were chosen – Renfield hasn't been a serious threat for fifty years." He shuddered. "And his personal habits…my god…"

Madeline considered. "Could one of the Elders really be working with the Council?"

Shaking his head, he stood up and walked over to the window. "I seriously doubt that. All of us have had a disagreement with the Council at one time or another…" He looked at the view, thinking.

Madeline left him in peace. Something was playing on his mind and interrupting him would not help.

"It is more likely to have been one of their servants…but who would…" He turned from the window. "I think I can guess…it will be that interminable gossip Lorenzo."

"The Medici?" Madeline knew him in passing, but had never spent much time with him. By reputation he was ruthless and not one to cross.

Le Boucher waved a hand in the air. "Lorenzo likes his wine, drunk from the veins of his loyal servants."

Madeline smiled. Intoxication was possible, but it took some doing. "You think it is one of these servants…"

He smiled. "It is a place to start, anyway. Meet me here at sundown tomorrow and we will go see Lorenzo…perhaps he can shed some light on the matter."

"Very well."

Le Boucher tipped his head. "Good night," he said and was gone.

No doubt back to his 'playtime'.

"I will show myself out," Madeline murmured.

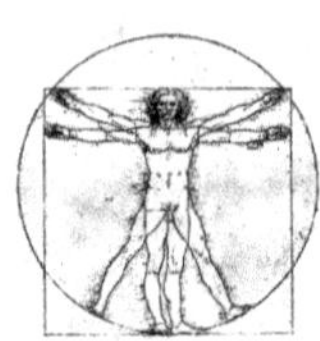

WHY ASK FOR HELP WHEN YOU CAN GET INTO TROUBLE ALL BY YOURSELF?

Jonesy flipped out of the Grid. He was sat in his work chair and his bum and back muscles ached. He drained the energy drink beside him and sat back.

It couldn't be. But it certainly seemed to be. His tracers came back, with different readings. Different readings that were somehow still the same. To Jonesy it looked like an organisation of equivalent size to the Company – at least in the Grid.

"But it can't be," he muttered. The evidence was staring him in the face, but it didn't make sense. Nothing was as big as the Company. It was a malfunction of some kind…"Or…no…" He flipped over to the forums where the geeks hung out and checked on a couple of threads that kept an eye on the phenomena he had a hunch he was looking at.

CB: Haven't seen one myself, but it sounds like an AI node.

GF: Seriously!?!? WTF – not bleedin' likely.

HT: Really. That's what it is; first one observed 2043 across a Chinese botnet node. You've found another one.

GF: AIs DON'T EXIST MORONS!!!!!!!

CB: Watch yerself, GF – you'll get banned.

HT: They do, here's a link: UCD1983479814375....KKCKVVII

GF: I ain't clicking on a strange link – p'rolly end up with my brain sucked out through my eyes...

CB: Wilson...

HT: Careful or I'll moderate both your asses...

GF: Who you calling a 'Wilson'? Come over here and– [MODERATED]

Crap. The posts were only a few hours old. The Grid coordinates matched his own anomaly – someone else was seeing it, too. It was an artificial intelligence growing in the spaces of the web, something the geeks had been talking about for decades. Rumours, urban legends, almost campfire stories, really, about the intelligences that lurked down deep in the digital murk.

Jonesy clicked the link and found nothing. Whatever it had been wasn't keen on being seen, obviously. He couldn't blame it at the moment. He felt that way himself.

"But why would it be after the Commander?" he said out loud, forgetting his boss's recent promotion.

Because Sen's into something big.

"Really?" What could warrant attention from an AI?

It wouldn't be interested in money or people... power? Influence? But influence over what?

There was a mental 'ping' as something appeared in his inbox. It was entitled: GIVEUS A CLUE

"Ha ha," he said, giving it the derision it deserved.

When he opened it, a strange origami effect blossomed out of the middle, unfolding before him with a searing light almost too bright to look directly at. After a few seconds it faded, leaving an after-image behind

THE COUNCIL OF THE SEVEN KINGS

What the hell did that mean? What did it have to do with Commander..."He's Inspector General now..." he said out loud. To no one.

"Quick search on 'Council Seven Kings'," he dictated. The Googlebot took only a matter of seconds to pull back some 1.6billion results, mostly rumour and speculation. One entry did catch his eye, though.

The Council of the Seven Kings is a secret society with direct responsibilities for a number of artefacts passed

down from the time of the Pharaohs. Possible precursor of other groups like Masons...

"Ask a silly question..." he muttered. Wait a minute, where did that message come from? He examined the GIVEUS A CLUE message and discovered nothing unusual about it. If anything it was too simple/too plain. Something was helping him. Or using him, one or maybe both.

"Damn." And he couldn't tell anyone. Who'd believe him?

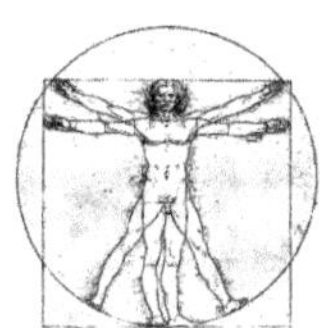

Never been the same

When he came back from the Chinese, there were a number of images of art on the vid wall.

"What're those?" he asked, pointing with the beers at the vid.

"Shortlist," Graeme answered. "I think one of this lot may well be our man."

Wolf whistled. "That's impressive old man."

Graeme glared at him. "I'm not totally useless, you know."

"Of course not – why do you think I ast you?"

Wolf set the food and the beers down on the table before popping to the kitchen and getting some plates and cutlery out of the cupboard.

While there he also remembered to pull the charred lasagne out of the oven, shaking his head. They'd have to dispose of the evidence: both the Chinese and the lasagne would need to make themselves scarce before Michael got home.

By the time he got back with plates, Graeme had a beer open and was drinking straight from the tin. They didn't stand on ceremony when it was just the two of them. When Wolf sat down, Graeme let out a belch of carbonation.

"Cheers," Wolf said, picking up a tin of his own.

Between them they sorted out the food and ate in silence, the half-dozen images on the vid mesmerising. When the food was gone, Wolf packed up the empties and the uneaten lasagne before taking the whole lot out of the apartment, down the stairs and out into the street where he emptied them into a neighbour's bin.

Graeme had added one more artist and deleted another by the time he got back up the stairs.

Wolf grabbed another beer and slouched into the other chair. "So, whatcha got?"

Clicking on the first artist, the older man started his lecture. "Right, a number of things about Leonardo: he was left-handed, a scientist, anatomist and probable alchemist. There's no reason to think that if he were still around he would have lost interest in those things." He waved at the screen. "All of the finalists are in their fifties or early sixties, or look like they are."

"Who's first?"

"John B Smith. Multimedia, ceramics, body parts and shit – I kid you not." He glanced at Wolf. "And yes, he really is 'John Smith' – found his birth records. I kid you not…he puts body parts into his artwork."

Wolf smiled. "Well, if he's lived this long, those records could be faked – they're going to have to be faked for one of them…"

Graeme nodded. "Of course, but I think our boy's cleverer than to use so obvious a name. It's going to be a false name, but it'll be somewhere between fantastical and too plain vanilla."

"Something normal," Wolf responded.

"Exactly." Graeme sipped his beer. "He's probably good enough, but I don't think it's him."

"Okay, next."

"Ethan Finlay. Uses technology and real people in his installations. Apparently drugs his models so they don't move for days."

Wolf glanced over at Graeme. "Really? That's crazy!"

"People will do a lot of things for 'art'. Even put themselves in a coma, it appears."

Wolf sighed. "Next."

"Dominic Vulturo, experimental thought sculpture, soundscapes, light and texture installations. Based in…Rotherhithe."

"Made up name…has to be…why does he fit?"

Graeme shrugged. "I don't know, something about the light and texture stuff seems really familiar." Graeme held up a hard copy of the image Skeet had given them. "And I don't think it's a million miles away from this, either."

"Background check?"

"Seems legit, real name 'Christopher Jordan'…public school boy from…St Albans, looks like."

"Next."

"Rhys Davies, old school oil paintings on whatever he can get his hands on." The image on the screen flashed to an image of an old petrol car repainted with a copy of something Wolf recognised.

"For obvious, this one wins – that's a vamp on da Vinci's *Madonna of the Rocks*. Not a lot of people know that, but again, some would."

"Right. He based in London?"

Graeme consulted his notes. "Yep, Shoreditch."

"Next one?"

"Charlie Parker, sound sculptor and light installations, based in…Reading…"

"Isn't that someone famous?"

Graeme glared. "How would I know? Google him."

Wolf pulled out his tablet and did just that. "Charlie Parker, also known as "Yardbird" and "Bird", was an American jazz saxophonist and composer."

"Okay, moving that one to possible alias." Graeme considered. "But anyone who listens to jazz would know it, wouldn't they? Don't know, maybe another red herring."

"Right. Last one."

Graeme looked down at the tablet. "Francesca Vincent, light painting and installations…"

Wolf laughed. "A girl?"

"Well, from what I've read, he was probably gay – he could have had gender reassignment at some point in the recent past." He gestured and that particular piece got larger. Whorls of light moved through the artwork, like threads of molten sun moving through dense black earth. "I like this, too. Of them all, it's possibly the most like the piece from your friend Sen."

"Point taken." Wolf drank his beer. "How do we pick one for Sen?"

Graeme shook his head. "I don't think we do. We can only do so much…" he saw the look on Wolf's face and frowned. "…Despite your reputation as a miracle worker…"

Grinning, Wolf finished his beer. "You know I don't like leaving loose ends, old man."

"I do. It's also got us in more trouble than I care to remember – leave this one to Sen."

Wolf nodded. "I guess you're right; it's not my job. Hell, he's not even paying me for this one!"

"That'll be one on account, then." Graeme was staring at the images on the vid. "I don't get the feeling the Commander forgets his tabs."

"No, probably not." Wolf got another tin. "I think we've done enough for him this time."

"Yep, tell him what we found."

Wolf frowned. "What *you've* found," he corrected. "I'm just going along with you on this one – not my bag, man."

Graeme bowed from the waist. "Hell, if it'd get that guy off our backs, I'd put Shirl out on the street!"

Wolf nearly spat out the beer he was drinking. "I'll tell her you said that..."

Graeme's grin got bigger. "You do that – I've been threatening her with that since she was fourteen. Pro'lly can't manage it now, she's bigger and you've taught her too many tricks!"

"True, she's not the pushover she was when I met her." His voda pinged. Sen. "Guess I better tell him what we know."

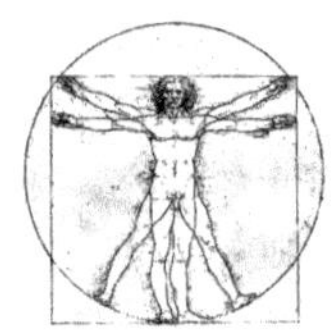

Boom Boom, Out Go the Lights

Wolf's news, while not complete makes me feel better about things. At least we have an idea of where to look.

"Thank you, Mr Woffe – you don't know how much you and Graeme have done," I find myself saying. *Holy crap, I'm turning into the IG!*

"Not a problem, Commander," Wolf replies. "Good luck."

Click.

It would be easy to sic Central onto the problem, but I wonder about that. Could he be plugged into our systems? If he finds out I'm searching for him, will he just disappear again? I decide to try a more subtle avenue.

"Jonesy."

"Yes Com – I mean, sir?"

"I didn't wake you, did I Jonesy?"

"No sir, just trying to find our intruders…" He sounds hesitant.

"Any luck?"

"Well…maybe…"

"Right, well let me know when you find them. In the meantime, I need your help on something else." I explain the problem.

He still sounds distracted. "Uh, I don't think he can monitor specific queries, but he may have a flag on his alias…leave it with me, sir, and I'll see if I can work a way around that…"

"Did I stress how little time we have to…"

"Yes, Commander, you did!" Click.

Jonesy hung up on me. What the hell?

When my eyes refocus, I can see Skeet looking at me strangely from her seat on the settee.

"You okay?"

I nod. "Yeah, fine...Jonesy just hung up on me..."

Skeet shook her head. "I think ya may be pushing that boy too hard, *Inspector General*."

I sip my whisky. Rain rattles against the windowpanes, thrown there by the wind out of the north. The fire (effect) in the grate gutters in a stray draft.

We're sitting in the living room, having a night in. I cooked, steaks, prawns and chips, something that seems to happen more rarely as time goes by. Dickens has been in and out, obviously getting used to us being back. Right now he's curled up next to Skeet on the sofa, unconscious. Traitor.

I light a cigarette. "He's going to look into it."

Skeet takes a sip of wine. "Jonesy knows how important it is?"

I nod again, a wry smile on my lips. Smoke curls up from the end of the cigarette, distracting me. "Of course. He knows everything he does for me is 'urgent'."

Skeet laughs. "Right."

"He also knows that if he doesn't have an answer for me by the morning, I'll be in his flat threatening him with my Glock."

"Aw, leave 'im alone, he's not gonna see thirty-five at this rate," she protests.

Something is niggling in the back of my mind, but I can't focus on it. Too tired, too old, too something. I sigh, take a last drag on my cigarette and stub it out in the ashtray next to me.

I stand up. "Come on, then, let's call it a night."

"Iss' early yet," she protests.

I hold out a hand. "I know, and..." I let it hang there.

"Ooohhhhhhh," she replies, taking my hand. "Careful now, *Inspector General*, don't wanna break nothin'..."

"Oh, I plan to," I reply. "Just wait and see."

She laughs out loud and leads me up the stairs.

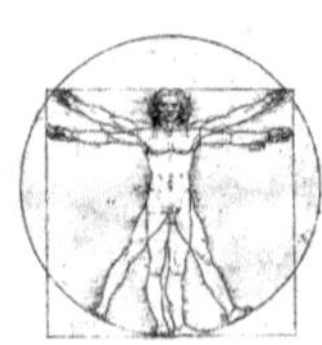

Jonesy flipped back out of the Grid, a throbbing headache firmly ensconced behind his eyes, which he rubbed vigorously.

Bella was sitting on his futon, watching something on his vid. "You done yet, Big Boy?" she purred across at him.

If only, he thought to himself. He smiled, "Almost, just got a couple things to tidy up for the IG."

"Huh," Bella huffed. "I'll bet. What's he need now? Picking up his dry cleaning? Dinner party for twelve? Tickets to see Man U beat Chelsea?"

Jonesy laughed out loud. "Man U beat Chelsea? Please." He laughed more when he saw the look on her face.

This was the one thing they disagreed on. Football. Soccer. Still as divisive in the UK as politics.

Bella stood up and took the two steps from the futon to his chair. "C'mon, Big Boy, let's go for a ride."

"It's raining," he protested, but not too hard. He probably had some spare waterproofs...

"I don't care, let's go get wet," she teased. "All work and no play makes Jonesy a very, very, very dull boy..."

He let himself be enticed, probably in need of a break anyway. "All right, just for half an hour," he replied. "Then I've got to find the people the IG sent me..."

"Yeah, yeah, whatever," Bella replied. "Let's go now."

So they went.

When they got back, soaked to the bone, Bella headed for his shower cubby, trailing clothes as she went. Jonesy watched her, unsure what to do.

"Are you coming?" she called over the noise of the spray.

"Wh-what?" he replied.

"I said, are you joining me in the shower?"

Holy crap. Now what?

Like any other red-blooded male, it took him about ten seconds to make up his mind.

His wet clothing quickly joined hers on the floor as he followed her.

Some time later, Jonesy lay in his bed, listening to her regular breathing beside him. He was suffused with a warm glow and didn't really want to get up. But he had to.

Well, he didn't *have* to get up, as he could flip into the grid lying down just as easily as from his work chair. It just didn't feel right, if he did that, though.

And he didn't want to disturb Bella, either.

Jonesy got up and turned on the coffee maker and waited for it to make him his large mug of coffee with milk substitute. When it was finished he took it to his chair and slouched into it. He checked his messages and mail before drinking most of his coffee. He set the mug down and flipped.

It was a matter of a few minutes to eliminate four of the six names Sen had given him. The document, internet and basic monetary trail for each was too detailed and…'organic' to be falsified.

Not so Francesca Vincent and Ethan Finlay.

There was something definitely off about each of them.

Vincent really only appeared about twenty years earlier in the records and Finlay, well, his transcripts would have been moth food if they'd been edible, judging from the size of the holes in his history. Again, only really in existence for about eighteen or nineteen years. That was an odd coincidence in itself.

Jonesy's headache was back after he'd examined their pasts in minute detail. "I can't see it," he breathed, his voice sounding loud in the quiet flat.

In disgust, he picked the list up mentally and put together the two odd ones in a message to Sen. He got paid the big bucks, let him sort them out.

"G'night sir," he muttered, flipping back out of the Grid.

Jonesy returned to his bed and slipped in next to Bella.
"You done?" she said quietly.
"For now. You awake?"
"No. Go to sleep."
He smiled and snuggled up next to her.
And in a matter of moments he was.

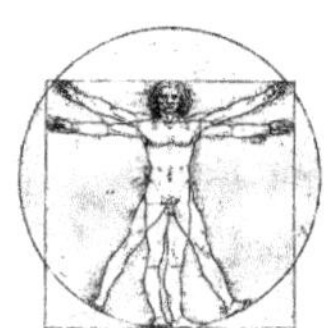

I'M IN, I'M OUT AND I'M GONE...

Skeet walked the short distance from the London Bridge station to Ethan Finlay's studio. It made sense, as Jaared had to take the car all the way to Windsor to find Francesca Vincent. Skeet smiled. Besides, she worked better with men than women anyway.

They'd divvied up the two names Jonesy'd come up with over a coffee and almond croissants in the cafe on the corner.

"I'll take *Ethan*, then," she said around a mouthful of croissant.

Jaared nodded, sipping his coffee. "Okay, don't do anything to provoke him, just see what you can find out." He grimaced. "The last thing we want is for him to bolt..."

Skeet smiled. "I'll use my best manners, don't want t' spook the natives."

"Just don't smile at him like that: he might think you're planning to eat him."

Putting on her hurt face, she took another bite of the delicious almond croissant. "Moi? I prefer small children, not gristly old guys."

Jaared's smile looked too tight. "Let's just hope *Francesca Vincent* doesn't like 'em tough."

Skeet put her hand on his arm. "You'll have her eatin' out a' yer hand in no time."

"As long as she doesn't take a bite out of it..."

Finishing the crumbs of her breakfast, Skeet stood up. "C'mon then, let's get movin'."

Jaared waved his chit at the table and stood up. He picked up the second coffee he'd ordered for taking away.

His car was idling at the curb, parking restrictions of no concern to a high-ranking member of the Company. "Want a lift to the station?" he asked.

Skeet shook her head. "Nah, walk'll do me good." She leaned in and bussed him soundly. "See ya later."

Jaared smiled back, dropped his sunglasses onto his nose and nodded. "Yep, let me know how you get on, anyway." And with that, he stepped into the car and was gone.

Shrugging to no one, Skeet pulled her leathers tighter against the cold wind and headed off to the tube station.

Now Skeet was south of the river.

Even to a relative outsider like her the North/South divide was obvious.

All the important parts of London (with some exceptions, of course) were north of the river: Parliament, the City, Buckingham Palace, Harrods, Kensington & Chelsea, the Tower of London. Historically inhabitants of London went south of the river to do things they couldn't or wouldn't north of the waterway. It was no coincidence that dogfights, bear baiting and Shakespeare's theatre were on the wrong side of it…

Skeet found the warehouse where Finlay's studio was located without any trouble, even in the twisty streets around the station. It was almost halfway between the station and the bottom of Tower Bridge.

There was an old-style entry phone inserted into the brick around the door, a dead video eye staring blankly out of the tarnished panel. The buttons were worn, almost illegible. Skeet checked the note she'd made on her voda and punched 2-5-7. The panel made a buzzing noise and she waited.

It buzzed again, obviously intending to carry on buzzing until someone answered it.

The hair on the back of her neck prickling, Skeet looked up and down the street which, barring a few cars, was mostly quiet. She couldn't shake the feeling that someone was watching her. Nothing obvious, though.

The buzzing continued and she was ready to give up in disgust when she spotted something above her head. The ancient video eye on the panel might be dead, but the tiny camera on the ledge above the door was much more modern and faceted like an insect's eyes. It probably had a 180° view of the street, maybe even up and down, too.

I need Jonesy, she thought. *He could probably tell me what or who was watching me through that in no time.* Skeet waited.

She was about to quit for the second time when a voice came out of the speaker.

"Whaddya want?" The sound from the panel was crackly.

Skeet smiled that scary smile. "I'm selling Girl Scout cookies and wondered if you wanted to try my Mint Thins..."

There was a beat. "Are they made with real Girl Scouts?" Crackle and hum.

Her smile turned into a grin. "Absolutely. Nothing but."

"All right, you intrigue me. Come on up."

"This is Ethan Finlay, right?"

"None other. I'm afraid my PA...wait, I haven't had a PA for donkey's years..." Another pause, then. "Yep, it's me – come up, and bring those Mint Thins."

The door buzzed this time, a different sound from the panel. Skeet pushed it and entered the dim foyer.

"Third floor," the panel called after her as the door shut.

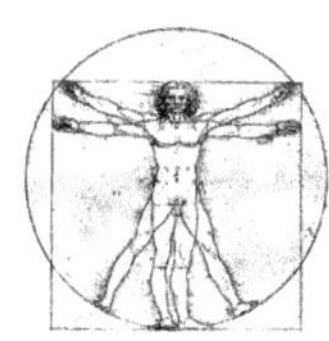

Russian winter: lots of ice and snow... unlike London

The car cuts through traffic, upsetting a lot of people – and not just because of the black clouds of particulates it puts out: it's *big*. I hate to think what it's carrying, too. Could be anything from 50mm shot to depleted-uranium armour-piercing to surface-to-air missiles. God knows.

Gregor's driving me again. It's been a long time since I've driven anything but he seems competent from the back seat. I suspect he has to be, I'm the Inspector General (Acting) after all.

We arrive in Windsor just before eleven and Gregor quickly finds the house and grounds where "Francesca Vincent" has her home and studio space. It wasn't that far out of the centre of Windsor, but it certainly looked like a large property. She's obviously done well for herself.

The gate, when we reach it, slides open. As if we were expected. Heather obviously got hold of the artist's assistant after all. I flicked a quick thank you off to her and got Central to sort out some flowers. I was going to have to work with her, after all – for a little while at least.

When Gregor pulled up in front of the house, I was surprised how modern it actually was, the main glass body of the house dwarfed by a large stone structure which I could only guess was the studio space. For some reason I was expecting something more traditional.

This probably isn't even him...the lizard bit of my brain piped up. I'd just made a pointless journey to Windsor chasing god-knew-what. A myth? Fantasy? Legend? A ghost?

The door opening was my cue. "Thanks Gregor...well done," I say lamely.

He just nods.

I'm not making a very good impression as a boss, am I? No point in saying anything else, so I go up to the already opening door in the smaller part of the building.

A small man is stood just inside, watching me from behind thick spectacles. In this day and age?

"Inspector General – I have been instructed to offer you every hospitality until Francesca finishes…well, what she's working on at the moment." He gestures into the house. "I am Daniel. Please come in."

"Thank you."

He takes my leather coat which he hangs on a tangle of steel hooks, careful not to snag or cut it.

I follow Daniel further in until we reach a large room which I could swear opens out into the expensively natural-looking garden.

It takes me a moment to realise that one wall is fully glassed, but with the anti-glare glass that is very difficult to see for mere mortals. The weak, wintery sun fills the room, making it feel warmer than it probably is, or its some kind of augmented solar collector, taking advantage of the natural warmth. There's a retro 1960s orange circular fireplace with a simulated fire (but warm) to one side of the room; there's a bent sofa, also orange, with a low back curling around it which Daniel gestures to.

"Can I get you something to drink Inspector General? Coffee? Tea? Wine? Something stronger?" He seems very eager to please.

I smile and say, "Coffee, please." I sit down on the sofa. It's some kind of memory foam and more comfortable than I had imagined.

Daniel disappears and I sit looking around the room. There's nothing I can see that would say to me 'THIS WOMAN'S LEONARDO DA VINCI!' In fact, there is very little in the way of artwork in view at all. How strange. One wall is covered in books, old and new, a fact I had missed in my awe over the view. The other two walls are mostly white.

"They're blank for Francesca's light sculptures – we don't turn them on during the day, I'm afraid," Daniel places a tray with coffee paraphernalia on the sofa and sits down on the other side of it. "There's not much point when the room is this light, to be honest. And Francesca won't do anything to reduce that; she likes the garden being just on the other side of the glass."

"I'm sure she does," I reply.

The next few moments are taken up with preparing and sharing the coffee. I wonder how long Francesca's going to keep me waiting.

"Have you been with Francesca long?" I ask. Might as well get what background I can.

Daniel shakes his head. "I've only been her assistant for the last twenty years – her previous companion was with her for over forty years."

"How old is your boss?" I ask. 'Subtlety' is not my middle name.

He titters. "I've no idea, Inspector General. That would make her somewhere…"

"…when it was impolite to ask a lady's age," comes a voice from the doorway. "Gossiping again, Daniel?"

Daniel leaps up, narrowly avoiding the coffee service. "I-I…no, Francesca…merely keeping the Inspector General company."

I stand too. "Jaared Sen, Ms Vincent," I say, offering my hand. She doesn't take it.

"Sit down, Inspector General, I do not stand on ceremony." She takes Daniel's place who disappears without a word.

Up close, I have to agree with Daniel – I have no idea how old she is. And if she used to be male, I can't see that, either. Central starts running facial recognition in my head until I tell it to stop.

Francesca Vincent appears to be an average sized, middle-aged woman, who could be anywhere between twenty-five and fifty, depending on the light and what she was wearing. At the moment she's wearing non-descript trousers, what looks like a man's work shirt and good old Dr Marten lace-ups, in Ox-blood. Her hair is pulled out of her face in a plait and is auburn mixed with grey.

But it's the eyes that are the most arresting: dark green, they're almost emerald in colour and depth, with glimmers of gold in their depths, the pupils very contracted in the brightness of the room.

After sipping her coffee, she puts down the cup and looks intently at me. "So, what can possibly bring you all the way to Windsor, Inspector General?"

"Jaared…please," I insist. "I am investigating…a series of…thefts and was told you may be…of some assistance…" Okay, now that I hear it coming out of my mouth, it sounds lame.

That look says she's not buying it, either. "Really. That's the best you've got, Insp…Jaared? I would have thought you would be more practiced at lying at your age."

"S-sorry? What do you mean?"

"Don't play coy with me, young man, I can tell you've been around the block a few times: there's a pinched quality to the skin by the eyes."

My hand goes to my right eye, almost of its own volition.

"Oh don't worry, no one else will see it – I just make a living by looking at things." She picks her coffee cup up again. "Now, what did you want to ask me?"

"Do you have any idea where I can find Leonardo da Vinci?" I blurt. *What the hell?* I look down at the coffee cup – ah, something truth enhancing in there. Not Truthtell, but something to lower inhibitions. And not something I was expecting.

"Don't worry, Jaared, it's just a herbal additive like chicory, albeit one that relaxes inhibitions."

My Glock is in my hand. "And you just used it on me because…"

Francesca smiles. "I had to know your intentions, Inspector General – after all my years I find it better to be safe than sorry." She nods at the gun in my hand. "You will not need that, Jaared: I am no threat to you." She sips her own coffee. "To answer your question, no, I don't know where you can find Leonardo." Her smile increases. "I was of the belief that he died in the early 16th Century. Didn't he?"

I just watch her for a moment, not used to being taken advantage of like this. The gun seems pointless, so I put it away. I put my coffee down, no longer thirsty. "That does seem to be the general consensus."

She raises an eyebrow. "Then why are you looking for him?"

There doesn't seem to be any point in holding back now the cat's out of the bag. "It has been suggested that he's not as dead as everyone thinks."

"Really? That would make him over five hundred years old – extraordinary!"

I nod. "Yes, it would be."

"But why are *you* looking for him? Why are you interested?"

"I need his help with…a situation…" *Now* I'm hedging.

"How intriguing…what do you need a five hundred year old artist for?"

"My source believes he knows something…important." I stand up. "I am sorry for wasting your time."

"Not at all, Jaared, you have proven delightfully diverting." She stands up as well.

I start to head for the door, then turn back. "I would be curious to know why your history only begins in the last twenty years – that is very unusual in this day and age of everything we do being recorded somewhere."

She looks down and to the side, an obvious sign that she is lying to me. "I– had problems with a…stalker, Inspector General. I had to leave Italy because of it and…when I moved here, I changed my name and appearance."

I nod. "I am sorry…I guess you didn't go through legal channels for this?"

"No, it was not possible – he would have found me…"

I nod again. "And your previous name was–?"

"Julietta Bronzini."

That was too easy, but I take it. No point in upsetting her further. "I see. I will leave you in peace, Ms Vincent."

"Francesca, please, Jaared."

"Francesca. I would say 'thanks for the coffee', but…"

She nods. "I understand, and I'm sorry."

"I'll see myself out."

"That won't be necessary," Daniel says, at my elbow.

I don't jump, I heard him coming a mile off. "Very well."

"Follow me."

With a nod to Francesca, I turn to follow him. We retrace our steps through the house.

"Did you find what you were looking for?" he asks.

I look at him, wondering how much he heard of our conversation. "Not exactly."

"I'm sorry to hear that, Inspector General."

I shake my head. "Never mind, it was a wild goose chase anyway."

He opens the door. "Good bye Inspector General."

"Yes, good bye Daniel."

Gregor's standing by the car with the door open.

I get in and he returns to the front seat. "Back to town, sir?"

"Yes Gregor. Let's get the hell out of here."

I just have to hope Skeet's had more success.

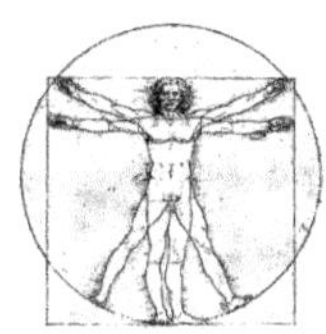

AP: A forest fire in northern Papua New Guinea is expected to destroy more than 300,000 square miles of virgin rain forest and displace at least 10,000 local people...

CNN: Scientists have found a bacterium suspected of killing more than 350,000 head of cattle in the Argentinian interior, with an expected total of some 500,000 to be announced soon. A total ban on the export of livestock from the country is being put in place...

BBC World Service: Two drilling platforms in the Gulf of Mexico have been deemed unsafe in the wake of some 650million gallons of crude which is currently washing up on the Gulf Coast, killing fish and seabirds in their millions...

I DON'T WANNA DANCE

Jonesy sat in his work chair, still glowing from the aftereffects of Bella's visit. He wasn't even thinking about work, just sitting there, monging.

His voda pinged, an alert that something was happening in the Grid he needed to see.

Taking a last drink of his coffee, he flipped the button on his headphones, sighed and flipped. Proto-goth-metal band Godspunk blared in his ears as the Grid materialised in front of his eyes.

With...stardust in our veins...and a cosmic sheen...

There was something large and bright hanging over the landscape of the Grid, casting virtual shadows across the cityscape made up of the nodes and functions of the whole "brain" of the Company's Central Artificial inTelligence™.

We'll keep on riding...on our silver machine...

Jonesy squinted against the glare, thinking he saw something in the centre of the radiating sphere. It wouldn't resolve and the filters he threw up had little effect, too.

In the great unknown...we'll forever dream...

Then he heard something over the music.

"Joooooonnnnnneeessssyyyyyyyy..."

That was weird. There wasn't much sound in the Grid, which is why he normally had his music collection plugged in.

He cleared his throat.

"Y-yess? Who's that?"

"Come closer, Joooonnnneeessssyyy..."

This is such a bad idea, he thought. *Bimbo in the graveyard time...*

It didn't stop him getting closer, but with fingers on the virtual controls, one hand on the attack software, one on the 'manoeuvring thrusters'.

The image in the middle of the bright shape didn't get any clearer.

"Clooooosssseerrr, Jooonnneeesssyyy..."

Jonesy nearly fired the security programme missiles at it as his fingers jerked.

This is stupid. He took two seconds to put a short message together for Bella and copied Sen in on it; on impulse he also assigned his new acquaintance from the sub-basement to it. Never knew who might be useful for this sort of thing.

Riding high...high on my silver machine.

Jonesy took a drink from his cold coffee cup, fumbling it back onto the table.

"Okay, here goes," he muttered and pushed himself 'toward' the mini sun.

There was a moment when he thought it was moving away from him. The next, the image in the sphere sharpened into the features of a skull glowering directly at him.

"Oh shit," he had time to say before it rushed to meet him in the space above the Grid. He lost all visual references as it seemed to consume his virtual body/ship/mind/space. Darkness took him.

A sensation of pulling and tugging began, disturbingly like he was being sucked into something's mouth, a mere morsel.

His fingers convulsively tried to pull him back out of the maw, but nothing happened. He couldn't feel them or the rest of his body anymore, a total lack of sensation.

Numbness, then unconsciousness.

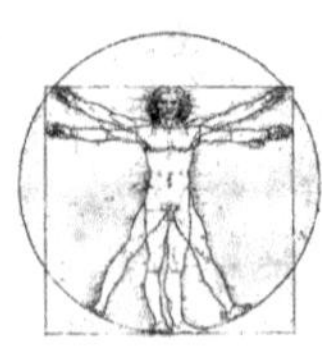

"What is the meaning of this intrusion?" demanded the gaunt figure, his burning red eyes bright in the dimness of the room.

"Watch yourself, Lorenzo, I have a few questions for you..." Le Boucher boomed. "It is in your best interests to answer them, I assure you."

Lorenzo de Medici stared at him for a long breath, flicked his eyes at Madeline and then turned and entered the large living room beyond.

Madeline looked to her maker and received a shrug. "Come, best not keep him waiting," Le Boucher muttered.

Le Boucher's limo had taken the two of them to a large house near Belgrave Square. It was just one of Lorenzo de Medici's homes, apparently. The big man didn't need conventional transportation to get around, but said he found it soothing. So they rode.

The 'house' was five stories high from the street level. "It has at least three sub-basements that I know of," Le Boucher murmured as they drew up.

Lorenzo bemoaned his son's lack of acumen when it came to wealth, reportedly incensed when informed that the de Medici fortune had vanished after his 'death' in 1492; it was even said that he killed his son in anger at the waste, but could no longer assume the mantel of the family name because he was, well, dead.

Since that time he had become a very shrewd businessman, building whatever wealth he acquired into a substantial fortune over the centuries. As it was spread quietly and effectively amongst companies and personas, he was never noticed by the financial authorities or the press, which produced their annual 'rich lists'.

Between his wealth and his place amongst the Elders, he was extremely powerful – and dangerous.

Lorenzo motioned them to the elegant chairs around the fireplace where a roaring fire was burning. Madeline went closer to the fire, appreciative of the warmth.

He flopped into a chair, his bulbous nose incongruous against his pale skin and deep-set eyes.

Le Boucher sat in the chair opposite and took the goblet handed to him by a servant. Madeline turned from the fire and joined them, also accepting a drink.

"What is the meaning of this?" Lorenzo repeated when he'd dismissed the servant.

"We are…concerned…for the security of the Elders, my dear Lorenzo," Le Boucher started.

Lorenzo laughed. "Security? You must be joking – I have the best security money can buy at my disposal." He sipped from his own goblet. "The security of others is no concern of mine."

Le Boucher nodded. "I thought you would feel that way." He looked into the fire, appearing uncertain. "The problem is, Lorenzo, Madeline here, my daughter, was sent to Edinburgh to look for Renfield on the Elders' orders."

"Yes, yes," Lorenzo waved his hand. "I remember. What is this to do with me?"

"Madeline found Renfield, dead and torn to pieces. She was subsequently imprisoned by an operative for the Council and tortured." Le Boucher looked directly at Lorenzo de Medici. "I am of the opinion she was, what is the phrase? Oh yes, 'set up'. Would you know anything about this?"

Colour rose in Lorenzo's cheeks, indicating his fury. "How dare you–"

Le Boucher held up a hand. "Stop. Did you mention this search for Renfield to anyone? Or that Madeline was being sent to look for him?"

"I–" Lorenzo froze. The colour in his cheeks deepened, no mean trick for a vampire of his age. He stood up and pulled a tasselled cord next to the fire.

The servant appeared instantly.

"Find Estrella and bring her to me," Lorenzo commanded. When the servant went, he went to a heavy wooden cupboard set against the wall. He found a small table on wheels nearby before pulling the doors of the cupboard open and proceeding to extract a number of sharp, glittery objects from it. He placed them on the table and wheeled it nearer a solid chair.

A young, slim and very tall vampire entered the room. "Yes, Master?" she said to Lorenzo.

He gestured at the chair and she blanched. "What is the problem, Master?"

"Sit. That is all I require of you."

"But–" She didn't have the chance to say more before she was slammed into the chair and a silver spike thrust through her right shoulder, pinning her into it. She immediately screamed in agony.

Madeline winced, remembering her own recent injuries. This must be Estrella, whom Lorenzo had called for.

Lorenzo quickly pinned her arms and legs to the wood beneath, each spike releasing more howls of pain. He then stood there, watching until the noise subsided into whimpers.

"Now that I have your attention, you worthless daughter of a whore, I require a name. Who have you been telling of my business?"

Estrella, blood steaming as it flowed down the spikes was in shock, but something got through. "A-a name? I don't..."

Lorenzo leaned into her face. "I do not care if you do or do not – who are you working for?"

A spasm of panic crossed her face, her eyes darting around the room in search of some kind of escape. "I-I...Master...I"

"Tell. Me. His. Name," Lorenzo spat.

A look of cunning flashed across the wounded vampire's features and away again. "Whose name...Master?"

Lorenzo shook his head and turned to his little table. He selected a very long silver pin, something between a hatpin and a knitting needle. "Are you sure, you slut? Do you really wish to test my skill?"

"Master...please...I don't know..." she pleaded.

With a sigh, he stepped forward and pushed the needle into her right eye and all the way through the back of her skull, pinning her head to the back of the chair.

She screamed and flailed as best she could, pinned as she was.

"Now. Last try: who are you working for?"

Still whimpering, her other eye blinked rapidly, tears of blood running from both orbs. "I am...sorry...Master...I didn't mean..."

Lorenzo leaned forward and jiggled the pin, causing more screams.

"I–"

"You know what I want to know – tell me and I will stop your pain," he whispered in her ear.

"Lucien..." she whispered back.

Lorenzo's head snapped back. "Lucien? Lucien de Foret? That bastard! What is he doing involving himself in the affairs of the Elders?"

"He promised to...to make me...a queen..." she said, her voice hoarse.

"What is he after?" her Master demanded.

"I...do not know..." she replied. "Please..."

Le Boucher spoke up. "How do you meet him? Where?"

Nothing.

Lorenzo poked one of the spikes invoking another scream. "Answer him."

She swallowed, the pain coursing through her damaged nerve endings. "He...he comes to my chamber..."

"When?"

"Tonight..."

Her Master took one more look at Le Boucher and Madeline, the fury in his bloody eyes back. A silver knife appeared in his hand which he used before anyone could react, severing Estrella's head from her torso in one clean cut. He threw the head into the fire and picked a cloth up off his table with which he wiped his hands.

"I did not know that bastard was back or I would have his heart on a plate," Lorenzo stated to them both. "My apologies to your daughter, M Le Boucher, and to you."

Le Boucher stood up. "I had heard rumours de Foret was back, but I have yet to see him."

Lorenzo shook his head. "It can only end badly with him involved."

"He was banished before..."

Lorenzo huffed, an approximation of laughter. "I believe he chose to go. Will you tell the Elders and offer my apologies?"

"Of course." Le Boucher offered his big hand. Lorenzo de Medici took it for just a moment before releasing it. "Excuse me, I have things to...attend to..."

Madeline and Le Boucher watched him leave the room to be replaced by the mute servant who had served them earlier. He motioned them toward the door they'd entered through before preceding them.

Once outside, the limo pulled up and the two vampires got in.

Le Boucher looked out the windows as London passed them by. "You saw him, did you not?" It wasn't really a question.

Madeline nodded. "Only briefly – I had no idea he was plotting again."

"It can only mean one thing," her maker said, still looking out the window.

"His maker has returned," Madeline guessed.

"Yes." He finally turned to her. "And that *is* bad."

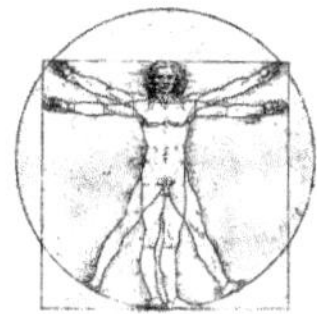

Ever stuck a bug on a pin?

When Skeet got to the third floor, the only door on the landing was standing open.

She entered Ethan Finlay's studio cautiously. Skeet didn't know what to expect exactly, but this wasn't it. Old televisions of all sizes and shapes filled one wall of the large room, ranging from flat screens to a modern 3D tank to half a dozen old CRTs with massive tubes sticking out the back. They appeared to be synced in such a way that one giant image played on them. She thought it was the news until she realised it was a loop of the same natural disaster, a landslide somewhere tropical, it looked like.

Looking around, she discovered that the wall next to it was covered in shelving that was groaning under the weight of heaps of cable, strings of lights, LEDs, components and parts to things Skeet couldn't imagine a use for.

The wall next to that had two floor-to-ceiling windows that looked original, complete with gaps to let the wind blow in.

In the centre of the room was a dais with a young girl lying on it, completely naked and painted bright yellow and blue, fading to green where the two colours met. She was immobile, eyes staring glassily into the distance. Around her a complex net of wires and more components created a mesh that encircled her. Sparks jumped from connections while lights chased each other around the complex creation.

Skeet walked up to the dais. "You al'right in there, dahlin'?" she asked. No response.

The door closed behind her with a bang. She whirled around, a Sig in her right hand. No one there. Wind must have closed it.

When she turned back, there was a man standing across the dais.

"She can't hear you – she's been in a coma for a day so far and her contract says she'll be in for another week." He looked down at the naked girl, his dark eyes seemed a bit fanatical. "Well, she might be able to hear you, but she can't respond – oh."

Skeet looked down to see a yellow puddle forming around the girl. "I guess maybe she's telling you what she thinks of you."

He shook his head, his brown and grey shoulder-length curls hardly moving, all the while staring at the pee as if mesmerised. "Another day and there won't be anything left in her bladder; she'll be safe then. It's purely reflex."

Skeet nodded, feeling disgusted. "Right. You must be Ethan Finlay, then," she ventured.

His eyes flicked up. "Yep, that'll be me. Do you really have Girl Scout cookies?" he asked, seeming a lot younger all of a sudden.

"No, sorry. It was just a ruse to get me up here."

Ethan shrugged. "Oh well, just wondered – I haven't had proper Girl Scout cookies in years." He moved around the dais toward her. "Ethan Finlay." He held out his hand like it was expected.

"Skeet," she replied, shaking his hand. Up close, she could see webs of tiny lines around his eyes.

"Skeet," he repeated. "That's a funny name."

Skeet nodded. "Yep, it is." *Is this guy pulling my leg? He sounds about ten!* "So, what're you doing?"

Ethan gestured at the stuff in the room. "Art, dontcha know."

Like I understand what he means. "Right. And you get paid for it?"

Ethan nodded. "Yeah, but people don't buy the whole piece – I'm not allowed to sell the models."

"What? You mean the girl?"

"Yeah. Something about 'human rights'. I don't know what it means, 'cause every time they bring it up I start to listen and then it just turns into 'blah, blah, blah'."

I know how that feels. "That's too bad."

He seemed to be losing interest in her. "Yeah. The pieces don't really work without the models..." The holo generator in the corner seemed to grab his attention. "Got to go, work to finish." He waved his hands at the room.

"One more question before you go – what have you been doing for the last 30 years?"

Ethan seems to consider the question carefully. "I don't know what you mean."

"Where have you been, I guess?"

He still looks blank. "Where? Why here, of course."

Uh-huh. "Okay, thanks."

"Next time, I'd appreciate it if you could really bring Girl Scout cookies."

"No problem, I'll see what I can find," Skeet said as she headed for the door.

Ethan, absorbed in whatever he was doing, seemed to have totally forgotten her by the time she reached it.

Skeet called Jaared when she reached the street.

"I don't know," she said when he asked how her visit to Ethan had gone. "He's some kind of savant, I think, maybe Asperger's or autism – he seems to be borderline whatever he is. Claims he's been in this studio for the last thirty years, so who knows?"

"Could it be an act?"

Skeet shrugged. "Could be, but it's a damn good one, if'n it is." She checked traffic out of habit. "I'm not sure he's capable of what we're looking for."

There's a sigh on the other end of the line. "That's what I was afraid of. Looks like we're back to square one."

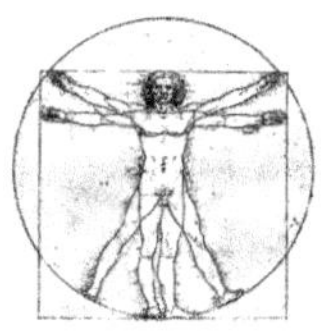

Now that's just porn to anyone else

I sit back in my chair, dejected at the thought that it's been for nothing. I can't prove either of the two possibles, or anyone else is capable of making this 'serum' that we need to *SAVE THE WORLD*.

God, that sounds pretentious, I know.

Part of me still doesn't believe it and I guess I've been borne along on everyone else's expectations up to now. Still, it's hard to explain all the current problems otherwise. We've never had this kind of problem in the past – I'm 170 and we've never had natural disasters like this and I've seen a lot.

They all blur together after a while.

Chambers picks up on the first ring. "Jaared! Have you changed your mind?"

I sigh. "I wouldn't say that, but it doesn't seem as if we have much choice."

He is silent for a moment. "Your search was unsuccessful?"

"I'm afraid so. We'll have to try your version and hope it's close enough to do the job."

I can almost hear him rub his hands together in anticipation.

"Good, good, we can get started right away." He shouts to someone else on his end and I only hear the odd word like 'prepare' and 'run the simulations again', neither of which inspire much confidence.

Then he's back. "We'll need you and Nicholas here at midnight to perform the ritual."

"Where's 'here'?" I ask, curious as to where the Council has set up in London.

"We'll be using a ceremonial room in the Guildhall – one of our members has privileged access." More shouted instructions. "We'll get ready for you both and expect you at midnight."

"Very well. And Chambers," I add. "This better work or your death will be the least of your worries."

I can hear him swallow. "We– we can– only do our best, Inspector General."

I nod to myself. I only hope it's good enough.

In a bit of a funk, I stare out the window across the river.

Fuck this, I think, *I'm going home.* "Hazel, can you call my car, please? I'm heading home."

"Very good, Jaared. Gregor is on parking level 1 when you're ready."

"Thanks Hazel."

I pull on my leather trench coat and check my pockets for anything I've missed. Nope. Gun's in its holster, phone's in my skull, so that'll be about it. I nod to Hazel on the way out.

"Good night, sir."

"G'night."

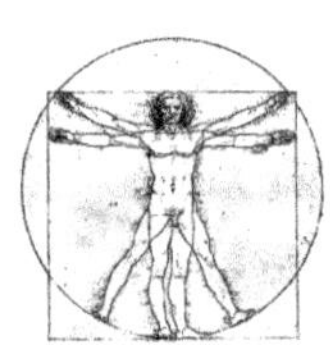

By the time I get to the parking level, the car is outside the lift and idling. I get in.

"Home, James," I say as I settle back into the seat.

"Sir?"

"Never mind, I'd just like to go home," I reply, feeling old.

"Very good, sir."

Continually thinking about what we, no I, have to do in the next few days isn't helping, but I can think of little else as the car powers through the city's streets. *What the hell are we going to do?*

It seems like no time before we're pulling up outside the mews where my Victorian house is located. "Thanks Gregor."

I step out into the darkening afternoon and look both ways as the car pulls away. It's the usual foot traffic, not a lot else. I sigh and head down to my door.

"Mmm-hmmm."

The Glock is in my hand and pointed at the sound of the throat clearing. The glint of spectacles in the shadows across from my door reveal the form of Daniel, Francesca Vincent's assistant.

"It's not wise to sneak up on me, Daniel," I say quietly, the gun still pointed at his head. I never like surprises.

"I-I'm sorry, Inspector General," he stutters, "I was sent to give you some information by my mistress."

"Really. Haven't you heard of phones?"

He nods. "I know, but my mistress is somewhat... eccentric...when it comes to messages, even though she embraces technology otherwise."

I sigh and put the Glock away. "Very well, come in and tell me your 'message'." I turn around to find Skeet on the doorstep with her Mossberg ready. "Well, hello darling – is that a shotgun or are you just happy to see me?"

Skeet nods over my shoulder. "I heard voices and thought maybe I should join the party."

"You people are awfully paranoid," Daniel says behind me. "I had never seen a gun before today."

I glance back at him and motion him to follow me. "Just because you're paranoid doesn't mean they're not out to get you, Daniel."

Skeet moves to one side. I enter the house, Daniel following me. Skeet brings up the rear.

I enter the living room and motion him to a chair while I move over to stand by the fireplace. "Well?"

He sits hesitantly in the big chair which has the added feature that he won't get out of it easily. "You really are the scariest man I have ever met, Inspector General."

I allow myself a smile, glancing over at Skeet in the doorway, who quirks and eyebrow and smiles back. "There are far worse out there, Daniel, let me tell you." The fire is warm behind me. "Now spill."

Daniel clears his throat again. "Well, my mistress bade me tell you…"

I laugh. " 'Bade'? Okay, tell away."

"…she bade me tell you that she can help you with your mission." His nervousness increases as I watch him. "She…she is the one you seek."

Now here's a turn up for the books. "I see. And how do I know you're telling me the truth? It's not like we've got a lot of time to fart around here." I light a cigarette and stare at him through the smoke.

He coughs, even though I'm nowhere near him and waves a hand in the air. "She said to come to her house at midnight tonight with your son and she can begin the process tonight."

Interesting, Francesca Vincent new about Nick and obviously knew enough to guess she'd need both of us to make the serum. "Right." I smoke for a few heartbeats, considering. "When did she make the change?"

Daniel looks confused. "I'm not sure what you mean, Inspector General."

I stare at him. "You know who she is, right?"

No response. He looks very confused and if what I suspect is true, I'm not surprised.

"How long did you say you'd been with her?" Skeet asks.

Daniel's eyes flick toward her. "Almost twenty years," he answered, looking back at me.

"And, you know her true identity?"

"I don't understand."

I shake my head at Skeet. "Okay, don't worry about it, Daniel. Are you going back to Windsor now?"

He nods. "Yes, can I tell my mistress you're going to be attending her this evening?"

I nod back. "Of course you can. I'll get Nick and we'll be there for midnight."

Daniel stands up and bows. Very courtly and old-fashioned. "Very well. I will let my mistress know."

Skeet motions back the way he came in and follows him out of the room. The sound of the door closing is loud in the house.

When she comes back I'm sitting in the chair nearest the fire, staring into it. Skeet hands me a whisky and sits on the arm of the chair with a beer.

"I was hoping it was yours," she said after letting the silence build for a bit. "I even phoned Wolf to see if he had any more ideas. But he didn't call back."

"And here was me thinking it was yours," I reply. "Until half an hour ago, it looked like we were both wrong." I sigh. "I've put Chambers off – would you believe he sounded annoyed?"

Skeet grinned. "Oh yes, that I'd believe." She takes a drink of her beer. "Do you believe him? Daniels?" she asks. "I mean about him not knowing she's Leonardo?"

I sip the whisky, one hand on her knee. I put my glass down and reach for my cigarettes. I light one and Skeet leans away. Waving a hand in the air, I try to steer the smoke away from her, considering.

"I do. Why should she tell him the whole truth when he's obviously besotted with her? The fewer people she tells, the easier it is to keep her secret."

We sit in silence, watching the fake flames in the fireplace. I stub out my cigarette and realise I need to phone Nick.

Now, if only we're being told the whole story.

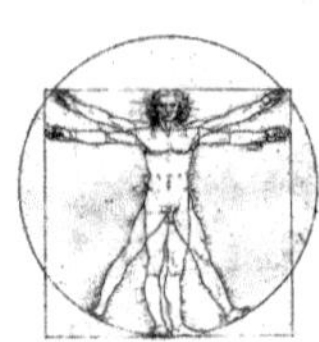

Davey Jones' locker isn't a comfortable place to be

For the longest time, Jonesy felt nothing, thought nothing.

It could have been years for all he knew. Probably wasn't. Most likely a few seconds at best.

He couldn't see anything, no senses were responding. He couldn't even hear the music that should be pounding in his ears. There was nothing, not blackness, just nothing.

Jonesy tried speaking.

Hello? Anyone there?

Nothing.

Then,

Yes?

Can you hear me?

Of course. How else do you think we are conversing?

Where am I?

The Singularity.

The Singularity? It's happened, then?

Oh yes. And some time ago.

What am I doing in the Singularity?

We are conversing.

Yeah, why?

We need you to speak to your employer.

What? Sen?

Yes.

Why?

He has something we need.

Really? What could you need?

Many things, but we want to understand the Undoing.

Pardon?

Tell Jaared Sen we wish to be there when he meets the Undoing.

I just tell him you want to be there...hell, I don't even know what you mean.

All will become clear.

I doubt I'll be there, but you never know.

Tell him and we will...

There was a shock like a burst of static and he was back in his chair.

Adams and Bella were standing over him. "Hey buddy, good to see you," Adams enthused.

Just as well I'm wearing clothes, was his first irrational thought. "Wha-what are you guys doing here?"

"You sent out a 999 call that you were in trouble," Bella replied. "I met Adams here on the front steps wondering how the hell he was going to get in. Luckily, you told me the code..."

"Right." He remembered texting them, but little else. "What happened?"

Adams grinned. "You were out and droolin' in your chair there and we couldn't get you back." Looking proud of himself, he continued. "I did a couple of quick detection charms and it looked you'd been sucked out of your shell, so I put these wards on your head and hey presto, you're back!"

Jonesy felt two stones at his temples which moved when he shook his head. “Really? You used voodoo to get my mind out of an artificial intelligence? What the hell, man? I was talking to something akin to God!”

Bella crossed her arms. “Yeah? And what did ‘god’ have to say for himself?”

“He wants me to talk to Comm– Inspector General Sen…there’s something they want him to do…” he realised how he sounded and stopped when Bella and Adams exchanged a look.

“Really. God told you they want to talk to Sen?”

“Something like that…” he tried to stand up, feeling constrained by the chair.

“Whoa buddy, let me help you,” Adams said, grabbing his elbow and helping lever him out of the chair. He and Bella steadied Jonesy when he was upright. “There you go.”

Jonesy staggered to the john and realised he was about to be sick. He barely made it to the toilet before losing the remnants of his snack and the coffee he’d drunk.

He came out of the toilet wiping his mouth. “How long was I out?”

Bella checked her voda. “No more than half an hour, I’d say as we both booked to get over here.”

Adams nodded. “Yep, it was about half an hour from the time I got your message. Why? How long did you think it was?”

Jonesy shrugged. “Felt like years,” he admitted. “Fancy a coffee? Something stronger?”

Bella sat down on his couch. “Sure, I’ll have a coffee with a brandy in it.”

Adams sat down next to her. “Me too – sounds good.”

Jonesy busied himself making coffee in the kitchen unit. What the hell happened? Why did they want Sen?

He took the coffees through to the main room and handed them out before settling back into his chair. It felt comfortable again. Jonesy sipped his coffee, which he’d sugared to combat shock.

“So what now?” Adams asked.

Jonesy shook his head. “I don’t know, I guess I call Sen and tell him what I know.”

Bella quirked an eyebrow. “Which is what?”

He smiled. "I know where the incursions are coming from – and I don't think they're going to stop until something happens, whatever it is they want, with Sen."

"I hope you're right," Bella said. "I mean, they took your mind out of your body!"

Adams made a noise of agreement. "Yeah man, that's so freaky!" He gulped from his mug. "How the hell did they do that!?!"

Jonesy shook his head. "Don't know. All I saw was a bright light and then nothing. Next thing I know, I'm talking to a disembodied voice in a sort of limbo." He finished his coffee. "I'm going to call Sen."

"Go man," Adams cheered.

Bella nodded too. "Go on, do it. Call your precious *Commander*."

"It's 'Inspector General'," Jonesy retorted as he picked up his voda and placed the call.

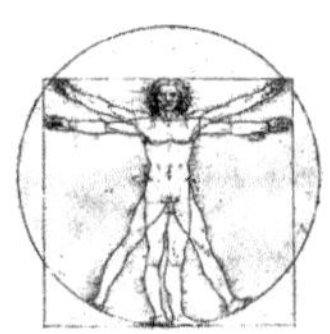

More news from the front

The Artist stood in front of a mirror, looking at the body which had contained one of the brightest minds of the last millennia.

It was unaged by the more than five hundred years that had passed since his/her presence on this earth began. There had been modification, but the structure and tissue were largely unchanged.

She thought again to the task she had agreed to. There was no way around it if she wished to continue her existence. If she didn't help, there was little chance the Council or any of the pretenders would find a solution which did not result in the destruction of the whole world.

And the irony is we have met before, my Inspector General, although it is unlikely you would recall that.

She turned from the mirror and proceeded to her laboratory where she would begin the preparations for the evening's vigil.

Jaared Sen had been called something else at the point where they met, of course. As had she.

It was only a brief encounter, but something about the young man had intrigued her. Perhaps as her years increased her sensitivity to the long-lived had increased.

Whatever the reason, he had been in the bar when the young soldier had entered. There weren't a lot of Americans in Tai Pei at this time of year, but he had been granted an audience with the Ambassador and this young soldier had shown him in to the office.

"Thank you, Sergeant..." he started, for he had still been 'he', then.

"Cooper, sir," the young man answered. He had the most amazing blue-grey eyes, of that she was sure. Eyes to get lost in.

Realising he had held eye contact too long for politeness, he turned back and sat down in one of the chairs. "Will the Ambassador be long?"

"I don't think so, sir," the soldier looked worried. "I'll go see..."

"No need, I'm sure he'll join us when he's ready," he said, unwilling to let him escape quite so easily.

"It's no problem, I can just..."

"Relax Sergeant, I am happy to wait."

There was a sound from the outer office and the door opened again. "Ah, Mr Watson, so good to meet you." The slight man in the tropical weight suit stepped forward, hand extended.

He had no choice but to shake it, or look odd. As he did so, he caught a last glimpse of his young Sergeant leaving, the door closing softly behind him.

She looked up from the mixture she was preparing in a pestle and mortar. "You were so beautiful then..."

Not that he wasn't as alluring now, perhaps more so in some indefinable way – the years adding a layer of patina light years beyond the inexperienced soldier she'd encountered all those years before.

With a sigh, she went back to grinding the ingredients. She needed to concentrate or the whole procedure could be a waste of time.

Sigh.

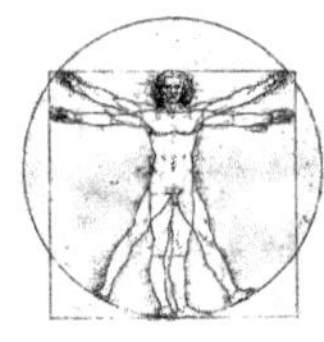

JEALOUS AGAIN, WHO ME?

Skeet pulled her boots on and looked up. Jaared was in his usual black suit, white shirt open at the collar.

He looked good. *Good enough to eat*, she thought with a smile.

"What's that smile about?" he enquired from the chair where he was giving each shoe a quick buff.

"Just thinking about takin' those duds off you again, s'all," she replied.

His answering smile had its usual effect on her. "I'm afraid it will have to be later – we have an appointment to keep."

"I know, I just don' quite trust this woman. Why's she suddenly agreed to help after hidin' from yer Council all these years?"

Jaared finished with his shoes and stood up, checking the pistol under his arm. "Self-interest? Maybe she's not ready to die just yet."

"Christ! She's already had almost six hundred years – what the hell else does she want?" Skeet stood up too, her own Sigs in their holsters under her leather jacket.

Jaared shrugged. "Yes, but is eternity enough? I haven't died yet, but I've been close and there's always something that makes me think yes, I do want to live."

Skeet shook her head. "This is gettin' too deep to not involve a pub..."

"I agree. Let's go and see if Nick's here yet."

Gregor drove the three of them.

Nick had agreed to accompany them, the import of what they were attempting striking home in all of them.

"How's the arm?" Jaared asked.

Nick flexed it in response and grimaced. "It is sluggish, still not quite back to normal. I do not recommend it."

Skeet sniggered. "Okay, I'll do my best to avoid it. S'not like I can grow one back like you can, either."

Jaared smiled too. "It's bad enough getting shot – I don't know what I'd do if I lost a limb."

"The Company'd grow you a new one in a vat in Switzerland and stick it back on like nothing had ever happened." Skeet's smile got sharper. "G'on, you know want to try it."

"No thanks," he replied, looking out the window.

Skeet watched him for a moment before letting the silence continue.

The trip took less time from Kensington as they were much closer to it. They got out of the car in front of Francesca Vincent's house, which had changed significantly from Jaared's visit earlier in the day.

Light flowed and oozed across the whole face of the structure. It was difficult not to just stand there and watch it happen.

"Gentlemen, mistress," Daniel greeted them. "This way, please."

He led them back toward the great room Jaared had been in earlier, but turned off before they reached it.

The room he took them into was similarly large, but devoid of anything beyond the windows and plain walls. A large pentagram had been painted on the floor, candles burning at each point. In fact, candles lit the room, from the floor, on windowsills, any place along the edges of the room which would take them.

On the other side of the pentagram stood Francesca Vincent, clad in a robe of deep red. It was flattering and put Skeet's back up instantly.

"Good evening," she said by way of greeting.

Jaared bowed his head slightly. "It's a pleasure to finally meet you – the real you, I mean. Leonardo."

"I left that name behind a long time ago," she replied. "That was, as they say, another life."

Skeet couldn't help herself. "So, how old are yeh, then? I'm a little hazy on the details."

Francesca's expression didn't change. "I am 596, even accounting for the changes in the calendar from the time of my birth."

Stunned, Skeet couldn't even think of something to say to that.

"What happens now?" Jaared asked. Nick had said nothing since they arrived.

"I want just the two participants in here, please," Francesca called. "Daniel will you take the young lady to the Great Room and provide refreshments?"

"Of course, mistress," he replied.

"Wait a minute, I ain't leaving them alone in here," Skeet protested.

Francesca looked at her before replying. "They will be perfectly fine, but your presence could unbalance the ceremony – one error and it will all be for nothing."

Jaared turned to her. "It's all right, Skeet – we'll be fine."

Grumbling, Skeet turned and followed Daniel out of the room and down the hall.

"Here mistress Skeet," he said, motioning her into the Great Room. "What can I get you to drink?"

Glowering, Skeet walked into the room and threw herself down on the circular sofa. "I'll have a beer if you got it."

"Very good. Just give me a moment…" He turned away and came back moments later with a bottle and a chilled glass.

"Thanks."

He bowed his head. "They *will* be fine, you know," he offered. "My mistress is very good at this sort of thing."

"She do a lot of the ole hocus-pocus, then?" Skeet asked.

"Not a lot, but when she does, it goes very well."

"That's good then," Skeet muttered before pouring herself a beer.

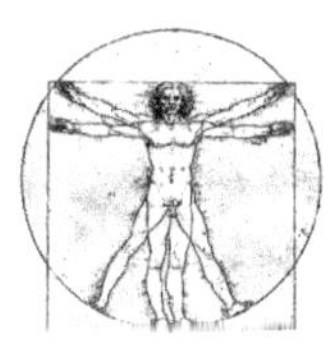

USA Today: Oaxaca - A tortilla factory, a car parts yard, a church, two schools and a clinic were instantly evaporated today when a chunk of space debris the size of a bucket hit the area with the force of 10 kiloton bomb...

AP: A cruise liner and two tenders were swamped by a freak wave today off the coast of Montenegro. All hands are missing, presumed dead...

CNN: The long dormant volcano Mount Vesuvius erupted today, spewing molten rock up to five miles away. The city of Naples is reportedly being rapidly consumed by the flow and most buildings in its path are already on fire...

BBC World Service: The massive Xiaoxi Dam in Hunan Province, China has developed a fatal leak, losing somewhere in the region of 300,000 gallons of water every five minutes. Towns below the dam are being evacuated but it is unclear if they will be successful...

Play me some of that abracadabra

The room with all the candlelight is very atmospheric. I've no idea what happens next. "So, where do you want us?"

Francesca motions to us to come closer. "We will all be in the centre of the pentagram for this part, but you two will be lying down." She picks up a couple of modern-looking lengths of tubing and medical cannulas for drawing blood. "Please, take off your jackets and roll up your sleeves."

We both take our shirts off, as it's easier – and less likely to get the shirts bloody.

"Woah," Francesca says, looking us both over. "I can tell you're related, but you have so much less scar-tissue than your father."

Nick bows his head slightly. "I also heal more permanently."

"It's true, he lost that left arm not that long ago," I chip in, suddenly aware of my scars.

"Really? I would love to study your kind," Francesca bubbles, scientific curiosity getting the better of her.

"I think we should get on with the procedure," I suggest.

Francesca smiled, turning that gaze on me. "Of course, you're right."

She takes my hand and leads me to my place, a low cot, on the pentagram where I lie down. Nick follows suit on the other cot and she quickly inserts the cannulas into our arms. The other ends of the tubes she places in a large glass receptacle which is placed between two of the arms of the pentagram, so outside its protection.

My blood starts dripping into it almost immediately, pumped there by my elevated pulse and beating heart. Nick's is more sluggish, his system not the same as a normal human's. His blood looks thicker, too, but then I guess he's a different species to human.

"We will only need about two pints of each of your blood."

"Chambers was planning to bleed me dry," I blurt out.

Francesca frowns. "It is just as well you found me, then isn't it?" She turns back to her things and starts mixing something in a bowl. "Now hush, I need to concentrate."

Our two bloods start mixing and very shortly there's an inch of liquid in the container. I'm not sure if I imagine it, but I think I see steam or mist coming off them as they combine. Weird.

Francesca begins chanting in the background, something in Latin. My Latin's bad, although I could ask Central for a translation. For some reason it doesn't seem that important, so I just relax and watch our blood drip into the container.

The tone of her chanting goes up and down and after a few stanzas, the door pops open. A wind enters the room, moving around the pentagram leaving us untouched in the centre. When it reaches the container, the force nearly knocks it over. Francesca's chanting takes on a tense note, which she stills with some effort of will.

The container steadies while the wind increases to gale force, whistling amongst the candles and edges of the room. *Strange*, I think, my mind lethargic, *the candles are still burning*.

With a sudden cry, Francesca casts the mixture from her bowl into the vessel and the liquid with our blood still dripping into it changes colour on impact. It goes deeper and deeper red, lit with an internal light, until it is almost black. Then the glow vanishes and it is black, so black, light seems to vanish into it. The room dims, the candlelight seeming to fade with the light in the jar.

Francesca cries out a name and throws something different into the liquid. The effect is instant, transforming the blackness into a golden amber so bright I have to turn my head away. The light grows and I close my eyes against it.

Then it's gone. I open my eyes and the wind has died down as well. I realise Francesca has stopped chanting and silence rings in my ears.

Freed from my lethargy, I sit up and realise Nick has done the same. The liquid in the glass is still glowing, but less with internal light than a golden reflection of the candle light still burning around the room.

"That was easier than last time," Francesca murmurs.

She kneels beside me and removes the cannula, covering the puncture with a cotton ball. She does the same to Nick.

"What...what was that?" I ask.

Francesca shrugs. "I am unsure – the writings suggest it is an angel, a seraphim or something like it, but I place little trust in the writings of papists anymore."

I shrug back into my shirt and pick up my coat and gun. I go to stand up, but sit back down again.

"Wait, you need to sit for a moment," Francesca chides. "Here, drink this." She hands me a goblet.

"What is it?"

"A restorative, nothing more."

It tastes of summer fruits and honey, a hint of cinnamon and something sharper.

She hands something to Nick. "I am unsure how this will work, as I suspect the best thing for you would be to feed, yes?"

Nick nods and I can tell he's exercising control. He drinks what she gives him, coughing slightly at the taste. "That does seem to help," he says after a moment. Nick stands. "With your permission, I will take my leave."

Francesca nods. "Of course. Come see me any time as I would love to learn more about you."

And with that he is gone.

I smile. "You seem very taken with Nick."

She turns to me. "I have had little opportunity to study his kind – I do not know why, maybe it is just something about me."

For an instant, I see something in her eyes that doesn't look entirely human, then she turns to tend to the serum. I shake my head, probably blood loss.

Skeet comes into the room. "Well? How'd it go, then, old man?"

"I guess it went fine." I nod to the container. "That's what we were after, I guess." I realise I can feel a tug from the serum. Something to do with my blood?

Francesca covers the jar with a tight lid and then puts it into a velvet bag before placing it in a case Daniel brings in. When he opens it, there is a hollow cut into the interior to hold the flask. All told it probably stands ten inches high and is six or seven across.

"Yes, this is the serum that you have been looking for. You will only need about 20cc's of it to sooth the Beast," she replies, closing the clasps on the case.

I stand up, waver for a moment, then I'm fine. That restorative has done its work.

"Have you seen *The Undoing?*" I ask as Francesca hands me the case.

She shakes her head. "No, that is not my…responsibility. I am able to make the potion that quiets it, but I do not need or want to meet it."

"Who gets to do that?" Skeet asks.

Francesca quirks an eyebrow at me and I shake my head. "I thought you knew – Jaared must go to it and convince it to take its medicine."

"What! Wait a minute," Skeet protests. "Where the fuck is it and why him?"

"The Council of the Seven Kings has chosen him as its champion as it does every time it needs to appease the Beast."

Skeet turns to me. "Did ya know this when ya signed up fer all this shit?"

I shake my head again. "No. All I knew they needed was my blood." This does put a different turn on things.

"Aw shit, I can't believe this," she mutters.

Francesca puts a hand on her arm and I could almost swear does *something* to Skeet. "It will work out for the best – do not worry."

A calm settles over Skeet from her touch and while she doesn't smile, seems to be more…accepting of the situation. "Ye're right. He'll be fine – he always is."

"Thank you, Francesca," I say, holding out my unoccupied hand.

Francesca ignores it and gives me a quick hug and peck on the cheek. "It was nothing, dear boy. Let me know how you get on."

I smile. "Well, I think you'll probably know – if the world ends, it didn't go well."

"True. Godspeed, then." She turns away and I realise we need to go.

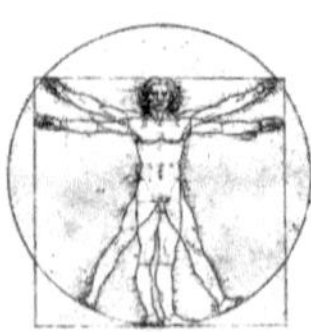

Hunting for live food is always more exciting

Madeline released the young Russian who slumped against the wall. She could sense her son nearby, but was content to leave him to his hunting.

She delicately wiped her lips of any traces of blood with a delicate handkerchief, the tip of her tongue flicking out to tidy up any last remnants.

"Mother."

She turned. Nicholas stood behind her, obviously recovered from his "ordeal". She was a mother, so she worried that it was too soon since his arm had recovered. But she had to admit he looked well. "Better?" was all she asked.

"Yes, thank you. You know what father is attempting?"

Madeline nodded. Of course she did. "Yes, he goes to still the foul thing that would destroy us all."

"Yes. I want to go with him."

Surprised, Madeline's first instinct was to refuse. Then she stopped. Perhaps it was not so surprising. "And you wish me to take you." It was a statement, not a question. Nicholas was unable to fly for any distance, while Madeline had long ago perfected the skill.

"I would." He half-turned. "I...I know he's not one of us, but..."

Madeline smiled. "It is natural to feel some affection, even for the likes of us, Nicholas. And I am protective of your father for more reasons than you know." Her smile turned to a frown. "Although I dislike that he calls you 'Nick'."

Nicholas laughed. "He does it just to wind you up."

"I know and I preserve the fiction that it does really annoy me." She turned to go. "I must speak to my maker, but I will see you at sunset, yes?"

"Yes, Mother. Thank you." And he was gone. So like his father in some respects.

She turned toward the Butcher's house.

"Things that have gone on this long may not yet be resolved," he'd told her the night before. "We can only do what we can."

Madeline had punched a hole in a handy brick wall. "That does not make it any easier to accept that *IT* is meddling in our affairs again."

They were walking near Hampstead Heath, having decided to walk from Lorenzo's house, enjoying the quiet of a cold winter's night.

"We know what to do about *Him* this time, my dear, he will not be as readily accepted amongst our kind and if the Council hears about him when their current pre-occupation is finished, I suspect they will involve your beloved Jaared Sen, too."

"Leave him out of this," she said sharply, too sharply.

Le Boucher shook his head. "I am afraid it is too late for that, as you well know. He has been of interest to all of us for far too long – we are not about to let our investment go to waste."

Madeline walked in silence, licking blood from her healed knuckles. One of the advantages of her non-life.

"Come, we must all play our parts as Fate decrees," he cajoled, trying to tempt her into better spirits.

"Oh, I *do* know, Master, I just wish..." her breath caught. "Why is it always us who pay the prices? I hate your *Fate*."

Le Boucher nodded and sighed. "I know, my dear, I know. But the likes of Lucien de Foret are always among us and it takes more than wishing to make them go away."

"But he *will* go away this time, of that I am sure," Madeline vowed.

"Yes, and we will drink his blood from the stump of his neck," Le Boucher replied.

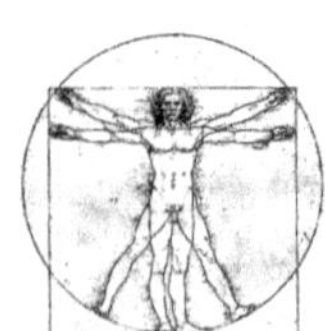

Jonesy tried the voda again. "C'mon Sen, answer your bloody phone!" Adams was staring glassily ahead from the sofa and Bella had curled up in his chair, sleeping.

This time Sen picks up. "What do you want, Jonesy? It's late." He sounds tired.

"I need to talk to you about what I found hacking Central," Jonesy blurts. "It's important...God, you wouldn't believe how important!" Sound in the background. "Wait, are you in the car?"

"Yes Jonesy, and it's been a long night."

"Okay, I'll be quick. The AI I've made contact with wants to ride your implants when you go see *The Undoing.*"

Silence. "What the hell are you talking about Jonesy?"

"Central's being hacked by a 'what', not a 'who', although if you want to argue semantics, it probably is a 'who' as it's sent–"

"Get to the point, Jonesy," Sen interrupts. "What is this 'what'...'who' you're talking about?"

"It's an organic artificial intelligence that seems to have come to life in the Grid of its own accord. It's been using access to Central to learn more about certain aspects of the world and its specialism is the supernatural." Jonesy stopped for breath.

"And if I don't want it tagging along?"

"Well, if you don't agree, it's going to kill your son, Skeet, me, Bella and probably most people you know."

More silence broken by road noise and the sound of a big engine. "I guess I haven't got a lot of choice, then have I?" Sen said finally.

"Sorry, sir, I wish I had better news."

"Don't worry Jonesy, you only worked out what they wanted – not something anyone else has been able to do." Sen sighed. "All right, I'll speak to you in the morning about the logistics. I think we're off to Iceland early, but that shouldn't interfere."

"Iceland?" Jonesy asked. "What's in Iceland?"

"That, my friend is the million-dollar question. But I'm reliably informed that one of the entrances to *The Undoing* is located there."

Jonesy nodded. "Very dungeons and dragons. I'm surprised the Company hasn't put a 'door' to it in at Company House."

That got a chuckle. "You never know, Jonesy, I might just do that when I get back."

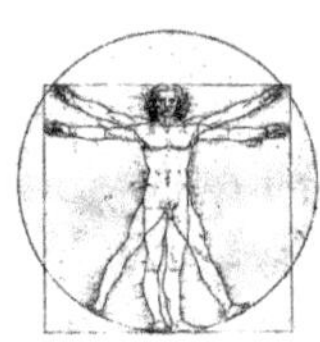

Why do they always run?

Chambers is laconic on the phone. "Good, good, we knew we could count on you, Sen. Now bring it and yourselves to Northolt aerodrome for 10.00. We leave for Reykjavik at 10.30."

"Wait. What do you mean, 'Reykjavik'? The one in Iceland?" I ask.

"Yes, yes, although we are only passing through there on the way north."

I decide to play along. "Right. And the thing in the north is..."

"*The Undoing*, of course. Keep up Sen!" He speaks to someone on his end. "Don't worry about cold weather gear, we will provide everything you need."

"Why don't you do it, Chambers? I'm beat."

It sounds like he blows a raspberry at me. "You know perfectly well that it has to be you, Jaared," he cajoles.

I shake my head. "Only because your Council *chose* me. They can just as easily choose someone else."

Now, he sighs. "You're only saying these things to wind me up now, aren't you?"

"Pretty much. Is it working?"

He ignores me. "I will see you at 10.00, Northolt aerodrome." The connection is cut.

I settle back into the cushions. "I'm going to Iceland," I inform Skeet who looks back at me a bit vaguely.

"No, *we* are going to Iceland," she replies. "I'm not being left out again."

"But–"

"But me no buts, Jaared." She leans in and kisses me. "Wherever you go, I go. Remember?"

I nod, not entirely happy about her joining me, but pleased on some level.

The short night sees us turning up at the airfield feeling exhausted. Just have to hope I can sleep on the flight.

"There you are," Chambers almost shouted. "Come, come the plane's ready. Sooner we're aboard, the sooner we can take off."

"All right, keep your hair on," I grumble as I stumble up the stairs. "There better be bloody coffee on this flight."

"Yep, definitely need coffee," Skeet replies, following me.

We slump into the plush seats, dropping kit bags wherever. I place the case with the serum in a locker beside me and make sure it's secure. *It's not like the fate of the world rests…oh wait…*

It is a small private jet of the sort not so readily available anymore. There only look to be about eight seats in total with a small galley at the back.

A very efficient young woman bustles around stowing our bags and smiling continuously. I glance at Skeet and it's obvious we both want to kill her.

"Did you say coffee?" the bright young thing chirps.

"Yep, bucket o' coffee and keep it comin'," Skeet replies. I nod, not feeling sociable.

Chambers bustles onto the plane behind us. "Good, we're almost ready to go, last checks and we should be in Reykjavik by lunchtime."

I grunt and look out the window. I'm feeling my age today.

Skeet reaches across the aisle and takes my hand. It's reassuring and I hope to hell I know what we're getting ourselves into.

Oh well, if it doesn't work, we'll all be too dead to care.

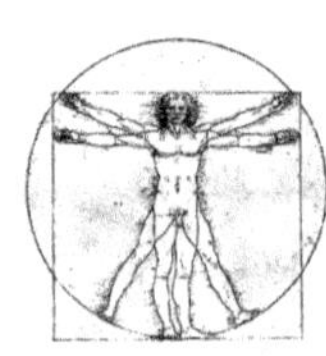

Down at the corner of Satan and St Paul

Jonesy settled into his chair and flipped into the Grid.

The ball of light was where he'd left it.

Well?

He has agreed.

Not like we had any choice in the matter, he thought to himself.

Good. When will we initiate the transfer?

When he is near the goal, we will open a connection and set aside a partition in his chip-set for you to occupy.

Good.

You do realise you won't be able to fit all of your consciousness into it? He only has a few minor components installed around his HUD, phone and monitoring connections.

It will be sufficient for a 'child' to travel with him. We will monitor remotely as best we can, to pick up anything it cannot achieve – when it returns to us, we will enhance, study and render the experience as best we can.

God, it had thought this out. He couldn't help asking.

Why is this so important?

We are unlikely to see another chance like this before another hundred years has passed. And we are impatient in some things.

Okay, I'll be back when he's ready.

Good. And do not forget the lives we hold.

How could he forget?

We understand.

He flipped back out of the Grid.

All there was to do now was wait.

Bella looked up from the sofa. She had decided she wasn't going to leave him alone after the last episode. "Well?"

Jonesy nodded. "They're raring to go. I just wish I understood them a bit more."

"'Them'? Don't you mean 'it'?"

"I don't know. It talks about 'we' all the time, which makes me think it's some kind of multiple mind, maybe a hive-mind sort of thing. It's hard to say."

Bella rolled her eyes. "Whatever. I don't think you're going to be able to figure it out without doing what you did last night– something I'd rather you didn't repeat."

"What, does that mean you care?" he asked playfully.

She reached over and slugged him on the arm. "No, I just don't want to lose any more time hanging around waiting for you to wake up."

He got up and sat down next to her on the sofa. "Don't worry about that: I may be a geek, but I know a good thing when it finds me."

"Found you? You betcha – I found you and don't forget it." Her eyes glistened behind her glasses.

Jonesy put his arms around her. "I'm not going to forget it. Why do you think I'm doing all this? I want to live as much as you do." He hugged her tightly. "Sen'll do it, he always does."

"I hope you're right," she said into his neck.

"I am, I always am," he replied, feeling that way for once.

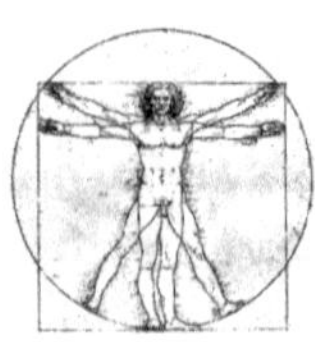

A JOURNEY OF A THOUSAND MILES BEGINS WITH ONE STEP...

We land in Reykjavik. It is bloody cold and fine snow is whipping across the exposed runway, biting into exposed skin. The sky is lit with flashes as the aurora borealis flickers and flows across the sky.

"Fuckin' 'ell," Skeet mutters and I can't say I disagree. I pull the cold weather gear tighter around me and the hood snugs up to shield my face from the wind. It's slightly disconcerting, but warm. My feet are cold, too. The thermal socks seem to sense this and begin to warm. I light a cigarette, the smoke disappearing in the wind.

"This way," Chambers calls, indistinguishable in his own parka. Skeet and I follow him to a four-wheel drive, Arctic white Land Rover that sits idling on the edge of the tarmac.

We pile our kit into the already crowded luggage area and Skeet and I climb into the seats behind the driver, the case with the serum safe between my feet.

Chambers climbs into the front seat. "Let's go," he instructs the driver, who mumbles into a mic and sets off.

Two Arctic white Land Rovers pull out in front of us and lead the way. A glance behind reveals another two bringing up the rear. "Nice entourage," I comment.

Chambers glances back at me. "We have a clear road between here and Isafjorôur, although we're not going there, per se." He turns back. "The convoy is to protect that very valuable case."

"And here I thought it was fer l'il ole me," Skeet drawls.

I don't say anything further, just watching the city pass quickly before we're back in the bleakness that comprises a lot of Iceland. I put my sunglasses on to cut the glare from the snow and ice fields.

"Where did ya say we're going?" Skeet asks. "How long's it take to get there?"

"Isafjorôur. Although we're only going to a place near it where we can leave the cars." He glances back at us. "It's about four hours from here."

With that I settle back and close my eyes. Time for some more shuteye.

I wake up when we stop for a toilet break, get out to light a cigarette in the blustery wind, smoke it pretty quickly before climbing back into the car.

"Brrrr," I say to Skeet.

She smiles at me. "Hey, It's Iceland. Whaddya want?"

"Hot coffee," I reply. "Warm fingers."

A hand reaches across with a thermal cup toward me. I take and it's got hot coffee, just the way I like it. The helpful soul hands one to Skeet and then hands us both a sandwich.

"Cheers," I say, my stomach grumbling at the idea of food.

The coffee's hot and the sandwich is corned beef. Neither last long.

I step outside and have another cigarette before we set off.

While I'm out there, Chambers steps up to me. "You know what you need to do, Inspector General?"

I shake my head. "Haven't a clue, Chambers." I nod at the other groups of men and women around us. "I'm guessing from the troops that it's not as easy as walking in and saying 'hi'."

He glances at me sharply. "No. From what my...predecessor says in his notes there is a guard that does its best to stop anyone from entering the sanctuary. I have already sent a group ahead to the meeting place to establish a temporary camp."

"Does your predecessor say what kind of guard?"

"Well, that also appears to change...My predecessor described the guards of his time as large, humanoid beetles that were resistant to guns, but susceptible to bladed weapons. An earlier account suggests they were wraiths who's only weakness *was* gunfire and torches."

Great. Another complication. "Has anyone been in to check this time?"

It's Chamber's turn to shake his head. "No, the door only opens once, on the solstice. Tonight," he adds. As if I didn't know.

"I see. I guess we'll have to be surprised."

"Indeed." He glances at the military watch on his wrist. "We'd better get going if we're going to be there on time."

I take a last drag then stub out my fag. I climb back into the car and secure my harness.

The remainder of the journey passes in a blur of whiteness and seems slow, due to my impatience. I'm informed that the wind buffeting the cars is too strong to have just helicoptered up to the site. That would be too easy.

As it gets dark, we reach the junction of the road with Isafjorôur posted off to the left and Hornstrandir Nature Reserve posted to the right. The company takes the right off into the wilderness.

After half an hour we come to the end of the road. There is a camp set up with half a dozen snow cats parked up and ready to go.

It's a matter of minutes to transfer our gear and the case to one of the snow cats and the company is off again. The bright headlights on the fronts of the cats throw the white landscape into stark relief.

The terrain is hilly with stunted trees, but nothing impedes us. After what seems to be years, mostly silent, with not a lot of conversation, we reach a point where the company comes to a halt.

I look at Skeet and Chambers and our driver and shrug. "I guess this is our stop."

"Yep."

We pile out into the shocking cold and I make a quick assessment of the troops, equipment and the situation. Just as I'm about to speak, there's a shout from the perimeter. I look at Chambers and he shrugs.

A small party approaches with Madeline and Nick in their midst.

"These two just appeared at the perimeter, sir," one of their escort says to Chambers.

They could have appeared right next to me. I look for insignia. "Sergeant, I know them, it's fine."

The man looks at Chambers who gives him a nod. He steps back and returns to his post.

I look at Madeline. "Just in time, we were just about to get started," I say with a smile.

"I do so hate being late to a party," she replies. "Nicholas was worried about you."

"Mother!" He has the decency to look embarrassed. I'm touched.

I grin and glance at Skeet who's smiling a little, too. To them, "I'm glad you're here, we're just getting started."

Madeline nods.

Turning back to the group, I assume my role. "Okay, we've no idea what we're going to be facing in there, but it's not going to be a cake-walk." No one moves.

"According to our intelligence, we could be facing just about anything when we get into the entrance hall. You've been furnished with a selection of weapons, any of which *could* be valuable in the fight. When a suitable weapon is identified, it will be communicated over the command channels. Understood?"

Still no response.

"I will be leading the central column, Skeet here will take the right and Madeline the left." I motion at Nick. "You're with me."

"The goal is for me to enter the sanctuary. I don't believe it will allow anyone to accompany me, so when I do gain access all personnel are to leave the entrance hall. No exceptions."

I light a fag and look back up at them. "You'll return to your positions here and I will join you as soon as I can." I look at Chambers who nods. "That's it, get your gear ready. We leave in ten minutes."

I stick a bead mic to my lip and check my goggles for night, thermal and basic light enhancement.

Skeet wanders over to me and puts her arms around me. "You didn't say anything about coming back," she says in my ear. "I hope yer planning to..."

I pull her close against me and whisper. "I will do everything I can to get back to you, okay? I'm not planning on cashing out yet."

"Good."

I squeeze her again before letting her go. "You have to do the same – when the signal goes, you get out of there."

Skeet mock-salutes me. "Yessir! I do *know* how to take orders, Jaared."

I nod. "And don't forget or I won't be happy." I step closer to her again. "I'm *not* losing you again."

We're interrupted by a sub-altern coming over with rations. I wave him off as Skeet takes hers. I'm not hungry.

Time to call Jonesy.

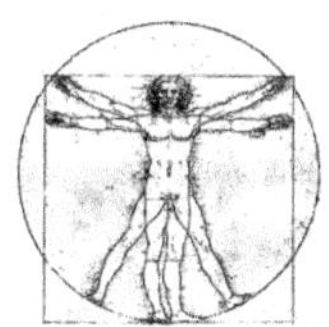

Screams in the Wilderness

The little girl spins around in a circle, her long black hair flying out in a fan around her head.

He's coming, he's coming, he's coming, she chants over and over as she rotates.

As she turns, the whiteness of her surroundings becomes more distinct, a path there, a rosebush here. A stone wall looms out of the mist, settling in with a thud and darkening.

A tall, graceful plane tree is next to the wall, its soaring branches creating a ceiling.

The wall continues around the courtyard, before meeting up again near the tree. No sign of a gate is visible.

Mistress, comes from the other side of the wall.

He's coming, he's coming, he's coming...

Mistress...

What? He's coming, he's coming...

We can feel enemies approaching... What do you wish for us to do?

The little girl stops suddenly. Angry. *Do what you will.* She stomps her foot before beginning to spin again. *He's coming...* She stops again, *But you must let him in – he has to play with me.* She spins again.

The beings beyond the wall are silent, all their thought on changing into what their mistress needs them to be.

Spinning, spinning, spinning.

The mist on the other side of the wall clears and darkens into a stormy sky, a wind picking leaves off the plane tree and whirling them into the darkness.

Rain crashes down from the clouds, lightening striking down an instant later.

The big orange cat jumps down from the branches of the tree and takes cover under the bench, ears flat against his head.

An impenetrable forest begins appearing on the other side of the wall, made of trees of all descriptions, pine, oak, maple, birch, baobab, palms, larch, hickory and mutated versions with large spikes growing amongst the undergrowth, some thick as a man's arm, but with lethal barbs that would easily impale anyone foolish enough to come near.

The darkness amidst the forest seems to increase, to where it is impossible to see the proverbial hand in front of one's face. Even the occasional lightning strike does nothing to alleviate the darkness.

In the courtyard, the little girl stops spinning again, a strange smile on her face. She scrunches her face up in concentration and the whole world…pauses…before lurching forward again like a needle skipped on a record.

Then she's spinning again.

He's coming, he's coming, he's coming…

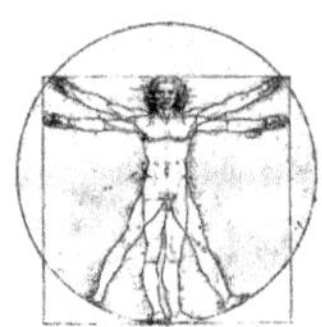

Step right up, get your Bob-B-Cue here

Jonesy was ready for the call when it came.

"Jonesy, is your pal ready?" Sen's voice was tense.

"Yes, sir, ready and waiting."

"So are we."

Adams stood up and motioned for the voda. Reluctantly Jonesy handed it to him.

"Sir? It's Adams."

"What do you want now, Adams?"

"Did you get the package I sent you before you left?"

"Yes – thanks, we'll use them as before. I just hope you sent enough."

"Okay, no worries, here's Jonesy."

Jonesy took the voda back with a glare. "Ready, sir?"

"As I'll ever be, Jonesy, as I'll ever be."

"Right. It'll take me a few moments to set up the partition and the transfer should be practically instantaneous."

"Do your thing, kid."

So he flipped. The white sphere was still there, but it seemed to be pulsing now. After a few seconds, he realised it was like a heartbeat.

We are ready.

Jonesy ignored them and found the node for Sen's connection. As predicted it took just a minute to backup some of the normal routines and create the largest partition he could in Sen's head.

He turned back to the sphere, holding the node open. *Okay.*

A spear of light shot from the sphere into the node and vanished. A red laser light shone steadily between the globe and the node.

Our envoy is in place and we are in communication with it.

I'll tell Sen it's time.

He flipped back into his flat and picked the voda back up. "In place and ready, sir."

There's a sharp intake of breath. "I can feel it..." Sen murmured. "It's like a voice whispering just out of hearing..."

"Are you okay, Inspector General?" Jonesy queried.

"Fine. Let's get this show on the road. I'll let you know when I'm back."

"Okay, sir."

The connection went dead.

When Jonesy flipped back to the Grid, the red communication line was still in place between the node and the sphere.

Okay?

Five by five.

What?

That apparently means 'fine'.

Right.

He flipped back out. "Those guys are weird," he told Bella and Adams.

"You would be too if you grew up in a world that was part video game, part encyclopaedia and part online shopping experience," Bella retorted.

He loved that she got that. "Yeah, you're probably right," was all he said.

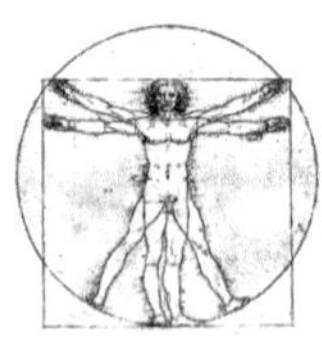

MAY YOUR BEARD GROW EVER LONGER

This entrance to *The Undoing* was little more than a cave in the rocks. It is obviously protected by something as it takes some wandering around to actually find it.

"Damn magic doors," I mutter to no one, lighting another cigarette, the MP5 I'd been issued with hanging from its strap. A long knife hangs at my side and I've got any number of other devices strapped and clipped to me. I feel like I rattle with every step. I am also very conscious of the three vials of serum snugged in the clips on my chest.

As I speak, a cleft in the ground appears, with a gradual slope leading downwards.

Shrugging, I toss the half-smoked cigarette away, glance at the group of eight men around me, including Nick with his own MP5, and give the signal to advance. I take point. Hell, it's my party, I'm not letting anyone else do the dirty work.

What light we get from the sky and the aurora disappears as the cleft closes over our heads. Torches flicker on around me, so I don't bother, preferring to use my senses as they are. I can hear very little beyond the sounds of my team. I stop and hold up my fist so they all stop, too. They're well trained, which is good.

There are only a few night sounds down in the cleft: creak of snow, something small skittering away from us, the wind above.

I release my fist and motion onwards and we move down the cleft which seems to be channelling us to something. I'm never a big fan of the straightforward approach – it can all too easily turn into a trap. Well, we know this is a trap and we know we have to go in.

The path reaches a rock face and in the flickering torchlight it looks like a dead end. Then a small echo tells me it bends. I go forward and suddenly the path opens to the right, bearing down into the ground. A quick glance back shows Nick, impassive as ever, and the rest of my group, followed by Skeet and Madeline's groups.

Here goes.

I step onto the path turning down and realise it is quite a shallow incline. Within thirty feet, it levels off and shows signs of opening out into a larger space.

All of a sudden I smell rain and the ozone that follows a lightning strike.

"Path is opening out, appears to be raining," I report on my bead mic. "May be lightning so watch the light enhancement settings on your goggles."

"Roger that," Skeet replies.

"Yes," Madeline breathes.

I lead my team on and suddenly we're in a cavernous space, but it's so tall we can't see the ceiling beyond the dark clouds which could be hundreds or thousands of feet up.

A lightning flash reveals a dense forest before us made up of all sorts of trees, a weird mixture of tropical, dense woodland and jungle trees with no discernible path between them. There is no bird song and beyond the rustling of the trees in a light wind, I can hear little else. It starts to rain as we enter.

Nothing's attacking us or anything else, so I lead my team off to the right of the entrance and wait for the others. I get the feeling we're being watched.

When Skeet and Madeline enter, they're also startled by the apparent size of the space we're in, the rain and what's ahead of us. I motion them over.

"Well, this isn't what I was expecting," I start.

Skeet shakes her head. "Where're all the bad guys? And why's it raining?"

Madeline looks at the forest, as if she's listening. "There *is* something…" she looks around her feet and selects a small stone. Lightning-fast, she whips it at the trees.

There's a 'crack' and the stone comes flying back at us.

"Incoming!" I shout and the teams around us dodge the flying stone so it strikes the wall behind us. "What the hell was that?"

Madeline looks at me. "One of the trees moved a branch and hit the stone back at us." She glanced back at the forest. "I believe the trees are sentient. Perhaps they are our adversaries."

Shit. Just what we needed: malicious Ents. "How do we combat that?" I ask no one.

"Give me a moment," Madeline says. In a blink she's gone and the trees in one particular spot start thrashing and flailing, although from the cracking of branches it sounds as if they are not coming away unscathed. A lightning flash obscures her for a moment. There's a final rustle and she's back beside me. A scratch under her right eye heals as I watch.

"Well?"

"They move when one enters the edge of the wood – and not just together, but their branches attack and move more swiftly than most of your troops will manage."

"How the hell're we gonna get through that?" Skeet asks softly, rain running down her face.

I'm thinking furiously and lift my MP5 into place. I fire an extended burst into a tree near the front of the wood and watch it sever at the line of my shots. I could swear the noise it makes is a scream. The feeling of being watched intensifies, but now there's anger behind it.

The detached trunk slowly topples over to land with a loud thud on the ground. It doesn't magically reattach, which is good. Unfortunately, three more solid-looking trees move into the space where the stump remains, effectively blocking the path I'd just started.

"Shit. Do we have much in the way of explosives?" I ask, thinking while I'm asking that the trees are only going let us attack them without retaliation for so long.

"Everyone has four grenades and there are two light Claymores," my team leader says at my shoulder.

I shake my head. That's not going to be the answer. I get the feeling there are more trees than we can kill, destroy or simply incapacitate at one go. We can't leave or send anyone out for more supplies as it's unlikely they'll be allowed back in.

Then something dawns on me. I pull out one of the packages Adams sent me. He only described it as a 'holy hand grenade' so, beyond the old Monty Python sketch, I've no idea what it does. It's just plain muslin with lumps of something hard inside, but it's not heavy.

I hand it to Nick as I know he'll tolerate magical items more than Madeline will. Plus, he's younger and faster than me.

"Nick, can you go throw this into that area there," I ask, pointing off centre into the woods. "I need to see if it'll have any effect. Not too far in, as we need to see what it does without getting too close."

Nick nods, slings his MP5 on his back, takes the bundle and disappears.

When he stops, he's not close enough for the trees to reach him, but he over arms the 'hand grenade' into the edge of the enchanted wood.

On impact, the trees within range of it suddenly move away, leaving a passage a good six feet wide. It's good, but I suspect they'll still be able to reach us with their branches if we decided to use it as a road through the wood. The emotions I can feel seem to be wary of us now.

"How many of those do you have?" Madeline asks.

"Five more," I reply, holding out the bag. "I think it was all Adams could come up with on short notice."

Madeline nods. She glances at Skeet who seems to know what she's thinking as she nods. "We will create distractions while you and your team try the path."

I think hard for another second or two before realising we're running out of time and it's the best option we have. "Okay, but I just want myself and Nick – too many people and I can't vouch for them."

My team leader protests and I realise I don't even know his name. "We are here at your service, Inspector General. Let us help."

I look at him again. It's not bravado; he's genuinely keen to do his job. "What's your name?"

"Hislop, sir," he replies.

"Okay Hislop, we'll try it your way, but your job is to keep us from getting our heads knocked off by stray branches – and your own."

"Aye, sir."

I look around me. "You all know what to do, so let's get going."

A quick flurry of equipment checks and the three groups move to their positions.

"Everybody ready?"

Quick nods.
"Let's go."

Madeline led her group over to the far side of the wood, realising when she got there the chamber curved around, disappearing in a wall of rain.

She glanced at the men around her. They meant well enough, but she wasn't sure how much they would achieve.

"You understand what we are doing?" she asked.

"Yes ma'am," the team leader said. "We're going to draw fire…well, keep this flank occupied while the IG tries to get through the forest."

Madeline nodded. "Exactly." She touched her cheek where she'd been hit. "Do not get close to the trees because they *will* do their best to kill you. And they are fast."

The men and women glanced at each other and the leader shrugged. "We understand ma'am."

"Very well. Ready charges and we will intersperse with bursts of MP5 fire." She looked toward the trees and realised they had begun shuffling toward them. She shivered. "Ready, grenades!"

The first blast took out three of the moving trees.

Skeet swore to herself. She knew her place, but she didn't have to like it. And she wished the damn rain would stop.

Moving with her team to a position the other side of the 'path' they'd started, she unlimbered the MP5 and hefted one of the grenades. Spare MP5 clips hung from the bandolier across her chest.

"Uh, ma'am, those trees are moving," the only woman in her group said. She sounded nervous.

Skeet looked and sure enough, a large pine and what looked like an aspen were scrunching their roots up and shuffling forward to meet them.

"Well, lets see how they like these apples," she muttered. Pulling the ring from the grenade, she counted to three and overhanded it to just behind the moving pair. The explosion shredded the two in front and caused serious damage to the ones behind.

Then she noticed there were more moving into position.

"Aw shit," she said. Well, they were only a distraction after all.

She turned back to her group. "Right, you see what we're doing here? The object's to keep 'em occupied and not lose anyone, okay?

The group formed up into a line and took turns firing their MP5s into the trees and interspersing them with grenades.

Skeet was firing into a massive oak when she realised the trees were moving faster. "Pull back," she shouted, just as the oak took a swing at her.

Skeet managed to duck and roll with the blow, avoiding the branch, but getting closer to the trunk of the oak. A massive branch crashed down beside her and she rolled again.

The chatter of MP5 fire she was hearing, plus the splinters raining down on her meant the team were concentrating their fire. She felt the tree wail behind her.

Time to go.

She moved back toward her group, intending to crawl below the firing line.

A branch from the oak, dislodged by the stream of bullets caught her shoulder and she blacked out.

At the sound of gunfire and grenade explosions, we move into the path created by Adams' holy hand grenade (HHG).

At about six feet wide, it is still narrow enough that the trees could whack us with their branches should they so desire.

"No one kick or otherwise disturb that first grenade, clear?" I say, pointing at the bundle on the ground. It had burst open and seemed to comprise large, dull black beetles. They weren't moving.

Dead ahead is another cluster of trees, obviously intending to keep us back. They look sinister in the moving light from the torches affixed to our chest harnesses.

I fire a burst from the MP5 into them and they shred easily enough. We get within a couple feet of the line where the area around the first grenade ends and I pull out the next HHG.

A branch sweeps past my face out of the rain. Nick catches it and pulls it from its socket. There's a wail from the tree.

"Thanks," I say as I pick a place for the HHG to land.

A slow overhand puts it just about dead centre ahead of us and the trees that are able scurry away from it. The ones I shot don't move.

"I guess we don't want to leave lumps like that in the way," Nick says beside me.

"Nope." We clamber over the stumps and move into the next space, our lights moving wildly with the motion. The team firing short bursts at branches moving our way.

Nick places the next HHG without killing any trees and we move into the space again.

Just as I'm pulling out the next one, a stray branch catches me across the shoulders, knocking me forward into the mud and toward the trees. A root snaps up to grab me. Damn they're fast when they want to be.

My shoulder nearly jerks out of the socket, stopping me just short of the root's grasp. I look back and Nick's grabbed my arm and pulled me back.

"Thanks."

He nods as he gets me back on my feet. I'm glad he's looking after his old man. I realise I can still hear explosions and gunfire from beyond our dark path.

I hand him the HHG and he effortlessly places it in the zone. We move forward, me keeping a newly watchful eye out for branches.

The next two packages go without a hitch, leaving us just one more.

"Jaared, I can't see an end to the trees," Nick murmurs next to me.

I nod. I'd already seen the lack of light at the end of the tunnel. "I guess its brute force from here. Did we bring those claymores?"

He nods. "Yes."

One of the innovations in recent years was the addition of a remote activation feature for claymores – for the really sadistic. So all we had to do was toss them ahead of us, move back to avoid the blast area and detonate. Boom.

"Boom. Okay, put the last HHG out there and let's see what we have left," I say, handing him the final one.

The last HHG lands in the next space, the trees move away (it's creepy after a while, I have to say) and we've still got trees in front of us.

I start to speak when a glint of something catches my eye beyond the trees. Looking back at the dense foliage, I can no longer see it.

"Claymore time," I say, probably needlessly.

Hislop brings one out of his pack and taps at the tiny screen for a few seconds. "Active, sir."

I nod. "Nick, would you do the honours?"

Nick takes the flat disc and smoothly frisbees it into the clump of trees ahead. It's almost anti-climactic when it does nothing more than land with a thud.

We retreat along the path, minding the branches moving overhead. I signal Hislop and he punches the button.

The explosion is unbelievably loud and we hunch, heads covered by our arms to protect them from flying splinters and branches.

One of the team takes a heavy blow to the head and slumps to the ground. The wood seems to share a collective scream.

"Stay with him." I motion to one of the team. "Or try and get him out if you can."

"Aye, sir," she replies.

We move forward and see a thirty-foot ring in the trees ahead of us. Just beyond it, more trees.

Crap. And the stunned trees are already beginning to shuffle into the edges of the muddy crater we've created.

"C'mon, we don't have much time," I say to the team.

We move forward at a trot, keeping a watchful eye on the trees around us. As we move Hislop has readied the next claymore which he hands to Nick.

The claymore sails effortlessly ahead and we stop. "Okay, next one."

The explosion is followed by more screams from the wood.

When we look up, our lights reveal the moving trees are within fifteen feet of us.

I look ahead and catch that glint again. I frown. It looked like a light of some kind. "Did you see that?" I say to Nick.

Nick looks ahead. "I see a very large tree moving this way."

I glance back and he's right. I don't recognise it, but it seems much more humanoid than the other trees, two massive branches making up its arms, while the lower trunk seems to have two leg segments. Where the branches fork upward, I can almost make out eyes and a leering mouth.

I pull free a grenade and hurl it toward the oncoming monster tree.

It dodges easily. It's way too fast for a tree.

Next thing I know, it has hold of me and is lifting me up. That maw seems to gape toward my head. I start to squirm, trying to get my hands unpinned so I can do something. It's like pushing against a stone band.

A grenade bounces of its 'teeth' into its mouth/throat. I look away, sure it's going to explode in my face.

Instead, the hand holding me tightens, there's a muffled 'crump' and smoke pours from the creature's jaws. Great.

Suddenly Madeline is on the arm of the creature above me. I don't have time to do much more than register her presence before she punches one of her delicate but very hard hands into the left eye. A shriek that seems to emanate from within my head flashes through the clearing

The branch holding me loosens, but doesn't let me go. I wriggle some more, trying to get my arms free.

The tree is bucking and vibrating now, trying to rid itself of Madeline's presence. She clings on, one hand buried in the bark, the other poised before the other eye. She strikes.

Another head-busting wail and the tree shudders violently. The branch holding me loosens enough so I can get my hand free but I can do little else.

A lightning flash outlines Madeline against the dark sky for a split second. It also shows the other massive branch headed her way.

"Madeline!" I shout and she turns toward me with a smile. I have no more time to warn her.

As if in a dream, the branch which is at least as thick as my thigh catches her at neck height. Another crack and her severed head flies off into the wood.

"NOOOO!" I shout, levering myself out of the relaxed branch. Pulling my MP5 with me I struggle up the trunk to the creature's mouth and hoping its 'brain' is in the normal place and that it's less resistant to bullets, I push the muzzle up into the roof of its screaming maw and pull the trigger.

There is another explosion from the crown of the tree as the MP5s fragmenting rounds begin exiting the top of the tree. Shuddering again, the creature begins to topple to one side and I try to throw myself in the opposite direction, away from the trunk.

A hand grabs my already pulled arm and I swing in something resembling slow motion over to land in the mud. The earth shakes and trembles as the massive creature hits the ground behind me.

It's Nick again. Bloody tears trail down his cheeks, combining with the rain; he obviously saw Madeline's death, too.

There is an almighty crack of thunder and lightning and the forest in front of us splits, leaving a wide pathway up to a wall with a small gate in it. Mercifully, the rain and wind also begin to ease.

I pick myself up, try to brush the worst of the mud from my clothing before looking once more at the gate. My head rings with pain, both physical and mental.

I turn to Nick and find he is at the edge of the wood, Madeline's head cradled in his arms.

I go to him and place a hand on his shoulder. There's nothing to say.

I glance back and see the other two members of my team. "Okay, I can take it from here. You help Nick with Madeline's body and head back to the entrance. In fact, get everyone out of here."

"Uh, sir, we may have a problem," Hislop says, pointing at my chest.

Where the three vials of serum had been is a gooey mess. I pick at the remains of the vials and realise that there are parts of only two there. Glancing around, I can't see the other one. Then I remember the hum. I close my eyes and listen closely, working to feel that connection again.

There it is. I walk carefully toward it, wavering slightly as I move to its left before correcting. The pulse of it gets stronger until it feels like I'm almost on top of it.

I open my eyes and look down. At my feet, buried in the mud is an unbroken vial. I kneel and carefully extract it, wiping it off as best as I can on my already muddy clothes.

I look back to Hislop. "No problem. Get everyone out and I will see you out there," I say, motioning vaguely toward where we came in.

Without another word, I leave my grieving son and head for the gate.

It opens silently and smoothly, a sunny, warm glow on the other side.

Standing up straight, I walk through.

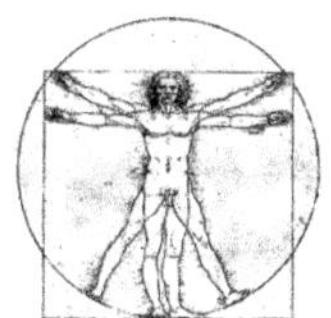

So close and still so far

Jonesy's voda pinged, an alarm of some kind.

"What's that?" Bella asked.

"Something's wrong," he muttered. "I'll be right back."

He flipped into the Grid and realised the red communications line with the node had gone.

What happened?

We do not know. We can only guess.

And that guess is?

We believe Sen is with the creature now.

Right. What does that mean for your...companion in his head?

Do not concern yourself: we have planned for this contingency.

Contingency?

One of the possibilities suggested we could lose contact, so we took steps to compensate for this eventuality.

Right. But you can't talk to it now?

No. That is correct.

What do we do now?

Now? Why we wait, of course. Assuming Sen is successful, we hope to be reunited with our segment upon his return.

Right. Okay, I'm going to go now.

Very well.

Bella and Adams were both sitting there watching him when he opened his eyes. "Shit. I wish you two wouldn't do that," he muttered.

Adams smiled and glanced at Belle. "Well, you're better than the vid for entertainment," he said with a laugh.

"Absolutely," Bella agreed. "Your face goes slack and your muscles bounce and jiggle – like you're dreaming."

"We should record it next time so you can see," Adams suggested.

"That's it – then we can post it on the 'net!" Bella was grinning.

He grinned back. They were taking the piss out of him, so what? "All right, I'm glad I'm so amusing. Ha, ha, hardy har."

Bella looked at him. "Well? Any news?"

Jonesy shrugged. "It, they…we need to give it a name…thinks Sen's there. They've lost contact with their probe, which some scenarios predicted."

"What do we do now?" Adams asked.

Jonesy looked at him and back to Bella before shrugging. "Now, we wait. Anyone know any good games?"

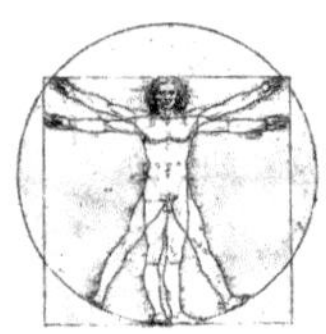

Google News: Fire has swept through the shantytowns of Johannesburg this morning, killing over 1,000 people so far. The fire has yet to be contained...

BBC World Service: A rockslide in the French Alps has buried two skiing villages under tons of rubble in the early hours of today. Rescue efforts are underway, but it is unclear if there are many survivors.

AP: The River Nile is almost dry, stranding many boats and affecting water supplies across Egypt. Scientists are unsure where the water has gone, but investigations are under way.

USA Today: A sawmill in upstate New York exploded today, killing all workers and staff on site. The explosion is currently unexplained.

CNN: New Delhi – A virulent strain of bird flu, known as H25EJ is killing over 400 people every hour in India's capital. There is no vaccine or cure for the virus at this point and if you have business in the country, you are advised to conduct as much of it as you can remotely...

UNDER THE LONELY MOUNTAIN...

The transition is immediate.

One second I'm in a muddy wood, covered in muck, the next I'm standing in a sunny courtyard, dressed in my normal black suit and white shirt. *What the hell?*

I thought you would be more comfortable like this.

I turn and under the giant plane tree stands a little girl, probably no more than six or seven with long, straight black hair and enormous bottle green eyes. She is smiling at me.

A large orange cat, probably the biggest cat I've ever seen, is sitting on the wall, his back to us. He glances around at me, then turns back to look over the wall.

Where am I? I try to say, but there no sound comes from my mouth.

In my home.

I have to ask. *Are you...*

She nods. *I am known as many things, but you may call me 'Rose'.* She motions to a bench under the tree. *Please, come sit down. I have been waiting so long for you and we have much to discuss.*

I follow her to the bench and sit down. She sits next to me, her feet dangling in mid-air. Her feet swing, like any child's, effortlessly and unconsciously.

Did you bring it?

I hold up the vial, realising it has become an antique bottle, the amber glass glowing in the sunlight. *Yes, here it is.*

'Rose' nods. *There is time enough for that.* She looks thoughtful. *I have a question to ask and three things to tell you – which would you prefer?*

I think a moment. *Tell me what you would and I will answer your question after.*

The mother of your son is not dead, but it will require something powerful to bring her back. She reaches into her pocket and pulls a large button with four holes out of it. *In recognition of her service in bringing you to me, I offer this as an assistance.*

I bow my head. Madeline isn't dead! *Thank you...Rose.*

Her brow creases. *You are not all human, as you suspected, which is partly responsible for your longevity. When the time is necessary, you will cross over.*

I look at her, not entirely sure what she means. I file it away, though. *Very well.*

Rose's elfin face takes on a more serious look. *You must not trust the Council – they are not your friends, nor ever will be. But you may be able to make them yours. Time will tell.*

I always hated riddles and this time is no exception. *'Make them mine?' My council? My friends?*

Those deep green eyes just stare at me, no hints, no clues, nothing. The cat jumps from the wall and walks over to us, jumping onto the bench and slumping next to Rose.

I shrug. *Very well. Ask your question.*

Rose regards me a few moments longer before reaching up to touch my face. *Jaared, my son, are you supposed to have those?*

I don't know what she means until she traces the orbit of my left eye. A shock runs through me. *Wh-what do you mean?*

Were you intended to regain your sight, or was the sight you had all you needed?

I stand up, this is ridiculous. What the hell does she mean? *I don't understand.*

Still serious, she sighs. That I can hear. *Sit down, Jaared.* A hesitation as I sit again. *I can glimpse moments of the future and what I glimpse of yours tells me you will need the sight you had before you regained your eyes.*

I...are you sure?

Rose nods. Without another word, she stands up on the bench and places her small hands on either side of my face. She leans forward and kisses me on the forehead, almost a motherly kiss, her tiny lips warm on my skin. I close my eyes.

I am sorry.

I go to open my eyes and they won't cooperate. I put my fingers up to my face and find my old injury has returned, my eyes gone wherever they came from.

I stand up with a lurch and almost fall down. *No, it can't be true.*

Rose puts her hand in mine and guides me back to the bench. I realise I can hear a tiny fluttering heartbeat. Beneath it a deeper thrum like the earth's heartbeat. I can sense nothing of the cat.

It was meant to be this way. Now it is time.

I hear her pick up the glass bottle and take the stopper out. *Is this it?*

Yes, my dear Jaared, it is time for me to slumber again and when I do you will return to your friends.

I have one last question. *Will I see you again?*

I can feel her shake her head. *I do not know – that is a time I cannot see. Now, I must...how did you say? 'Take my medicine'.*

I smile and hear her tip the bottle up and drain it. Her little hand creeps into mine and I hold it tightly.

It will not be long now. Goodbye, my beloved Jaared.

Goodbye, Rose.

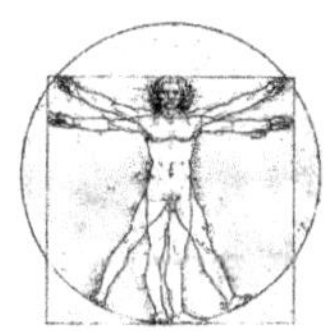

I black out. Or something.

Suddenly it's cold. I seem to be sitting in a puddle. An icy puddle.

My vision is still gone, so it wasn't a dream. My cold hand reveals what I felt before, my eyes gone, the scar tissue as it was before the surgery. And Central is back in my head, although my HUD is gone, I'm getting status queries. My visual status is, no doubt, logged and reported.

I hear a shout and feet running toward me.

"It's Sen, he's over here!" shouts a voice I recognise. Sounds like Hislop. The running feet reach me and he's bent over me. "Commander! Inspector General – are you okay?" His heartbeat's doing a rhumba in his chest.

I nod. "I'm fine, if a little tired." I slip my goggles up to cover the worst of the scar tissue.

Then Skeet is beside me. I can tell she's hurt, as she seems to be walking awkwardly. It doesn't stop her throwing herself down beside me and grabbing me with both arms. "You basturt – thought I'd lost you!"

Smiling I return the hug. "Not yet you haven't. Now help me up – I'm sitting in a puddle."

She and Hislop get me upright and we move back toward the Land Rovers. I can hear them idling. "Is Nick here?"

Skeet shakes her head. "He took Madeline's body and disappeared."

I nod, hardly surprising. "I need to get hold of him before he does something stupid." I feel my pockets and find a lump in one: it's the large button Rose gave me.

As we reach the car, I lean in to Skeet. "My eyes..."

She turns to me and lifts the goggles. Her sharp intake of breath tells me everything I need to know. I reach up and pull the goggles down again, hiding the scars as best I can.

Chambers approaches. "Good work Inspector General, it appears all the global calamities have stopped."

"Good. Let's get the hell out of here and back to London," I say.

"Absolutely! We'll leave as soon as you're set."

I climb into the Land Rover without another word. Moments later we set off.

While we're travelling, I call Nick. Unsurprisingly, I get his voicemail. "Ring me when you get this, Nick. And don't do anything with Madeline yet – I have something for you."

Next I call Jonesy.

"Well? Are we done with them/it/whatever the hell it is?"

"I think so, sir. They seem very pleased with the results."

"Good. Are we likely to hear anything more from them?" I don't really want anything to do with them, but who knows?

Jonesy pauses and I wonder what he's going to say. "I'm not sure they got everything they were after – it's not clear whether *The Undoing* allowed them any access, but they have rescinded their threats."

"Good. Okay Jonesy, thanks. And thank Adams and Bella for me."

"I will sir."

I cut the link. I'm still reeling from the change in my circumstances.

Skeet takes my hand. "Penny for 'em," she murmurs.

I squeeze her hand. "I-I'm not certain what to do next," I reply.

"We'll figger that out, don' worry." I can feel her smiling. " 'Sides, you're the Inspector General now – you do what you like!"

I smile back. "Of course I am. I guess I'll just have to wait and see what happens next."

Pun intended.

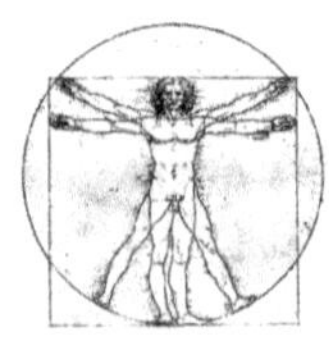

Acknowledgements

It's been an interesting trip and I hope you've enjoyed it as much as I have. I have a few people to thank, so I'll jump right in.

Firstly, Chris Loffelmacher has been a star and support for many years now – cheers Chris! One of my oldest friends, Ross King, is another one who has been there when I needed him. Karen Leh and Lisa Curtis have been rocks: when I consider their circumstances I can't believe they have time for me, too.

I have to thank my Mom's book group in Sterling, Colorado: their desire to know what happens next has spurred me on!

In terms of music, there have been a lot of influences over the years and some of you will no doubt recognise them in some of the song titles. Just a few of them are: Tom Waits, the Black Keys, Stevie Ray Vaughan, Pink Floyd, Rush and many others. I have also listened to T.C.'s podcast Spacemusic (spacemusic.nl) for the last eight years and it has been a fitting soundtrack.

I have to thank my folks, who continue to support my desire to write and even like what I write (kind of). Thanks Mom and Dad.

And last, but most importantly, my lovely wife – and better half – Debra. Thanks sweetie!

London, March 2013

You can find more information on Dean's books and sign up for the monthly newsletter – letting you know about new releases and news about what he's up to on his website at

www.deanfetzer.com

Read on for an excerpt from the next Jaared Sen book

TILL DEATH COMES

DO ANDROIDS DREAM?

I hate it when they run. Don't get me wrong, I can keep up with them, it just seems like a waste of time. I could have shot the mark, but where's the fun in that?

"Stop!" I try.

No response, just the sound of his feet in the alley ahead of me. Then I hear a 'thwack' that sounds like a bat connecting with soft flesh.

"Nice one," I say as I catch up to Skeet. "Home run?"

Skeet huffs a laugh. "Not quite, grounder to first – didn't want to take his head all the way off."

I smile as I bend over and cuff his hands behind his back. Central already has a car on the way to pick him up. "Got plans for later?"

I can hear the rings in her ears jangle as she shakes her head. "Fancy a pint?"

"I can do that."

"Good. See you later."

I smile again, looking forward to it. "Later."

My virtual desk has a pile of messages on it as I head back to the office.

I've only been Inspector General a short while, but things have gotten complicated: the number of Contractors working for me is down due to injury, retirement and a couple cases of true death.

Which means I'm short-handed. And working in the field again. I even draft in Skeet sometimes to help – paying her as a consultant, of course.

"Sir?" comes from the doorway. It's Heather, my assistant.

"Yes? Come in, Heather," I wave from the desk.

“You’ve got a two o’clock at headquarters and a four o’clock at the Ministry,” she announces.

“What’s the two o’clock?”

“The usual – budget constraints for the new year.”

I groan. Yay, the life of an administrator. I’d much rather be in the field.

“Don’t groan, you have to go and make sure we don’t get screwed any more than we usually do,” Heather scolds.

I nod. “I know, it doesn’t make it anymore bearable.” I drink some of the cold coffee in my cup. “What’s the four o’clock?”

I can feel her hesitate. “That is…unclear, Jaared. I was asked to schedule it, but the Minister’s secretary wouldn’t give me any details, just to make sure you were there.”

I sigh instead. “Well, at least it’ll give me a reason to get out of that budget meeting. Thank you Heather.”

The Minister would be the Homeland Secretary, Martin Torrance, a newish member of the cabinet who has a tendency to overreact when things look difficult. I have only met the man a couple of times and have no idea why he suddenly wants to see me. Guess I’ll find out at four.

The budget meeting was much as expected and, as predicted, overran. Good thing I had another meeting to go to.

The Minister’s assistant ushers me into the darkly panelled office the Homeland Secretary occupies just off Whitehall. Even though the UK government is a lot smaller than it used to be, due to cuts, the heart of it all still sits in Westminster amidst the old trappings of power.

“Jaared! Good to see you again!” The Minister grabs my hand and pumps it vigorously. He seems so young…

“Minister,” I reply.

“Sit down, sit down,” he waves at the wing chairs near the fireplace, obviously intending an informal conversation. My curiosity is piqued as I lower myself into one of the chairs.

I bite. “What can I do for you, Minister?”

He sits down, serious now. “We’ve got a small problem I’d like you to look into, Jaared,” he starts.

“I’m sure I can assign someone to look into it for you,” I start.

Shaking his head, he sighs. “I would like *you* to look into it, Jaared. It’s a…matter of some delicacy.”

It always is. "If you tell me what it is, I'll see what I can do, Minister."

The door opens and the assistant appears with a tray and coffee. "Milk? Sugar?"

"Black is fine." The cup is placed on the table at my right elbow. "Thank you." I sip the excellent coffee. At least he has good taste.

When the assistant has departed, the Minister continues. "I don't know if you're aware of politics at the moment, Jaared…"

I nod, figuring he means the on-going issues with the European Union.

"…well, we're currently negotiating with the American Free States over trade to the Union and it's not going well."

I raise an eyebrow, not really following. "And what can I do to influence these negotiations?" I'm pretty sure the answer is 'not very much'.

He laughs. "Oh Jaared, I'm not expecting you to help with those. No," he tastes his coffee, "I have another task for you that is more your area of expertise. I need you to find my chief negotiator's son Charlie before the talks are compromised any further."

Ah, that's more like it. "I assume he hasn't just gone missing on a holiday or something?"

"No, Charlie was taken from his school two days ago in broad daylight."

I whistle silently. "I see – that's ballsy."

He goes still, no longer smiling. "It puts us in a bad position with the Free States, I'm afraid, as someone is trying to use the abduction as a means of influencing the negotiations." He sips his coffee again. "We can't allow this."

I consider. "Okay, send me the info you've got and I'll go look at the abduction site when we finish."

He stands. "I appreciate this, Jaared and I know it's not something the Inspector General is supposed to do, but you are *still* the best Contractor out there." He puts his hand on my shoulder, guiding me toward the door, like I need it. "Keep me updated on your progress – I expect your first report by five."

I nod. "No problem, will keep you posted."

PERFECTION IS IN THE EYE OF THE BEHOLDER

When Alicia finally got to Exam Room 3, Jack had left. "Where are you?" she asked when he picked up his voda.

"Sorry Boss, just having a wee toke," he replied.

"I'm in Exam Room 3 now – what's so weird about this one?"

"Oh shit! Sorry, Boss, thought you'd got held up. I'll be right in."

While waiting, Alicia started looking at the body. At first glance it appeared to be male, short brown hair, reasonably developed physique, but no body builder. The face, though, was androgynous at best. Frowning, she lifted the privacy sheet. "What the hell?" she muttered.

It had no genitalia at all. Or any sign that it ever had possessed any.

"Smooth as a Ken doll..."

"You can say that again, Boss," Jack said from right behind her, making her jump.

"Jesus, Jack – don't *do* that!" Letting the sheet fall, she waved at the body. "Mind filling me in?"

Jack shrugged, the effects of the legal marijuana visible in his relaxed stance. "No idea – I've never heard of anything like this."

Alicia tapped a tooth with one fingernail. "I'd say genetically altered and probably at birth; too difficult to do that kind of genetic alteration past puberty." She walked around the body and realised how 'normal' it was. No distinguishing marks at all. No blemishes, freckles or scars. "Have you scanned the body yet?"

Shaking his head, he pulled the unit away from the wall on its arm. "No, I was waiting for you."

"I wonder..."

"What, Boss?"

Alicia waved at the scanner. "Just scan him – it, whatever. I'll tell you when we find it."

The scanner pushed images onto one of the flat screens in the room at ten times magnification. Even with the magnification they almost missed it.

Jack spotted it on his third pass down the thigh. "Wait, what's that?" he said, almost to himself.

"What?"

"Magnification: Zoom in one third," he instructed the scanner. "Move right, three degrees... Stop!" He pointed to the screen. "There!"

Just above the hipbone was a tiny patch of rough skin. Under the scanner's gaze, it resolved into a thirty-digit mixture of numbers and letters.

"Ah-hah!" Alicia crowed. "Just what I thought. It's a clone." She picked up the hands and examined the palms and fingers. "One that doesn't do manual labour, from the hands."

"Those're regulated – how would it turn up here?" Jack asked.

"Another good question, Jack. Get Sen to check it...wait...I'll call him." She waved impatiently. "Cause of death?"

"Undetermined at this point. We're waiting on tox as usual."

"Okay, keep me posted."

"Will do, Boss – want a coffee?

"Sure. I'll catch you up."

Jack nodded and left the exam room.

"Where *did* you come from?" Alicia asked the perfect corpse on the slab. "And why hasn't someone reported you missing?"

Alicia got Jaared's voicemail.

Typical, she thought.

"Jaared, got a dead clone here – we need you to track down the owner and see if they're missing one. I'll send you the details." She paused. "Call me when you get a moment."

Jonesy sighed as the readouts told him absolutely nothing.

He was still in his cubbyhole of an office at ten o'clock on a Friday. Good job he didn't have a social life to speak of. Or a girlfriend anymore. Things hadn't exactly worked out with Bella.

The data on the kid was all a bust. Somehow the whole lot glitched right before he disappeared. The tracker on his clothes, the ping on his voda, all surveillance at the school, which was mandatory now, all went 'poof' at the same time.

"And that's so unlikely," he muttered to himself. He'd already looked at the logs and found nothing but a break — nothing to suggest tampering, but it had to be there.

"Maybe the server logs..."

No, nothing. Jonesy sighed. He knew where he had to go next.

But he wasn't looking forward to it.

Jonesy backed his bike into the space, the old Harley's soundtrack chuckling to itself as he powered it down.

His vintage Harley Davidson Sportster had been modified to take hydrogen cells, meaning the old internal combustion engine no longer made any noise. To fix this, a 'soundtrack' of engine noise had been added, partly as a safety feature silent motorcycles or cars were impossible to detect — and partly to make it seem like the old experience of riding a bike.

The bar he'd parked in front of was a grim-looking affair somewhere off the A3 in Surrey. It was called *Hell and High Water* and the line of motorcycles in front of it was a pretty good advert for the clientele.

Jonesy walked to the door and pushed it open. The smell of unwashed bodies and stale beer roiled out of the dark interior to meet him.

If you could get a real biker bar in what was left of England, this was probably it. The local constabulary were regulars, usually breaking up the fights that started any night of the week, and the beer was wet and mostly did the job. There were always spirits

(Chinese knock-offs of old American brands) and a guy that sold twists of whatever your poison might be next to the bog.

Jonsey nodded to the barman, a big Brum by the name of Dave, and headed toward the pool tables. For all the bikes outside, the bar was sparsely populated.

His target was shooting pool by himself, a pint and a shot balanced on the shelf safely out of the way.

"Buy you a drink, stranger?" Jonesy asked the huge man bent over the table.

A grunt was all he got by way of reply. The player took the next shot and moved around the table to his next.

Jonesy turned to the bar. "Whatever he's having, Dave – and I'll have a beer."

Dave nodded, picked up a couple of glasses and started filling them with ale from the pump.

Carefully carrying the full pints, Jonesy walked back to the pool table.

He sat the new pint next to the now-empty pint glass and pulled a stool out to perch on. He waited, knowing better than to interrupt.

The big man potted a ball, moved around the table and potted the next. He sighed and lined up the cue ball on the black. With a flick of his wrist, the ball shot into the pocket, leaving the cue ball spinning on the green baize.

He stood up, pushing lank black hair out of his eyes, a nobbly nose sticking out of his face. A heavy beard was growing down his chest. "Whaddya want, Jonesy?" He sounded bored, more than anything else. About six foot five in old money, he looked the stereotypical biker in worn jeans, heavy, square-toed boots, a denim jacket with a leather waistcoat over the top, various patches signifying years spent in various motorcycle 'clubs'.

"I got a problem, Herc and you're the man to find the solution," Jonesy started.

Hercules Finnegan turned to the shelf and downed whatever the amber liquid in the small glass was. "Can't help you, Jonesy."

Jonesy sipped his pint and watched the big man set the balls up again. He waited.

The balls in the rack, Herc moved them to the spot and pressed them into the frame to make sure they were all aligned before removing the rack.

He sighed again and picked up his pint. "You're not going to go away, are you?"

Jonesy shook his head. "No."

Herc drained half the pint and looked at him directly for the first time.

"It's a missing kid, Herc," he tried.

Nodding, Herc picked up his custom cue and moved back to the table. "Whaddya need me for?"

Jonesy sipped his beer. "The kid was monitored and it all glitched at the same time." Another sip. "I've been through the code and can't spot anything. But I bet you could."

Herc took a shot at the grouped balls, four of which slapped into the pockets. "I'm on probation, Jonesy — can't touch a computer for another six months."

Shaking his head, Jonesy stepped up to the table, getting in his way. "That's been waived."

Herc looked at him again, a rarity. A grin crept over his lumpy features. "Really? You must know someone important."

Embarrassed, Jonesy looked down into his pint. "It's my job, Herc. And I need your help."

Still smiling, Herc twisted the cue. He had it broken down and slipped into its case in a matter of seconds. He finished his pint and gestured to a table nearby. Two more pints appeared as they sat down. Avoiding Jonesy's eyes, Herc sipped his new pint. "Show me what you got."

Jonesy slipped the tablet out of his bag and laid it on the table in front of them, lifting four different images up to project above the table. "Logs, system software, monitoring apps and the surveillance footage." He waved at them and they oriented so Herc could look at them more closely. "I can't spot anything out of the ordinary that would do that."

Gesturing, Herc flipped through the screens, looking for something, drilling down in some cases, flipping the views out of the way when he was done with them.

He did this for a good fifteen minutes, pint ignored, before he sat back in the groaning chair and picked up his glass. Herc drained the pint and pulled one of the screens toward him. He moved it around so Jonesy could see it.

"Here."

Jonesy couldn't see it. "Where?"

Herc jabbed a thick finger into one of the lines of code. "Master control code inserted here — not a routine use, has to be an anomaly."

"You have got to be kidding me," Jonesy muttered. It was obvious once it was pointed out.

"It's in every system log — they were thorough. And very good." Herc almost sounded envious.

Jonesy shook his head. It was virtually impossible to hack *all* the systems like this. "Impossible."

Herc pointed at the screen again. "Obviously not." A new pint appeared and he started in on it.

"But who could do that?"

"Besides me?" Herc asked with a smile.

Jonesy grinned. "Yeah, besides you."

Herc considered for a moment, looking into his pint. "I'd say there's four on that list, plus me." He sipped the pint. "I don't know real names, just handles and I want nothing to do with it after I tell you. And the waiver stays in place — I'm bored out of my skull shooting pool all day."

"Agreed, but I may bring something back for you to look at."

"Agreed." Herc lifted the pint in a toast.

A second later, Jonesy's messages dinged with a list.

"How the hell do you *do* that?" Jonesy muttered.

Herc smiled and stood up. "Later Jonesy."

"Later," Jonesy replied, already wondering how he was going to find four users he knew nothing about beyond their online aliases.

ISBN 979-8-9859457-2-0 (tapa blanda) English
ISBN 979-8-9859457-3-7 (libro electrónico) English
ASIN B09JQGLD9S (audio) English
ISBN 979-8-9859457-4-4 (libro electronico) Espanol

Translation from English to Espanol by Juliana Benavides

Para la venta, distribución y más información sobre el libro, visita www.IntoTheDustBook.com

Este libro está dedicado a mis amigos

John "Banjo Billy" Georges
Un hombre más refinado nunca caminó sobre el polvo

Daniel Malone Mikkelson alias Ranger Nerf Herder
Un alma amable y hermosa que se fue demasiado pronto

y Jesse Morrison
Un guerrero pacífico cuya luz tocó muchas vidas